NOT IN THE PLAN

DANA HAWKINS

Storm

To request permissions, contact the publisher at rights@stormpublishing.co

Ebook ISBN: 978-1-80508-204-0
Paperback ISBN: 978-1-80508-206-4

Cover design by: Leah Jacobs-Gordon
Cover images by: Leah Jacobs-Gordon, Shutterstock

Published by Storm Publishing.
For further information, visit:
www.stormpublishing.co

To my forever. You are the espresso to my Americano, the oat milk to my latte, the whipped cream to my hot cocoa. You make everything better, and nothing is complete without you. I love you.

ONE

CHARLIE'S DRINK SPECIAL: DAILY GRIND DRIP

The Colombian dark-roast hazelnut aroma jostled Charlie from early morning brain fog.

Nestled on a stool in the cramped storage room, she blew into her red-lipstick-stained rainbow mug and indulged in a grateful sip. The caffeine danced on her tongue before it left a trail of heat down her throat.

Coffee. Her true love.

She trailed a fingertip over the freshly inked butterfly on her inner wrist and flinched from the sharp burn. A few more days and her final freedom branding should heal. She drew a tiny heart on June 10th on her motivational quotes calendar, marking Sugar Mugs's official six-month anniversary. Her dream of creating a safe space where kids, queers, and grand-parents could all hang out was finally a reality.

For now.

A brown leaf from her bamboo plant on her bookshelf caught her attention. She moved to pluck it, then pried open the blinds to peek at the few regulars waiting on the sidewalk. Maybe today would be a good day.

Scratch that. *Manifest. Focus.*

Today would be a *great* day.

Over her shoulder, she called out, "Ready, Peaches?"

Ben stood up from the corner table. "I'm caffeinated, moisturized, and having a good hair day." His inky-black hair was perfectly pomaded, as usual. He was *always* having a good hair day. He pointed double finger guns at her with an exaggerated wink. "Open."

All morning a steady stream of customers filtered through Charlie's neighborhood coffee shop. Each time the door opened, the unusual Seattle heat whooshed in carrying lavender scent from her outdoor plants. As her fingers tapped the order screen, stress evaporated.

"Really? Five pumps of regular vanilla and one pump of sugar-free?" Ben muttered a couple of hours later, his saltiness reaching max level. "What the hell's the point?"

"You burnt out?" Crafting coffee drinks was physically intensive, but Ben normally held on for at least three hours before they rotated. She bumped him to the register and swapped places with him at the espresso machine.

"I'm hangry. And my abuelita sent a huge dish of arroz con gandules, and I can't eat it." He wiped his hands on the towel and rang up the next customer. He scribbled the order on the cup and pushed it towards her. "Cleansing sucks."

"When did you start a cleanse?" she asked while pumping the espresso into the portafilter.

"This morning." He turned his attention to the man who approached the till. "What can I get started for you?"

"Drip with room."

Perfect. A proper order, highest profit margin. He was probably a purist at heart, just like her.

I'm so glad I opened this place.

"Excuse me!" The shrill voice erupted behind Charlie. "I said peppermint. *Not* vanilla."

I should've never opened this place.

"Oops! Sorry 'bout that. Let me redo it for you." She winced as she tossed the botched drink down the drain and mentally calculated the cost of her error.

An hour later, the rush slowed and Ben handed her a short Americano.

"A vendor dropped these baked samples off earlier." He dug a banged-up white pastry box covered in masking tape from under the till. "Twenty bucks says they taste like hell."

"I'm not even taking that bet right now." She took a quick sip and relished in the welcome reprieve of the chaotic morning. "It's like they didn't even try."

He ripped open the box and handed her a droopy, pink-cream-topped muffin. "Bottoms up, baby." He bit into the muffin and faked a gag.

She poked at the crusty frosting, sniffed it, and took a tentative lick before sinking her teeth into it. "Eww. This tastes like feet." She threw her dehydrated muffin in the compost bin. "Wait, I thought you were on a cleanse?"

"I'm already over it." He clapped the crumbs from his fingers.

"Thank God," she said. "When you keto'd last month, all you did was death-glare the doughnuts."

"It takes a lot to maintain all this." He rubbed his hands down his chiseled belly. "Hey, you ever hear from your dad last week?"

"Nope. I still only get a birthday call when he's sober." *Or needs cash.*

Being her bestie since junior high, Ben had witnessed it all. He nodded in solidarity.

"And nothing else from Jess?"

"Just that text I showed you." Charlie wiped the steam wand with a wet towel. Her ex-wife refused to allow the scabbed-over wound of their broken marriage to fully heal, and never missed an opportunity to send well-wishes or trip selfies from God-knows-where.

Last week, Jess had messaged:

> Happy Birthday, You! Hope you have an amazing day and splurge on a slice of Swedish lemon cake from your fave bakery in Queen Anne ;-)

For a split second after reading the text, a tiny lump grew in Charlie's throat. But soon after, irritation took over.

"Do you have any idea how many regulars check you out? You should jump on that." A few rogue coffee beans scattered across the counter as Ben poured them into the industrial grinder. "Maybe there's actually light at the end of your celibate tunnel."

"I'm not giving up a sale for booty." She snapped a garbage liner in the air and stuffed it into the container.

"Whatever, princess."

Charlie grabbed the sanitizing spray bottle from the cleaning station and wiped down the tables as Jess's voice swirled in her head.

Babe—we're talking about Spain! How can you pass this up?

Belize tickets are practically free this time of year.

Fiji, Charlie. Come on. You know you want to...

The bell over the door jingled, and the mail carrier marched toward the register.

"Eddie!"

"Afternoon, Charlie." Eddie handed over a stack of mail to Ben.

She snatched it from Ben's hands before he could look as her neck grew warm. "Did my invite to Macklemore's birthday party arrive today?"

"Not today. It'll happen." Eddie adjusted the strap on his mailbag.

She pouted. "Five minutes alone with him and we'd be best friends."

"Hey!" Ben snapped a towel in her direction.

"Next to Benji here, of course." She grinned and held the mail to her chest like a shield.

"I believe in you." Eddie nodded at Ben, who handed him a complimentary cup. "Did I tell you I used to deliver in his neighborhood in West Seattle?"

"What? Did you see him? Is he nice? Are you kidding?"

"Sure am," he said with a chuckle, and slammed his iced coffee.

"Dang it. I thought you'd have an insider tip. Guess I'm back to square one, manifesting my dreams with crystals tonight."

After Eddie left, Charlie flipped through the mail. "Ugh."

Ben stopped stuffing the napkins. "Chucky? You good?"

"Yep, for sure." She forced a smile and prayed that Ben's spidey sense was off today. "I'm gonna run upstairs for a bit. You okay on your own for a while?"

"Seriously? Go. I got this."

She bumped him on the hip, flashed an even worse fake smile than before, and raced up the stairs to her loft. Careful not to trip over the half dozen shoes and scattered packages inside the front door, she made her way to the shoddy desk tucked in the corner of the living room. She flung the two sweatshirts draped on the back of the chair to the couch and used her elbows to clear a space.

Her hands trembled before she slipped her finger under the envelope flap.

"Nope. Not today." She stopped mid-tear and pressed her palm over the seal, like the insides contained a poisonous gas she could contain if she kept it closed.

Today, she couldn't open the letter. Tomorrow she'd look. Or the next day. Or maybe this weekend she'd officially open them all. She yanked open the dresser drawer and stuffed the unopened envelope on top of the stack of mail containing the exact, bold red, two-letter words: *Final Notice*.

TWO

MACK'S DRINK SPECIAL: FLUSTERED FRAPPE
WITH A DRIZZLE OF HOPE

The chill in the night air suffocated me and

Nope. She tried again.

The freeze in the air matched my heart

Absolutely not.

The briskness of the oxygen

Seriously?

Mack slammed her laptop shut. She pushed her palm into her chin and inhaled a shaky breath. Even the circling scent of flowers and ferns from her parents' guest bedroom open window, combined with the spectacular view of the sunrise over the Olympic Mountains, couldn't inspire her.

She hospital-edged the sheet and smoothed the comforter. After double-checking that her T-shirt was still crisply ironed from her middle-of-the-night relaxation technique, she began her escape.

The hardwood floors squeaked as she tiptoed down the hall. She eased the rental car keys from a hook and crept to the front door.

"Mack?"

Ugh.

She spun on the balls of her feet. Seeing her mom's formerly straight, thick, long black hair now short and wispy dropped Mack's heart into her stomach. Three years since they found the lump, two years since treatment stopped. The hair would take another year to get used to.

"Hey, Ma."

Narrowed, dark-circled eyes glared at her.

"You leaving?"

"Yeah." Mack's shoulders stiffened. "Needed some coffee. Didn't want to wake you and Dad."

Caffeine was a solid excuse. Her mom didn't need the entire truth this early.

"It's barely after six." Lines cut across her mom's forehead. "It's still dark."

Extreme worst-case scenario was her mom's favorite sport. She was probably going through an itemized list of things that could hurt her twenty-six-year-old daughter, ranging from a rabid raccoon to an escaped serial killer. And people wondered where Mack got her storytelling gift.

"I'm good, I promise." Her mom had been through enough in her lifetime. Worrying about her daughter was the last thing she needed.

Her mom's slippered feet padded across the cherrywood floors, and she plopped onto a kitchen chair. "Wanna talk about it?"

Talk about why Mack hadn't visited her parents for a year and then called eight hours ago from the Seattle airport letting them know she was in town? No, not really. "I'm kinda tired right now."

"Shocking, since you've been up since three."

"You heard me? Sorry, I didn't want to wake you. I just wanted to—"

"Iron. I know." Her mom jutted her head toward the corner

of the room. "I'm the one who put the iron and board in your room for you."

Mack's heart softened. "Someday I'm gonna craft a personal essay on the joys of midnight ironing. Reduction in heartrate. Satisfaction of a job well done. Waking up sharp and fresh."

"Mackey."

"What?"

"You're avoiding." Her mother tightened her frilly pink robe around her willowy frame.

Mack brushed her palm across the tiny hairs poking out from her freshly buzzed undercut. "Can we just say it's been a hellish week and leave it at that?" Words congregated on the tip of her tongue, begging for release. "I gotta go."

Her mom shook her head. "You can't go traipsing around in an unfamiliar city. You know, I saw on *Dateline*, or maybe it was one of those Netflix true crime stories, about this writer who—"

"Ah, come on. I travel all the time for work." She laid a quick hand on her mom's arm. "I'm gonna head out. I'll see you later this afternoon."

Her mom sighed and leaned into the touch. "It'd be nice to have breakfast with you... I, we, haven't seen you for so long."

Her mom's words landed with a punch.

"You trying to make me feel guilty?"

"Honey. I'm trying to make you feel *loved*."

Less than eight hours with her mom, and Mack pulled in two different directions. Option one, rush into her mother's arms and cry it out. Option two, run like hell.

Her money was on bailing the F outta here.

"I'm sorry. I know. There's just... a lot." Mack waved her wrist as if that would magically explain everything that transpired in the last few months. "We'll chat later."

Mack darted down the hall before her mom could speak. She hit the elevator button multiple times before the door opened. After she verified no sketchy white van was parked near her rental car, she hopped in.

Inhale. One, two, three, four. Hold. One, two, three, four. Exhale. One, two, three, four. Repeat.

Minutes later, her heartbeat slowed. She rolled her windows down and took off for any place but here.

Seattle air was different from New York's. The city smelled like the color green. Ripe. Meadowy. Invigorating. Clean. Made her want to breathe and meditate. And forget the scene twenty-four hours ago when she raced around her apartment, stuffed her military-style folded clothes and anxiety meds into luggage, and rushed to the airport.

She needed to figure out a plan—and fast. The countdown clock ticked toward a looming deadline. *What am I gonna do?*

Two hours later, her head feeling clearer, the rental car shook with the infinite potholes as she headed downtown. The fuel gauge indicator verged just above half. No way would she break her own rules in a different city and let it dip any more. She pulled off the highway and followed her navigation to the closest gas station.

"*Jesus.*" Was the apocalypse happening? Every pump was full.

She white-knuckled the unfamiliar steering wheel as she snuck in between two SUVs. Before her smartwatch could warn her that her heartrate was too high, she deflated into the seat and took a breath.

Moments later, she exited the car and swiped her card. The machine beeped in response.

Card error. Please see attendant.

Seriously? She swiped a second card. The same message flashed across the screen with the same shrill buzz. She glanced up at the person pumping gas next to her, who was for sure judging her incompetency.

"Broken machine," Mack muttered with a weak smile.

The woman gave her an uninterested nod.

A pit formed in her stomach as she entered the store. Social Interaction 101: stay calm, maintain eye contact, don't fidget. "Um, the machine outside isn't taking my card."

The man behind the plexiglass security wall stopped stocking vapes. "What pump?"

"Pump five." Tiny beads of sweat formed on her lower back.

A customer stood behind her, tapping their foot. More sweat pooled and her increased heartrate thudded in her neck. The front door opened, and two additional guests entered. Was everyone staring at her?

The attendant pulled down the skinny microphone above his head.

Oh God, not the microphone.

"Jimmy! Can you come up front? Customer having a credit card issue."

Every eye in the convenience store bored into her.

"Machine issue... not credit card issue." She fanned the lower part of her shirt. *Don't they have air-conditioning around here?* She placed her hands on her hips—an over-heating preventative measure while she waited for the manager. Was everyone still staring? They were probably angry she caused them a delay. She stumbled a bit to the side to allow other customers to come to the front, and froze her gaze at some random tabloid, pretending it was the most fascinating thing she'd ever seen.

Ten minutes later, with her tank full, her hands still clammy, and a logged mental note to never buy gas in the morning, she exited off I-5 in search of coffee.

Her phone buzzed.

"Ugh." She sent Viviane, her literary agent, to voicemail. A minute later, she tapped the phone to listen to the message.

"Mack. You know it's serious when I'm leaving you an actual recording like it's 1995. Pick up your damn phone.

Listen, lady, I respect and appreciate your creative process, but I've got multiple people waiting for a status update, including me... Send proof of life, or I'm organizing a search party. Your Instagram posts of books don't count. Love you. Byeee."

She's pissed.

Mack swerved left to avoid entering what she thought was one-way. *Goddang Seattle drivers.* People parked on whatever side of the street they wanted and faced whatever way they wanted, and it was totally disorienting.

Her GPS rerouted, and when a car honked behind her, she panicked. The drivers here almost never honked and gave constant "thank you" waves. But the guy behind her was obviously in a hurry, and her GPS was frozen, so she took another left and parked.

Exhaling, she reached for her phone.

> Mack: I'm alive. Just head's down, finishing up.

> Viviane: Send proof of life. You may be a kidnapper.

Mack sent a picture of her middle finger.

> Viviane: Much better

> Viviane: Wait, are you driving a car? In Manhattan?

> Mack: Went to see my parents in Seattle

> Viviane: Are you kidding me? You weren't going there for a few weeks yet for the book signing

> Viviane: What's going on?

Mack could picture Viviane's smiling, smooth brown face morph into flatlined lips and a scowl.

Viviane could *not* know Mack was nowhere near delivering her overdue first draft, nor that Viviane wasted months busting her butt to secure a totally undeserved advance for Mack's sophomore book.

Viviane's name flashed across the screen, and Mack declined the call.

> Viviane: you know it's crappy when you're texting with someone, but they send your call to voicemail.

> Mack: Sorry, I know. Bad service. I'll call later.

No way would Viviane believe that excuse. She silenced her phone. Needing some air, she exited the car and wandered the neighborhood. Mid-century homes with lush greenery gave her the illusion she was no longer in the city.

"What the..." A rainbow flag—always a comforting hug—flew outside a small brick home in the middle of the block. A sign on the door displayed *Sugar Mugs*.

Perfect. A quick cup would jolt her from her funk.

The shop captured the ambiance of a warm living room. Beautiful hardwood floors, shelves overflowed with books and board games, and plants. So. Many. Plants. On the wall hung photos of Seattle-based musicians Macklemore, Nirvana, Pearl Jam, Dave Matthews, Jimi Hendrix, and Foo Fighters.

Mack froze when she turned her focus to the woman at the counter.

Thick, curly red hair framed a freckled face with equally red plump lips. A floor-length flowy dress completed the modern-day Renaissance look. Full. Curvy. Round. *Stunning.*

Oh, holy hell... who are you?

THREE

CHARLIE'S DRINK SPECIAL: MEET-CUTE MACCHIATO

Charlie stared at the striking woman with an undercut, skinny jeans, and the whitest T-shirt Charlie would never brave wearing at the counter. A new customer! She didn't remember every face that passed through Sugar Mugs, but she would've remembered this one. After a terrible night's sleep where the bills she shoved in her desk yesterday morning haunted her, this was a perfect distraction from her sleepy gloominess. "Hey there, what can I get started for you?"

The woman shoved her hands in her front pockets. "Can I get a short drip?"

"For sure. Room for cream?"

"No, black."

My kinda woman. "Gotcha. Anything to eat?" Charlie poised her marker over the cup and waited. And waited some more. "We've got fresh blackberry scones, coffee cake, brownies..."

The woman cleared her throat. "Ah, just a plain bagel."

"Toasted?"

A smirk flashed above a sharp jawline. "No self-respecting New Yorker would ever toast a bagel."

That voice. She had a velvet rasp like she could probably karaoke the hell outta Stevie Nicks. "New Yorker, huh?" Charlie lifted a brow. "I thought I sensed an accent. You on vacation?"

A blush swept her cheeks. "Not exactly."

Ooh. Mysterious. I like it.

The woman stuffed a ten-dollar bill in the tip jar and moved to the pickup area.

Charlie was a sucker for accents. She wiped a phantom spot on the counter in front of the New Yorker, hoping to scrape out a few more words. "If you need any good recommendations for non-tourist, local stuff, let me know."

The woman lifted her eyebrows. "You get a lot of tourists around here?"

"The city does, for sure, especially in the summer. But this place here"—her multiple beaded leather bracelets clicked when she waved her arm to the shop—"it stays pretty local."

"Short drip and bagel." Ben slid the items to the holding spot.

Damn it.

"Thanks." The woman pulled up a barstool next to Charlie's working station.

Yes!

The doorbell jingled. Erica and Amanda, her favorite mother-daughter duo, burst through the doors.

"Hey there!" Charlie waved. "Awww, look at you, Amanda," she said to the bouncy nine-year-old. "I'm totally getting a glitter unicorn T-shirt for myself this weekend."

"Charlie, watch this!" Amanda flipped the sequins on her shirt with her palm to display a different color.

"What? Awesome. I'm so jealous. Now I *really* want one." Charlie grinned at Erica. "You want your usual?"

"Sure do," Erica said, and dug her wallet from her purse.

Amanda rocked on her tiny feet and touched her double braid. "And a chocolate chip cookie."

"Why aren't you in school? It's after nine," Charlie asked as she scribbled *vanilla steamer: Ms. Amanda* with a balloon and smiley face on one cup and *peppermint mocha* on the other.

"I went to the dentist." Amanda pointed a tiny finger at her teeth. "Mom said if I didn't have any cavities, I could come here for a drink and cookie reward."

"Reward. Bribe. Depends on your definition." Erica patted Amanda on the back.

"Hmmm. No cavities means you get sugar? Suspicious." Charlie recited a silent prayer to the universe that Amanda would realize how lucky she was to have a mom who cared.

"Get any new inventory this week?" Erica eyed the Sugar Mugs community bookshelf.

"Actually... I just finished a Ruth Ware mystery last night." Charlie nodded toward the bookcase. "Second shelf, the one with the blue cover."

"Any good?"

"Do you even have to ask? All her stuff is good." Charlie grinned. "Feel free to take home. When you're done, we'll totally have to compare notes to see who we thought the killer was."

Erica put her wallet back in her purse. "I swear I never see it coming. Every time I'm shocked."

"Me too." Charlie stole a glance at the New Yorker and caught her doing the same. They exchanged a brief smile before Charlie returned her attention back to the other customers and the woman shifted hers back to the bagel.

Amanda and Erica waved goodbye as a petite woman with an impressively high ponytail approached the till.

Charlie grabbed a pen from her apron. "Hey, there. What can I get started for you?"

"Can I get a half-caf, three-pump sugar-free vanilla, one

pump hazelnut, almond milk latte? No dairy. Oh, and lots of foam."

Contradiction order. As a purist, Charlie would never put so many conflicting ingredients in a cup. But she admired her customers' creativity.

"I'm not sure how foamy I can get the almond milk," Charlie said. "For a foamy dairy alternative, you might wanna try oat milk."

The woman stared at her phone and didn't answer.

Charlie swallowed back irritation. *Shake it off. You need the customers.* "Just double-checking. *Full sugar* hazelnut?" She was not about to waste the supplies redoing a six-dollar drink when she had a pile of unpaid bills stuffed under the till.

The woman nodded without looking up.

Ben shot Charlie a cocky grin. Cranky white suburbanites, the *basics*, as Ben called them, were his catnip. She tapped him on the shins with her Doc Martens and gave him *the look* as the milk steamer screeched.

"Order up!" Ben slid the cup in front of High Ponytail.

She yanked off the plastic lid. "I said extra foam."

Grrr. You also said no dairy. Charlie choked on a string of F-bombs.

"My bad," Ben held out his hand and flashed his infamous ultra-white smile. "Let me top that off for you."

Her lips flatlined. "Just put whipped cream on top, and it'll be fine."

A delicious passive-aggressive comment taunted Charlie's tongue. But not even this woman could ruin Charlie's day. An intriguing New Yorker with a killer accent sat at the counter, and more customers visited today than yesterday.

After the dairy/non-dairy woman left, New York muttered, "Some people."

Customer solidarity for the win.

"Hey, do you have Wi-Fi here?" the woman asked. "The spinny blue ball of death shows I have almost zero cell service."

"Yep," Charlie said. "Password #Mack4Ever with the number four instead of the word 'for.'"

The woman froze. "Did you say Mack4Ever? Like M-A-C-K?"

God, that voice. Brooklyn? Maybe Bronx? Whatever it was, the honey sandpaper tone slid into Charlie's ears and traveled down her chest.

Ben looped his arm through hers. "Yep. Ms. Charlie here has an obsession—"

"It's not an obsession." She nudged him with her elbow.

"Okay, a *delusion*... that she and Macklemore are destined to become best friends."

"I like saying manifestation over delusion. It's a much prettier word." She unhinged her arm from his and reached for a coffee cup. "I call him Mack so when we meet in person, I'll already have become accustomed to his nickname, and we can skip all the *getting-to-know-you* formalities."

The woman's deep brown eyes narrowed and she tilted her head.

"You know who Macklemore is, right?" Charlie pointed to a framed photo on the wall from when she was an extra in his video filmed downtown. "You know, 'Thrift Shop,' 'Same Love,' 'Can't Hold Us'? The rapper."

"Yeah, I know who he is." She kept her gaze on her fingers tapping against the coffee cup. "My name's Mack, so it threw me off for a second."

Charlie smacked her hand on the counter. "What? No. Really? No." Did all her manifestations get cross-wired during Mercury retrograde, and the universe brought a beautiful visitor instead of the rapper?

The woman ran her fingers through her hair and grinned.

"My real name's Mackenzie, but the only person who ever used that was my mom when I did something wrong."

Whoa. Charlie could get lost in those dimples.

"Well, huh." Charlie leaned over. A mingling of sea salt and blackberry scent reached her nose, and she *had* to google this heavenly fragrance later. "By default, you'll have to be my runner-up bestie."

"Hey!" Ben called behind the counter.

Charlie rolled her eyes. "Sorry, second runner-up."

"Deal." Mack chuckled.

Charlie indulged in Mack's deep, throaty laugh that should be bucketed and released on a dark day. "As much I'd love to stay and chat, the tables aren't gonna clean themselves."

"And this bagel won't eat itself." Mack's mouth twisted. "That sounded way better in my head."

Charlie giggled and moved back to the storage area. The stepstool squeaked as she stretched to reach the top shelf and slid a few boxes out of the way. A cup of water that had been sitting there for God knows how long knocked over and trickled down her arm. *Really?* She wanted to blame it on Ben, but he was the only reason Sugar Mugs stayed even as tidy as it did.

"Don't hurt yourself," Ben joked as he reached for stevia packets. "You're not always the most graceful ballerina in the world."

"You suck." She flicked him on the arm. "Here, grab this for me." She handed him a box of sanitizer and hopped off the stool.

Where is it, where is it? She lifted stacks of paper and boxes. Opened and closed desk drawers. Finally, tucked underneath some towels, she found her yearly goal notebook. She flipped open to the fifth page and grabbed her pen.

#137 Be a better organizer. You got this!

The landline rang, and she shoved the notebook back under the towels.

Ben grabbed the phone and she snatched it from his hands.

He flung his wrists. "What the—?"

"Sugar Mugs."

"Hi, this is Jared calling from Pacific Northwest Collection and Debt Consolidation—"

"Wrong number." She slammed the phone down and turned her back towards Ben until her pained expression changed. Exhaling, she faced him with a forced grin.

He narrowed his eyes and leaned against the counter. "Been a lot of wrong numbers lately."

She swallowed. "So annoying, right? I must've gotten on some list somewhere."

"Yeah. Some list..." He pushed himself from the counter and reached back for the sugar packets.

When he walked away, she exhaled. She loved him, of course. But she refused to burden him with the mess she'd created. She rubbed her thumbs against her lucky charm and moved back to the floor room.

No way could Ben find out the truth.

FOUR

MACK'S DRINK SPECIAL: VANILLA INSPIRATION
CAKE AND AVOIDANCE AMERICANO

The barista—Charlie—floated in her shop. How do some people converse so effortlessly with others? Social suaveness was an underrated and highly coveted skill. She asked a guy about his corgi, high-fived a little kid, and recited one-liners from movies. She was so fluid and joyful in her movements like she was dancing in a ballroom instead of ringing up orders. Even her fingers had flair when writing on the cups.

Her fingers danced in anticipation... Wait! Mack could use that line. *The sound of laughter bounced against the hallowed walls...* She could use that, too. *The dark red lips hid something, a secret she was willing to die for...* All of these could work. She swiped open the note app on her cell.

Two coffees later, Mack melted into the chair. Everything about Charlie was a beautiful contradiction. The feminine makeup and hair set against the multiple piercings and tattoos. The '90s grunge songs she sang while working in her Renaissance-style dress. The gentle voice escaping from deep red stained lips.

The more Mack observed, the more she thought about her main character, Shelby, in her newest book—a young suburban mom by day, drug runner by night. *Breaking Bad* x *Queen of the South* x *Good Girls*, who used words like *fudgesicle* instead of the f-word but also ordered a hit on a rival. Maybe Shelby could have hidden tattoos, flowy dresses, and a butterfly purse to carry her 9mm.

Mack's thumbs flew across her phone but weren't fast enough. "Hey, do you have a paper and pen by chance?"

"Yeah, one sec." Charlie dug underneath the counter.

Mack shoved her phone in her pocket but picked it back out when it felt too bulky. She crossed her arms but remembered her agent said not to do that because it made her look standoff-ish. She awkwardly stuck her hand in her front pocket and committed to keeping it there while she reached for the over-sized dragonfly pen with her free hand.

In her zone, Mack barely registered when the male barista asked if she wanted another coffee, when her mom called for the third time, or when the shop's volume went from active to quiet with rotating customers. The black ink turned gray and she asked Charlie for another pen.

She flexed her cramped fingers, then handed the pen back to Charlie. "Thanks for this."

"Looks like you're working on something important, huh?"

"Yeah. And I think I found my new spot to work." She gathered her items. "Hey, I didn't catch your name."

Lies. But she wasn't about to tell Charlie that she'd committed her name to memory the second the mother/daughter duo walked in.

"You can call me Charlie, Cherry, or Cookie, but I draw the line at Kitten."

The tiniest tingle in a spot that had been dormant for a few months activated. Maybe not all hope was lost. "No Kitten? Guess there's no point in saying anything at all, then." She held out her hand. "Nice to meet you, Charlie."

Tomorrow she'll think I've come back for coffee.

. . .

After Mack returned to her parents' condo, she stacked a few pillows on her knees and rested her laptop on top of them in a pitiful attempt at a makeshift ergo station. She descended into the hypnotic, hazy world of fiction writing, as her mind over-layed words and images that she translated into her computer. Her fingers pounded against the keyboard until her stiffened legs screamed at her to move. She moved her cursor to the document title, deleted it, and gave her manuscript a new working title—*Charlie*.

Her phone buzzed.

> 🔥: Hey you! Cue up all the stalker vibes. I sent you a few messages. Did they come through? Just wondering if you'd like to catch a drink in the next few weeks? I'll be back in NYC for work and would love to see you!

> Mack: So sorry. I thought we were on the same page

Delete.

> Mack: Hey, sorry, in Seattle. Maybe see you next time I'm back in the city

Delete.

> Mack: I really hope I didn't give you the wrong impression. I genuinely thought

Delete.

Her fingers hovered over the block contact button. This was the fourth message she'd received, and if she had any integrity at all, she'd stop ghosting. Does a two-hour long, sexual yoga session before Mack slipped out of the hotel room constitute a conversation? Blocking felt gross, but they hadn't even exchanged names. Wasn't that a universal sign for no follow-ups required?

The other women these last few years seemed to understand that one night, maybe two, was the max of their relationship. Her books would always come first. Words were her spouse. The other women were distractions.

Ugh. She didn't want to deal with this right now. She dropped her fingers from the block button and silenced her phone instead. The whirlwind of the last thirty-six hours lurked behind her, puckering up to bite her in the ass. She yawned, twisted until she cracked her back, and headed for the kitchen.

Leaning against the counter, she took a moment to appreciate her parents' upgrade. The vaulted ceilings, open floor plan, and hardwood floors was a stark contrast to her childhood dishwasher-less apartment in New York. Even the water tasted better, although having it trickle through a filtered stainless-steel fridge instead of the '70s style faucet may have helped. She swiped a napkin across the counter to clean the drops that fell from her glass when the front door swung open.

"Jesus, it's hot today." Her dad removed his Mariners cap and dragged his forearm across his misted forehead. "You look less salty than what Mom said."

Whatever. "Yeah, must've been the jet lag." He didn't need to know the real reason.

"We're gonna catch the Mariners game tonight." He reached into the fridge and pulled out an IPA. "Want me to see if we can score another ticket?"

"Traitor. You haven't even lived in Seattle a decade and you've turned your back on the Yankees."

"Not true, kid. You know they're my first love. But I'm a sucker for overpriced hotdogs, beer, and ball. No matter who's playing." He picked the beer label with his thumb. "You been here all day?"

"No, I got lost and ended up in a random coffee shop."

"Which one?"

She dug into the candy bowl and popped a chocolate in her mouth. "Uh... I think Sugar Mugs or something?" Of course she knew the name. But she didn't need any invasive questions from her dad, who could sniff information out of her like a bloodhound. Right now, Charlie was a surprising lifeline sent to Mack from some literary god that had taken pity on her. She wasn't going to ruin any inspirational magic by talking about her in any detail.

"Oh yeah? I've been there. Good blackberry scones. Did you try one?" He tore open a cracker box and crumbs littered the counter she'd just wiped down.

"Nah. I just asked Charlie for a bagel."

He wiggled his brows. "Charlie, huh?"

Oops. She popped another chocolate in her mouth and did her best to ignore her father.

"Well, it's good having ya here." He crunched into a cracker. "This move's been tough on your mom. She really thought you'd come with us when we left."

And here it comes.

"You should visit more."

She exhaled. She *did* visit the first few years. A lot if memory served. But her mom getting sick changed everything.

Not wanting to kill her lingering afternoon word-count thrill, she softened her words. "You guys couldn't turn down the opportunity to take over Grandpa's business. And look"—she jutted her arm toward the living room—"look how far you've come. It's pretty freaking amazing."

The condo door flew open before her dad could respond. "Mack."

Tossed keys landed on the counter with a heavy clank and she flinched.

"I called you at least a dozen times today to see if you were alive." Her mother bored her gaze into Mack.

"I know. Sorry. I was super busy, but I texted you." Mack forced calmness into her voice. "You know, I manage just fine every day living in New York. I think I can handle Seattle."

A heavy sigh escaped from her mom's mouth. "I just worry. West coast is different than back home, and you have no idea if—"

"Some pot-smoking, hemp-skirt-wearing grandma is going to jump out of the bushes to force me to eat homemade gluten-free granola with organic dried beets," Mack said. "I know, Mom. I have the same fear."

"You suck, you know that?" Her mom shook her head with a grin.

Mack needed to focus on anything but her parents' faces. She shuffled through the fridge drawers looking for something resembling a snack.

"You're almost done with the book, right?" her mom asked.

"Yep." *Lies.* "Should be done with my first draft by the end of the week." *More lies.*

"When does the movie deal come in?" her dad asked as he slapped his flexed biceps. "I need to up my game at the gym so I can be camera-ready for the premiere."

Mack shut the fridge door with a heavy thud and rolled her eyes. If her dad spent any more time at the gym, he'd need custom-fitted shirts. "I don't even think *I'd* get to go to the premiere. A comped ticket is probably all. Besides, it's never going to happen, so let's forget it." She licked the yogurt lid and scanned the room for a garbage can.

He opened a cabinet under the kitchen island and pointed. "Not true. Look how close you got to a movie deal on your last book. Keep applying yourself, kid. Work hard, and it'll happen."

The bite from the studio passing on adapting her book into a screenplay still stung. With everything that happened these last six months, the very last thing she wanted to do was relive that moment. "Doesn't really work like that. But I appreciate the optimism."

"Optimism? It's fact." His proud smile sucker-punched her. "My daughter. Best-selling author. About to have another bestseller."

If they only knew. Mack struggled to swallow the yogurt that now tasted dry.

Her mom popped bread in the toaster. "Drew, leave her alone. She hasn't even been here a full day yet."

Her dad grabbed her mom by the waist and kissed the top of her head. "Have I told you that your mom is the most beautiful woman in the world?"

Her father. Master deflector. *Thank God.*

"You realize I'm a woman, too, right?" Mack grinned.

"You know what I mean," he said. "Hey, not sure how many days you plan on being here, but you might want to grab some headphones for the night. Or I'll leave a sock on the door handle for fair warning if you're out."

"Andrew!" Her mom pushed at his arm.

Mack shook her head. "You're seriously so disgusting."

"I better shower up. I'm filthy as hell. Here, give me your arm." He grabbed Mack's wrist and pretended to swipe it across his sweaty forehead.

"Eww, no," she squealed like a twelve-year-old, and yanked her arm back. "God, you're gross."

Once her dad left, the silence turned heavy as Mack concentrated on avoiding an awkward conversation. "I really like your new condo," she said after too many moments passed of nothing but breathing.

"I can't believe we've been here for almost a year, and this is the first time you've seen the condo." Her mom's voice was flat as she scraped her forefinger across the crust, clearly more interested in picking at her food than eating it. "Your dad really misses you."

Mack raised an eyebrow. "Just Dad?"

"Oh, stop. You already know I miss you." Her mom exhaled her usual *I'm-done-talking-about-this* breath and scooped Mack in for a hug.

Her mom's body was still a bit frail, but she'd at least bulked up a bit from when Mack visited last year. Her grip was tighter, her signature pink soap and apple shampoo scent had returned.

Thank God.

Three years ago when Mack flew in after the diagnosis—the week chemo started—the smell threw her off. Did cancer actually have an odor? Or had she made it up? A sharp, acidic, maybe even metallic scent evaporated off her mom, and imbedded in Mack's nose for weeks after she'd returned to NYC. Like a pharmacy, plastic facility, and bleach mated.

"I can't wait until your next book releases so I can finish decorating." Her mom waved towards the living room with multiple copies of Mack's book prominently displayed, including a framed cover that hung above the fireplace.

"You know it's tacky to have my book in the guest bathroom, right?"

"I have one in every room. Why would I leave out the bathroom?" She grinned and bit into the corner of the toast. "You're always so secretive about your projects, but I'm dying to know something. Anything."

"Hopefully, it'll do better than the last one."

"Stop that. You were on the *New York Times* bestseller list. New. York. Times. Isn't that like a huge deal in your world?"

Mack scooped the last bit of yogurt onto a spoon. "Yeah, but it wasn't number one."

"What number was it?"

Six. But she didn't want to say it out loud. Because it wasn't number one.

Her mom rinsed off her plate. "Don't most authors dream

about this? I don't understand why you're always so hard on yourself."

She rubbed a thumb into her temple to stave off the slow hum of a headache. "I better get back at it. I need to finish up that final piece."

"You'll have plenty of quiet time when Dad and I are at the game tonight. Good luck with it."

"Come on, Ma. Who needs luck when you've got this?" She tapped her head with a forced cocky grin and left. Once she shut the bedroom door, she leaned against the wall to center herself. She hated lying to her mom about her book. *Hated. It.*

She slid the patio door open and slumped on the wicker furniture. Her shaky thumbs scrolled through her contacts. Viviane's name on the screen felt like a noose. She exhaled and tapped call.

"So you *are* alive."

"Sorry, Viv. I know, I know." She shielded her eyes with her hand against the late afternoon sun. "I would've called earlier, but..."

"Listen. You need bouts of silence to get into your creative zone. I get it. I've worked with plenty of authors that do random stuff," Viviane said with a hint of annoyance. "I even had one that wrote in the nude. Couldn't stand any distractions, including clothes."

"Oh God, it's Dylan, isn't it?"

"I'll never say." Her voice softened just enough for Mack's guilt to thicken. "Point is, I really do understand. But you *have* to communicate. You should've given me—at minimum—a partial first draft a week ago. A little more time, fine. But going dark like this, it's not good. Leaves me squirrely. Leaves the editor squirrely. And if the director knew, he'd be super squirrely."

"Are you saying no one wants to be a squirrel?"

"Mack."

For someone who made their living on the English language, Mack could formulate exactly zero letters to relay the message that she was *horribly, desperately, achingly, dreadfully...* at a complete standstill.

"Look, I don't want to spook you, but I had a call with the CEO last week and he was asking about your progress. I told him everything was on target, but is that the truth? We're closing in on six months and I haven't seen a single line."

Heat burned Mack's stomach. She opened her dry mouth to speak but snapped shut her lips. She knew the deadline—Viviane didn't need to tell her. Every second of every day she saw the minutes deplete and her timeline shrink. And she knew *exactly* what would happen if she broke her contract and couldn't finish the book in the next two months—including paying back the advance she already spent. "The manuscript's, ah... not flowing as well as I'd hoped."

"What exactly do you mean, not flowing?"

She plucked at her jeans. "My focus is not up to par, and the words are, I guess, tripping over themselves and—"

"Are you saying you have writer's block?"

The heat of the sun matched her shame. She stood and turned her back to the horizon when her dad walked across the living room.

He pointed a V at his eyes and then hers, and mouthed, *I'm watching you*, with a dirty grin.

She flipped him off with a smirk.

"You should've come to me. We could brainstorm, talk to other authors, review the outline again, role-play, massages, therapy, whatever. Writer's block is not uncommon, but you have to tell me." A heavy exhale sounded through the receiver. "Don't worry about it, though. We got this. What's your word count?"

She coughed and put the phone down until the spasms stopped. "Fifteen K."

"Did you say *fifteen*? Like fifteen thousand?"

"Yeah."

Another long, uncomfortable silence followed, and she could almost hear mirrored thoughts running through her agent's head: contracts, deadlines, publishers, editors, money, negotiation.

"But! I wrote eight thousand of those today." *Thanks to gorgeous red hair and an easy laugh.* She burrowed the tip of her toe into the wood railing. "I'm on to something. I started feeling better this morning. The trip out here, the new scenery, is helping."

"In this business, you're not going to get this type of chance on a third book if we screw this one up."

Trust me, I know.

"You're brilliant, talented, and a helluva storyteller. But you'll have to keep proving your worth. *I* know your worth. *You* know your worth. But they... they'll need reminders."

She shoved the phone under her chin to shut down the tiny trembles that threatened to increase.

"So whatever gave you that spark today," Viviane continued, "you seize on to that like it's a lifeboat saving you from a sinking *Titanic*. Got it?"

Failure was not an option. Going back to temp jobs or waiting tables was not an option. Living outside of her fantasy world, detaining stories in her head when they were painfully demanding to escape, was not an option. Mack had to do this. She *would* do this. Viviane had spent four years dedicated to Mack's success. Her parents sacrificed *everything*. She refused to disappoint them.

"Whatever I have to do," Mack said, "I'll do it."

FIVE

CHARLIE'S DRINK SPECIAL: SUGARLESS SELF-DOUBT SMOOTHIE

Charlie scoured the supply inventory audit against the wrinkled bill for the third time. The numbers *couldn't* be right. Sure, she'd been a little scattered lately, but this? She slid her finger across the paper and reviewed again, one by one. She obviously made a big, fat, rookie mistake and just needed to calm down.

A box cutter landed next to her with a loud, metallic clank, and she nearly smacked her head into the counter. "Dude! Really?"

"Sorry. I thought you heard me behind you." He reached behind her for a marker. "Is there something in the air? Between you and Remi, I don't know which one of you has been the crankiest lately."

Ben's roommate, Remi, had her salty moments, but she'd just gone through a terrible breakup and was working out her wounds in her own way. "Give Remi a break. She's had a tough go lately." Charlie slammed a box into the corner with her foot.

Ben's eyebrows bunched. "What's wrong?"

Everything. "Nothing." She repeatedly clicked her pen.

Ben yanked it from her hands and tossed it in a container. "Go trim your bush."

"Really?" She was *not* feeling his jokes today.

He pulled out her bonsai-tree pruning shears from the drawer under the till and stuffed it in her palm. "You're stressed. Go trim your weird-ass bush."

Oh. "Fine. But not 'cause I'm stressed." The yellowing tree in the corner begging for mercy caught her eye. "It's because it looks sad and neglected. Like your soul."

He grinned and pushed her towards the windowsill.

The coziest spot in the shop—the lime-green sitting chair with the throne back—was perfect for the activity. She picked the tree from the bookshelf and sat down. The gratifying crunch from snipping branches liberated the strain from her body. After several minutes her breathing slowed. "The paper-napkin supplier increased their costs by twenty-five percent this month."

Ben hoisted the recycling bin from the covered container. "Did they send you an email or anything?"

Maybe?

The dead leaves fell to the table as she pictured her over-flowing drawer stuffed with unopened bills, the multiple unanswered emails from the remodelers, and the declined phone calls from unknown numbers.

Probably.

When her aunt Rosie left Charlie her house in her will, Charlie had ached to recreate the love that Rosie had vacated and began her mission to convert the main living area into a coffee shop. But the countless hours spent researching business permits, food handler licenses, insurance, and building accessibility—on top of exploring the best coffee beans and local bakeries—was clearly not enough. The names of remodelers, lenders, and business loan officers blended like a rancid cocktail and slammed against her skull.

"I gotta go back and check," she finally said, and swept the trimmings into her hand.

Next month she'd catch up on the stifling paperwork when she hired another staff to focus more on management. Or maybe the following month, so she could save a little longer on labor costs. Or maybe never, because her house would be repo'd by then, she'd be on the street with nothing but her favorite pink dinosaur slippers and yellow duck robe, and none of this mattered anyway.

Her phone rattled against the counter. She raced from the nook and knocked over a cup of pens reaching for it. They scattered across the desk and fell onto the floor with a clatter. *Breathe.*

The name flashed across the screen and her neck pulled tight. "Hey, Pops."

"Well, what do you say, there, princess?" Her father's characteristically chipper voice boomed through the receiver. "Did ya have a good birthday?"

She mouthed, *Five minutes,* to Ben and transferred the phone to her other ear. Conversations with her father could go one of two ways: laughter or tears. Potential customers didn't need to be scared off with tears. She stepped out the back door and angled her face towards the sun. "Yep. Ben took me for Puerto Rican food at his aunt's place and I took myself for a manicure."

"Quarter-century old. Who woulda thunk that? Sure does make me feel like an old man."

Her shoulders deflated. "I turned twenty-seven. Not twenty-five."

"I'm just pullin' your leg. I know how old ya are."

A long silence followed. She pictured her father scratching the scruff on his face with a smoke dangling between his teeth. Probably sitting on a busted-up recliner somewhere, flipping through basic cable TV with a bowl of generic chips on his stomach, wiping his greasy fingers across his T-shirt every few bites.

"You taking care of yourself?" Digging her knuckle into her temple, she attempted to stave off what would undoubtedly become a gnarly headache by the end of the call. "Haven't seen you for a while."

"Sure, sure. Ya know me, always doing this or that. Takin' a break from work right now. I told that no-good manager to shove it last week. I ain't putting up with him no more."

Same words, different day. Did he ever realize that all their conversations were on repeat? A sad soundtrack of someone doing him wrong. His ex-wife, his ex-girlfriends, his ex-bosses. He never realized he was the constant in the equation, and she'd long ago given up trying to convince him otherwise. "Did you find another job?"

"Just takin' it easy for the time but got something lined up."

Her mouth drew into a flat line. Like on autopilot, she knew exactly where this conversation was headed.

"Say there, kid, I think I'm gonna have to stop by soon."

I knew it.

"Ya know, just to make sure you're stayin' outta trouble."

His visits were never about her well-being.

"You up for seeing your old man?"

No. "Of course, Pops. Anytime. You know where to find me."

Her heart sunk into her stomach. She stuffed the phone back in her pocket and returned to the shop. For so many years, her father had been a flashy, shiny object that was *just barely* out of reach. If she were more accommodating, if she were quieter, if she were *better*, that shiny present might be attainable. Even though she forgave her father years ago for his addiction, it didn't always lessen her frustration with him.

She pinched the bridge of her nose, wishing *so hard* that Rosie was here. Rosie always knew what to do. Like the time when a whispering chorus of *that poor girl* floated around her as her dirty, stumbling, apologetic father was escorted out from her eighth-grade choir concert by her classmate's dad. When Charlie flew into Rosie's house that night and bawled into her musty sunflower couch pillows, her aunt tugged Charlie to her feet and told her to get in the car.

Nuthin' that a makeover and hot chocolate can't fix, Rosie had said, clutching her Marlboro Red between her dragon-long, neon pink fingernails, her frizzy blond perm bouncing as they drove to the salon. *Just remember, Charlie-girl. The longer the nails, the bigger the hair, the closer to God. We'll get all glammed up, and you'll forget all about today.*

Charlie never forgot. But she loved Rosie for trying.

"Back bar's stocked," Ben called out. "Let's get a drink."

She wandered to the front of the shop to water her overgrown plants, push in the plush rust-orange chairs, and ignore the knots in her belly that it was only 11:15 a.m. and they hadn't had a customer for almost an hour.

"You glad the semester's finally over?" She released her heavy bun from the ponytail holder and massaged her scalp.

He lined up two shot glasses for espresso. "You have no idea. I'm doing a full-on hot boy summer this year before things gets serious."

"Unlike other summers?" She rewrapped the ponytail holder tightly around her hair. "Do you think you get so much action 'cause you're pan and poly, or 'cause you're so damn cute?"

"I'd like to think it is because of my charming personality and incredible abs." He tapped the ground beans against the knock box. "I still can't believe I graduate next semester."

Her eyes dropped to the cup he handed her, and she ignored him tapping the side of his mug to hers. The rising aroma of warm, fresh brewed grounds didn't make it any easier for her to choke back a sip.

The glass clanked against the counter when Ben set it down. He reached for her shoulders and lowered his face to meet her eyes. "Hey, you know I'm never gonna leave you, right?"

She nodded.

"I'm obviously not going to work here when I get my job at the hospital. But I'm never leaving *you*."

She both loved and hated that he knew she had to hear this.

Wrapping her arm around him for a side-hug, she breathed in the smell of coffee beans and his spring-meadow soap. "Yeah, I know, Peaches. Just not going to be the same without your wiry ass hanging around, getting all up in my business on the daily." She forced a grin. "Where else am I gonna find a hot, twenty-six-year-old, fresh-faced dude who likes dirty jokes and fuzzy slippers?"

He kicked out his slim, muscular leg and rotated it like a display. "These are Uggs."

"It's June."

He snorted. "And my ass is more bubble than wiry, thank you very much."

She grabbed the clipboard to review the audit list again when the front door rang. A hipster strolled in looking like a human mullet. Business suit pants, a meticulous man bun, and exactly one-quarter rolled sleeves showing just enough of appropriated tribal tattoos to let people know that underneath his perfectly conditioned beard, he was a *really cool* guy. If this guy was with a group, he'd be the best tipper of the day. Flying solo, she was almost guaranteed nothing.

"Hey, there. What can I get for you?"

"Tall macchiato," he said. "Less foam the better. I don't like head."

Ben leaned into her ear. "Said no man ever."

She pinched his arm, thankful the man had on AirPods, and felt an odd satisfaction in her expert observational skills when he marked $0 for the tip.

Several respectable drinks later, she rotated the bakery

items when the bell jingled. Mack stood in the doorway with her subtle-yet-edgy energy, short, inky-black hair, and rocking *the hell* out of skinny jeans and a white T-shirt. *Oof.* Charlie's mood lifted from zero to ten.

"New York. Welcome back." Charlie gravitated towards her like a magnet with a hum vibrating in her lower belly. "What can I get started for you?"

"Tall drip." Mack dug into her back pocket for her wallet, stretching the fabric of her shirt against her chest.

Stop looking. Rude. Charlie forced her focus to the ticketing screen.

"And apparently, I'm supposed to try your blackberry scones."

"Yeah?" The idea that people talked about her coffee shop gave her the mist of hope needed to lessen her drought of despair. "Is there some Yelp review I should know about?"

"My dad's been here before and said they were amazing." Sitting at the same spot at the bar as yesterday, Mack threw her bag across the chair and pulled out a laptop.

"Ah." Charlie scribbled the order on the cup. "Good to know I've impressed Papa New York."

Charlie put Mack's order in front of Ben, who had a hint of a lifted eyebrow, and she fought the urge to poke him. Ben would get none of her attention right now. All her attention was on this mysterious out-of-towner with the curious smile and haunting doe eyes.

Mack captivated her. Quiet, yet engaged. Fidgeted a lot. Seemed to observe, maybe even study, her surroundings with the way her eyes moved deliberately across the room. Had a New York ruggedness to her when she spoke, firm and direct, but the tone tiptoed on hesitation.

"How's Seattle treating you so far?" Charlie's throat turned thick, and she had to clear it.

"It's pretty here." Mack swiveled her chair to look outside. "Like someone plopped a city in the middle of a forest."

"Agreed. And the air feels different than other places. Anytime I leave the city, I miss the smell of ferns and weed in the air."

Mack laughed. "There *is* a distinct smell of marijuana in the air. And patchouli oil. Swear to God it's being pumped through the vents in the lobby of my parents' condo."

"Patchouli. Gross. I hate that smell. Pretty sure half the city bathes in it."

Ben approached from the side. "Tall drip and blackberry scone." He glanced at Charlie through his peripherals and whispered, "Meow."

She glared and shook her head, grateful he said it low enough that Mack probably didn't notice.

Mack took a small bite over the plate and dusted off her fingertips. The bell chimed and Charlie's attention diverted to an arriving customer. Just her luck—hardly any customers all day and the moment Cutie McCuterton popped in, the place starts hopping.

What was it about this woman that was so intriguing, anyway? Mack was stunning, yes. Had a killer jawline and sexy-as-hell, apple-plump cheekbones. Dark-as-night eyes that Charlie could get lost in. But it was more than that. Maybe living in the perpetual Seattle Freeze, as the locals called it, where people in the city really didn't talk to one another, this was a refreshing, easy flow of conversation. Maybe she missed having a woman to bond with, commiserating over cramps and talking about burning down the patriarchy while choosing the perfect shade of MAC lipstick. Maybe she was lonelier for a partner than she'd ever admit to anyone, including herself.

All she knew was that she'd never gone to bed thinking about a particular customer.

Before this one.

SIX

MACK'S DRINK SPECIAL: GETTING TO KNOW YOU GREEN TEA

The barstools at Sugar Mugs perfectly cradled Mack's ass, so much that she sat still for over an hour until her lower back nudged her to move. Watching Charlie interact with customers superseded any need for physical comfort. Mack peeked up from her keyboard while dictating everything—the flow of Charlie's corset-backed dress that hugged every curve like it was painted on her, the gentle smile with the cutest gap in the middle of her front two teeth, the tug on her lip during a customer downtime, the sweep of her long, beautiful neck.

Jesus, I'm not writing a romance novel.

A pinch in her lower back burned, and Mack dug her fist into her hip to release the pressure. She may not be writing romance, but all these observations creatively moved *something*. And right now, she'd take creative movement of any kind.

Birkenstocks slapped the hardwood floors, and a man wearing board shorts and a canary yellow polo shirt strode to the till.

"Hey there, what can I get started for you?" Charlie smiled at the customer.

"A buttered croissant and cappuccino with no milk."

Charlie cocked her head. "Did you want a milk substitute?"

"No, just a regular cappuccino with no milk." His thumbs tapped across his phone screen without looking up.

Mack hid her smile. Even she knew a cappuccino was literally espresso and steamed milk.

"So, you want a shot of espresso?"

The man lowered his phone. "No. I want a cappuccino with no milk. The drink's very popular in Italy."

"Gotcha." Charlie's brilliant smile returned, and she scribbled the order on a cup.

"Ben." Charlie set the cup down on the counter behind her. "Cappuccino no milk."

"So you want—"

"Yep, cappuccino no milk."

The two communicated between themselves with the tiniest raised eyebrows when Ben moved to the espresso machine. The water hissing through the coffee grounds infiltrated the otherwise quiet café.

Charlie glanced at Mack with the slightest smirk, and something about being included in the cool kids' club with their silent communication warmed her insides. This guy reeked of dickweedness. How did Charlie keep her placid demeanor? If they swapped positions, no way would he be on the receiving end of any smiles.

Oh! Smile variations for Shelby. Might be a good detail. Mack returned to her keyboard.

The ghost of my father settles in my ear. "Shelby, baby, your smile holds the strength of a million men. Use it." No doubt he's smiling in hell right now that I'm working one of his tricks.

So, sure. I'll flash a grin, show my dimples, even throw in a little lip lick for good measure. I don't care how many teeth I need to display. I'm not leaving here until they can guarantee me a kilo by Friday.

Three pages written later, Mack interlaced her fingers and

stretched her arms, catching Charlie's eye. "What did you end up making Mr. Cappuccino-With-No-Milk?"

Charlie tossed her head over her shoulder at Ben as she wiped dried milk flakes from the machine. "Ben, did you get Salty Britches an Americano?"

"Salty Britches one or two?"

"Two." Charlie leaned in Mack's direction. "We rank our naughty customers each day."

A faint scent of rose and vanilla drifted off her, and Mack dug into the chair to keep from leaping forward. "Ah. Good to know if I hear you refer to me as a number."

Ben stuffed the towel in his apron and sipped from his straw. "Yeah, an Americano."

Ben was intriguing and a great character study: a beautiful man with stellar dimples and a white smile who reminded her just a touch of a much shorter, much younger Ricky Martin. He had an easy laugh and deep sexual energy that even Mack picked up on. But Ben would have to wait. All focus was on observing Charlie.

"Does that happen a lot? These interesting customers?" Mack asked, fishing for a story she could use as a springboard. The publishing walls closed around her, and the conversation with Viviane yesterday expedited the panic.

The barstool squeaked across the floor as Charlie dragged it from under the till. She sat down and fluffed her bright mint dress—a hideous color that no human should've looked good in, but, somehow, she pulled off. "I'm seriously so grateful for ninety-nine percent of the customers. But some are... more unforgettable than others." She looked at Ben. "Remember at Red Lava Café when that guy clipped his toenails in the lobby?"

"I almost caught shrapnel and freaked out." Ben joined Charlie, who scooted over so half his butt could rest on the stool.

An unforeseen pang of jealousy ran through Mack. No one existed in her life who she had this level of obvious closeness with, and no amount of hot-yet-soulless one-night stands made up for that lack of intimacy. She was the school kid whose words formed quickly in her head but not on her tongue. She'd avoided most adolescent interactions, eating in the library instead of the cafeteria and burying her nose in a book during recess. As an adult, no matter how tight she and Viviane were, it wasn't *touching-butt-cheeks* close.

"You guys worked at a different café together?" Mack asked.

Charlie peered over her cup at Ben. "Yep, we've been working together since we were what, sixteen?"

"Fifteen if you count the summer we mowed lawns."

"Damn. Lawncare was really good money," Charlie said. "If this coffee shop ownership doesn't take off, I should open a landscaping company. Why did we quit that, anyway?"

"Because you hate spiders."

"Oh yeah..."

Fear of spiders. Mack should've used that in her outline. Not spiders, per se, but *something*. Building Shelby and the other characters outlines took a full week: wants, goals, obstacles, and fears. But the fears were sweeping themes, like failure and disrespect. Maybe she should add something small, like mice or bees or clowns. She typed *spider* into her open document.

Mack rested her fingers on her lap. "You two have known each other a long time, huh?"

"Since we were in junior high," Ben said.

The ice clanked against the side of the plastic as Charlie shook the cream to the bottom. "But our relationship has steadily declined since senior year when we were both up for the president of the Queer Club, and Ben refused to admit defeat."

"It was a tie, *Charles*." Ben rolled his eyes. "Why should I have given up that spot?"

"A tie? How'd you settle it?" Mack's eyes flickered between the two of them, chewing on the delicious confirmation that Charlie was queer.

"We decided on a co-presidentship." Ben twirled the straw in his cup. "Which I'm still ticked about because if Ethan had been there on voting day, he said he would've voted for me."

Charlie abandoned her drink and grabbed a paper towel and sanitizing spray. "He told me the same, *Bernard*. Next year's our ten-year reunion. We're having him settle this once and for all."

If it weren't illegal, Mack would record this conversation and listen to it later for tidbits. The inflections of their voices. The tightened facial expressions mixed with relaxed postures and jovial, amplified energy. Everything about their interaction was gold.

She could pull this into her thriller—hone in on her main character feeling like she has a superpower by watching micro-expressions. She opened the note section of her document:

He thinks he's clever, doesn't he? With his smug little smirk and his stupidly shiny shoes. I'm oddly fixated on his blinding gold watch that he probably thinks makes him look like *a real player* (his term, not mine) but, in reality, accentuates his skinny wrists. I swallow the over-whelming urge to point this fact out to him.

But he doesn't realize that I've studied him like a dissertation these last two years. He clicked his fingernails against his cuff links twice and his ears raised when I mentioned the shipment date. He's nervous. And now I'm in the lead.

Dammit. No more words came out. She sat back and tapped her fingers under her seat. She needed more. "Of all the years in this business, what's the craziest experience you've had?"

Charlie stopped mid-spray and looked at Ben when they simultaneously said, "Browniegate."

"Browniegate?"

Charlie set the spray bottle on the counter. "So, this guy comes in and tells us he's gonna propose to his girlfriend and hands me his cell phone to record. Then he orders a brownie and stuffs the ring in the middle, which I thought was a terrible idea—"

"*We* thought it was a terrible idea," Ben interjected.

"Okay, *we* thought it was bad. But what can you say? He was so excited, and it was super sweet." Charlie moved closer, her voice speeding up. "The plan was that Ben would deliver the brownie, and I'd stand in the corner filming. So Ben saunters over, and without any hesitation, this woman takes a huge bite, and her boyfriend leaps out of the metal chair, which flies into another chair, knocking it over, and it was so loud when it banged on the ground. He starts yelling at her—"

"And I'm standing there in shock while this girl starts coughing all over the place, and brownie chunks are flying everywhere—"

"And I drop the phone, and the screen shatters, and now her boyfriend gets behind her and is smacking her on the back, and I'm screaming at him that he'll make it worse—"

"And Charlie stomps in like a badass and gives her the Heimlich, and nothing's happening. Charlie's literally lifting this girl off her feet until *bam*—"

"Brownie chunks *and* the ring fly out of her mouth and hit Ben right in the face—"

Mack laughed as her eyes ping-ponged between the two of them.

"I was so pissed," Ben continued. "I started yelling—"

"*Screeching*, Ben, not yelling. Like a cat stuck in a dryer. And while he's slapping the heck out of his face to get the brownie chunks off, he accidentally kicks the ring. The guy ditches his girlfriend to tackle the ring, and Superman-slides across the floor on his belly."

Ben let out a deep, throaty chuckle. "Such a disaster."

The burn in Mack's core from laughing so hard spread to her chest, and she relished the rare moment as Charlie and Ben caught their animated breaths.

"And that... is the story of Browniegate." Charlie grabbed the wadded-up paper towel from the counter and rehung the spray bottle. "Ben's getting his Master's in nursing, but he can't handle bodily fluids."

A devilish grin flashed across Ben's face. "Some bodily fluids I don't mind."

"Benjamin!" Charlie smacked him on the shoulder. "Dirty boy. Not in front of the customers."

The two of them resumed their restocking and lightness seeped into Mack. God, it felt good to laugh. Since her book launch, deadlines and expectations clouded every day. Charlie and Ben were the type of people she needed in her life—ones that helped her forget she was buried in a coffin of indecisions and self-doubt.

Her fingers hovered over her keyboard while Charlie stuffed cardboard cup holders into a container. "It'd be so fun to work at a job with your best friend and laugh all day. Even when I worked in an office, I never had this type of camaraderie."

Charlie's arm strained to reach the lids tucked in the corner. "What is it that you do?"

Mack swallowed. She wanted to be the one asking questions, researching this woman's fluid movements and effortless sexiness. Not answer personal questions. She shoved her hand under her seat to stop herself from scratching her suddenly itchy skin. "I'm, ah, a writer."

"Oh yeah?" Charlie's face lit up. "Anything I would've heard of?"

No matter how many books she sold, conferences attended, or podcast interviews given, the imposter syndrome demon hovered like a shadowy figure. "Um... maybe?" She put the back of her palm up to her mouth to conceal a cough. "I only have one book. A thriller."

"Really? Thriller is my favorite genre."

Those eyes.

"Mine, too." *Duh.*

Charlie dug a box from the cabinet. "What's the title?"

Mack had her fair share of bad reviews. Some gut harder than others. Some she brushed off because people are jerks. But it'd make this entire interaction awkward as hell if Charlie read the book and hated it. "*The Edge of the Shadow.*" Fire spread up her neck.

Charlie stopped stuffing straws into the holder. "No."

What did *that* mean? "Yeah."

"No effing way." Charlie marched to the bookshelf and plucked out a book. "You're 'M. Ryder'?"

Mack nodded hesitantly, forgetting the word one used to confirm a suspicion was correct.

Charlie flipped to the back jacket cover and held it up, looking between Mack and the author's photo. "I can't believe this. I *loved* this book. Ben! Come here!"

Mack was still irritated that Viviane convinced her to wear a blazer for that headshot. But soon, a tingle spread in her chest. She'd heard people say they loved the book before. During interviews, the host always started by saying how much they loved the book. People at writers' conferences and book signings told her how much they loved the book. Her family screamed from their rooftop, *literally*, how much they loved the book. But something about Charlie saying this with her silky tone sounding all genuine and warm was almost too much. Mack wanted to hear it one more time while hiding under the chair.

"What?" Ben entered from the back room and shoved the box in his hands to the corner.

Charlie smacked the back of her hand on the book. "Mack wrote this!"

Every last one of Mack's words escaped. *Yeah, that's me* or *Sure did!* seemed like odd responses. Her face flushed and she gulped lukewarm coffee.

Ben grabbed the book from Charlie's hands and his eyes narrowed on the jacket cover. "Wait, is this the one you said I had to read this summer? The one about the small-time criminal who sells goods on the black market?"

"Yep!" Charlie bounced. "But she only does it because her sister was kidnapped. And there's a robbery that goes wrong, someone gets killed, and even though she didn't do it, they blame it on her, and she goes on the run. And that plot twist. Holy damn, I did *not* see that coming. Effing. Brilliant."

Mack's insides flamed from the praise.

Ben handed the book back to Charlie. "Charlie's not just blowin' smoke. She genuinely didn't shut up about this book."

"Well, thanks." Mack reached under her shirt to fan it away from her body before it stuck. "It was fun to write."

Charlie cradled the book against her beautifully ample chest. "Okay, I gotta know. Are you in Seattle writing a new novel?"

Trying, not writing, was the more accurate word. "Yeah."

Charlie's eyes grew wide. "Ooh... can you give any hints?"

Mack looked behind her shoulder at the empty café and curled her index finger in the "come here" motion. "You know that phrase 'I'd tell you, but I'd have to kill you'?"

Charlie nodded and gripped the book tighter.

"Well, that doesn't work in this case because it's publishing and no one's gonna die." Mack grinned and leaned back. "But I'd have a super pissed agent and probably be sued by my publisher if I said anything."

"Dammit! I was *this close.*" Charlie shuffled her fingers in her pen holder container, the utensils clanging against one another until she snatched one and held it out. "Autograph?"

"Are you serious?" Mack thought her tone was joking, but Charlie's smile vanished. "I mean, of course. Yeah. I just..." *Always feel like an undeserving fraud.* "I never have anything clever to say. Ironic, isn't it? Words are my best friend and worst tormentor."

Charlie's smile returned. "I get it. Don't stress over it. Just put down the first thing that pops into your head."

Her head was currently a vacant black cosmos. The plastic pen clicked against Mack's silver index ring as she rolled it between her hands. She hooked her finger in the neckline of her T-shirt to pull it away from her neck.

"How about something like this," Charlie said. "'Dear Charlie, even though we've only known each other a few days, you are by far the best barista I've ever met, you have fabulous hair, and it's painfully obvious that you are smarter, funnier, and cuter than Ben.'"

"Rude," Ben yelled from the storage room.

Mack opened the book. "I think I have all the inspiration I need."

Charlie,

Thanks for the Seattle caffeinated dreams, evergreen smiles, and anti-patchouli oil bonding. It's been a latte fun (see what I did there?) ;-)

Mack Ryder

She slid the book back across the counter.

Charlie bit her lip as she scanned the page. A blush swept across her cheeks, and she looked at Mack. "It's perfect." She returned the book to the shelf, and her finger lingered on the spine.

Mack swiveled in her chair to avoid staring and analyzed why she felt like she had intruded on a daydream. She *had* to concentrate. Sure, her creative energy spiked these last two days, *thank God*, but she cusped on disappointing every person she cared about and producing a heaping pile of garbage. The countdown clock's pedal to the ominous deadline was accelerated to the max.

Her fingers tapped across the keyboard as she laser-focused to capture the flying brownie chunk story, hoping for a nugget she could pluck for her manuscript. Her mind got lost in the hallucinogenic writing world for the next half hour until the bell jingled, and a postal worker walked in.

"Eddie!" Ben yelled.

Charlie scurried from the back room right when Ben reached for the mail. She seized it from his hands with a possessive yank and tucked it tight under her arm. The kindness in her smile was a sharp juxtaposition to her flushed face and rigid backbone.

Hmmm.

A mysterious envelope. That could be added to her story. And maybe a short scene of the interaction with the postal carrier and kidnapper. Maybe the postal carrier could be an unwitting participant in delivering a message.

Mack glanced back up at Ben's worry line that cut across his forehead. Clearly, the envelopes contained something unpleasant. Whatever it was, it was none of her damn business. She returned to the keyboard flushed with the adrenaline of drafting a fresh scene.

SEVEN

CHARLIE'S DRINK SPECIAL: NAKED CAPPUCCINO WITH FAIRY DUST SPRINKLES

Charlie's eyes glazed over the bills scattered across her desk. *Final Notice, third time trying,* and *sending to collections* screamed at her. All the financial planning articles she'd devoured over the past two years in preparation for opening Sugar Mugs battled one another for space in her head. Pay off the lowest bill first. Pay off the one with the highest interest first. Consolidate. Move money. Invest in your business.

God, she missed Rosie. After running a successful insurance company out of her home for forty years, Rosie knew everything about small businesses. It would've taken Rosie exactly ten minutes to look through the bills and give Charlie solid gold advice.

She misted the air with the lavender calming spray she kept in her desk drawer for a temporary reprieve. After paying each company a little bit, hoping to buy time before the creditors confiscated everything not bolted down, she closed her laptop and exhaled.

Let it go. She refused to allow the impending threat of her life crumbling around her take away from glitter, naked bike riders, and funnel cake.

In the bathroom she wiggled into her rainbow fairy wings for the Solstice Parade. After an extra dash of cheek glitter and heavy eyeliner, she confirmed in the mirror her look was complete. She turned sideways to avoid crushing her massive wings against the narrow door frame and headed for the café.

Ben's freakishly loud, high-pitched sex whistle cut against the empty shop. "Aren't you just a bucket of fabulousness? You look like Tinker Bell's sexy lesbian older sister."

Charlie twirled and held out the side of her dress for a curtsy. "I'd dress like this every day if I could."

"I actually believe you."

"You have everything you need, right?" She sifted through her silver crossbody for her flaming magenta lipstick. "I turned my cell to max volume. Promise you'll call if things go sideways."

"Seriously? Go. I got this. Lena's coming in about ten minutes." He grabbed a dark chocolate muffin and peeled the paper back. "She told me yesterday she'd wanted more hours."

"She told me the same." Ben's younger cousin was on the docket if Charlie ever had the means to hire. But for now, Lena would have to settle for Saturday morning shifts only.

"Everyone's gonna be at the parade anyway. A break's good for you. Working seven days a week isn't healthy. Pretty soon, you're gonna get all cranky and stressed and do something stupid like think bangs would work with your face frame and curly hair."

"You're such an ass." She threw a straw at him. "For the record, I like being here. Besides, I have limited time with you and want to squeeze every last drop." She pinched his face like a baby.

"I smell bullcrap."

It wasn't *all* lies. Her lifelong quest for a sense of family was like trying to capture steam in a mug. The small community she built with her regulars helped fill that void, and she woke up more grateful every morning than the previous day.

Besides, if she didn't keep working daily to pay bills, the contractor was gonna rip out her flooring.

"Does it feel weird going to Solstice without..."

He didn't need to say who.

She focused on her bright orange nails, not the dull ache that, for the second time in a decade, she'd be flying solo at the parade. "Nah, it'll be fine."

"Do you think you'll run into her?"

"According to her latest post, she's in Prague right now."

Ben stopped mid-bite and lowered his sugary breakfast. "You haven't unfollowed her yet?"

She shrugged. "Why? It's not like we hate each other."

Bad blood didn't exist between Jess and her, other than she'd been proven right that she shouldn't trust anyone besides Ben. Everyone else in her life disappointed her on a macro level. Her mom, whom she hadn't seen in twenty years. Her dad, who looked her up every few months and asked her to spot him a fifty. Jess, who fell into another woman's bed the moment Charlie suggested they think about a family.

"Real talk for a second, 'kay?" Ben set the muffin on a napkin.

Nooooo. Talking about feelings with Ben was as pleasant as a steam burn. "Okay."

"Should you try dating again? Even just casually?"

"Swiping through an app like I'm looking for a puppy sounds terrible."

She'd been with precisely two women in her life, one of them being a rebound right after her divorce. A blurred memory of frantic hands, a quick and dirty orgasm, and sobbing afterward while the nameless brunette awkwardly patted her on the back before reaching for her shoes and calling an Uber.

"I don't feel like I'm missing out on anything by not being in a relationship." The shoulder strap of her fairy wing loosed, and she tugged on it to tighten. "Isn't there a bumper sticker that says *Solitude equals safety* or something like that?"

"Guaranteed that bumper sticker doesn't exist."

"Whatever. Besides, I got you."

Ben tore the muffin wrapping into scraps and tossed it in the trash. "You should just get laid, then. You're so fricking tense all the time."

She cringed. "No way could I do casual sex. I'd probably propose right after we banged."

"You're such a hopeless romantic."

Hopeless romantic? The inability to have casual sex had nothing to do with romance, and everything to do with *finally* discovering the beauty in healthy boundaries. When she and Jess were together, Charlie had an obsessive need to take care of her wife. She could see now that it was an attempt to bury her own feelings, and the darkness that hovered anytime she was alone. Nearly a year passed after their divorce before Charlie understood how deeply toxic her codependency was with Jess. If she slept with someone, who knows if that compulsion would return.

Her clunky platform sandals—totally impractical for a parade but darn cute with her gold-and-silver-sequined minidress—clicked across the hardwood floor. She took a bottle from the water cooler and zipped it in her purse. "You're right, though, about me being in a funk. Running this place takes more than I thought, and all the paperwork and stuff stresses me out."

Ben whipped up his head. "You good?"

"Nothing I need to worry about right now." Her phone buzzed with an unknown number. She clicked it off. "Hey, if Mack stops by, you could mention the parade." She attached a purple-and-jade sparkly butterfly clip to the side of her hair and hoped Ben didn't notice the slight shake in her voice. Only two weeks had passed since she first met Mack, but she had gotten weirdly used to having her at the shop, typing away at the laptop.

"Mack, huh? Ooh… does someone have a crush?"

"What? No. I just, you know, she's new in town." She had the distinct urge to smear chocolate frosting across his cocky smirk. "I don't have a crush."

Okay, fine. Maybe a tiny one.

The packed metro bus dropped Charlie at the corner, and she walked two blocks to the parade. Mini-doughnuts, perfumed bodies, and marijuana blended in the air, and she stopped to take two full, delicious breaths before moving on. She shielded her eyes against the sunbeams ricocheting off the metallic floats shooting multi-colored rays like fireworks.

Laughter, bells, and the methodical heartbeat of the drums infused the air as she navigated through swarms of people and searched for an open spot where she could appreciate the Mardi-Gras-plus-nudist-colony-style parade.

"Oops, sorry," said a purple-haired woman who bumped into her as the throbbing of drums amplified.

Stretching on her tiptoes, she hoped to get a better look at the body-paint-covered naked bike riders. Fern leaves, strawberries, and cherries strategically covered breasts. Angel wings swept across bare backs. A Pokémon covered, well, everything.

"Charlie?"

Charlie's head snapped so fast that she almost slapped her cheek against her fairy wing. She blinked multiple times as her heart thudded in her ears. "Mack?" *No way! She's actually here?* "Hey!"

They both opened their arms for a hug, but Charlie flash hesitated since they'd never touched. Mack's face seemed to register the same thought because she stopped and stumbled, but now Charlie committed to not making this any more awkward and dove in sideways to not poke Mack's eye out with a wing. A beautiful combination of crisp sea salt and blackberries wafted from Mack's neck, and Charlie turned to Jell-O at Mack's firm embrace.

Mack released. "Look at you, all festive and sparkly. Pretty sure I've never seen this outfit on you before."

"This old thing?" Charlie tossed her hands up and twirled. "I wear it the first Sunday of every month."

A group of G-string-clad folks with masquerade-ball masks and rattling tambourines passed them with several people bumping into both Mack and Charlie. A small scowl inched across Mack's face and she squeezed her arm tight against her side. "Who's running the shop?"

"Ben and a part-time employee." Charlie fanned her face and cursed herself for not bringing a sunhat. "I've come here every year since I was a kid. No way was I giving this up for mocha-seeking urbanites."

"I get that. Lot of people, though, right?" Mack scanned the crowd. "Might even be more colorful than New York City's pride parade."

Pride parade.

"Mack!" A broad-shouldered, taut-chested, perfectly five-o'clock-shadowed man trotted towards her with a wide grin.

Mack gave off a queer vibe, but maybe Charlie's gaydar was faulty. Didn't matter, though. Mack was a fun little crush, nothing more. Charlie's healed heart had no desire for a fresh crack.

"Sorry, the bathroom lines were outta control." The man tugged his baseball hat a little lower. "Who knows what sort of shady shit was going down in there. *Shady. Shit.* Get it?"

Mack nudged the man with a groan. "Charlie, this is my mortifyingly embarrassing dad, Andrew. Dad, meet Charlie."

Her *dad?*

He grinned. "From the coffee shop?"

Holy cannoli, she talks about me.

Pink blushed Mack's cheeks. "Yeah."

"Nice to meet you, Charlie." He held out his hand and shook hers with a firm, warm grip. "Sounds like you've been keeping my baby girl company lately."

Mack rolled her eyes. "Seriously, I'm twenty-six."

He bent down to eye level with his daughter. "Look at how cute you get when you're annoyed."

Charlie stifled a giggle at the death glare Mack threw her dad.

"Hey, you girls thirsty? I'll grab us some bubble tea." He bumped Mack with his elbow without waiting for a response and walked away, ripping off the third-party comfort blanket.

"Sorry about him." Mack pushed her sunglasses higher on her nose as the crowd chattering around them morphed into white noise. "Everything about him is a little extra."

Charlie's gaze followed Mack's father as he weaved through the crowd. "That's your dad? Like your actual dad?" *Good looks clearly run in the family.*

"Yeah."

"He looks like George Clooney. *In his prime.*" Charlie switched her attention back to Mack, admiring the sun's glow on her skin and briefly wondering how soft it was.

"No chance I'm ever telling him that." Mack laughed and put her hand on Charlie's forearm before whipping it back.

But not before a trail of goose bumps flew up Charlie's arm.

"It'll go straight to his head."

"He legit looks like he's thirty."

"He turned forty-two this year. But every year, his maturity level rapidly declines."

"Whoa. Forty-two? So, he was like sixteen when you were born?" Charlie nibbled on this crumb of insight and wanted more. "I can't imagine having a kid so young. All that responsibility. I'm a half-assed plant mom at best."

"Same. Couldn't have been easy juggling parenthood and junior prom. But they did all right." A side smile grew on Mack's face. "Kept me fed, watered, and fully annoyed."

Teenage parents. Charlie had so many questions but asking about family dynamics while body-painted nudists circled them didn't feel right. Sugar Mugs was her turf, full of necessary distractions if a conversation turned too personal. Questions about the ex-wife? Tables needed wiping. How does it feel to be a child of an alcoholic? Coffee beans needed opening. Why are superficial conversations safer than talking with a friend? Cups needed restocking. Without the cover of the shop, there was no deflection guarantee.

Mack, who'd been so quick with questions last week, scratched the top of her arm and gazed into the crowd, silent. Her lips twitched into a short smile when she caught Charlie's eyes, then refocused her gaze on the ground. Until a lime-green-painted seventy-something-year-old man—wearing nothing but a frog cock sock and a smile—waved at them. Then turned and bent over to look at handmade jewelry.

Bent. Over.

"Oh my God," Charlie whispered, and gripped Mack's arm.

Both their eyes grew wide, and Mack smacked her hand over her mouth.

Charlie looped her arm through Mack's to remove her from the eye carnage. When they were a safe distance, they busted out laughing.

"I will never be able to unsee that." Mack swiped a laughter tear from under her eye. "I mean, all the power to him, but... *ewwww.*"

"You do you, boo. That's my motto. But that's for sure gonna turn into a core memory." Charlie pointed to a shaded black park bench. "After that, I gotta sit down."

They zigzagged through the thumping throngs of parade-goers and past the vendors to their spot. Charlie sat carefully on the bench to avoid crushing her fairy wings.

Mack laid her arm across the back of the bench, removed it, and pinched the tips of her fingers. "I've never seen anything like this parade." Mack wiggled in her seat. "The naked bike riders, though..."

"Right? Do you wonder what their bike seat looks like when they stand? I feel like all of them would leave a puddle of sweaty paint on it and walk around like one of those red butt monkeys I see on the Discovery Channel."

"I'm dying. I just can't." Mack chuckled and pulled her hands out from under her. Shifting on the bench like she had zaps of energy poking at her, she finally turned her body. Their thighs met and Mack's sporadic movements quieted.

Charlie froze to elongate the touch. The tingles spreading up her leg were probably more intense than they should be after only knowing someone a short while. It felt good—a little *too* good. She shifted her body to break the contact.

After several minutes of admiring various stormtroopers, Harley Quinn, and Deadpool body art, she leaned toward Mack. "I bet your dad's happy you're here. He probably misses you."

"Yeah, both he and my mom are. I miss New York, though, and I've only been here two weeks."

"Oh yeah? What do you miss the most?"

Mack plucked at her jeans. "Hmmm. My bed. My own space. The bagel vendor two blocks from my apartment."

"Rude." Charlie's playful voice masked her heart dropping.

"Wait!" Mack smacked her palms on her thighs. "Your bagels are a close second."

The competition bagel wasn't what made Charlie's heart drop. It wasn't like she didn't know that... *this*... was temporary. This level of negative reaction upon being reminded that a *customer* was in town on a visit shouldn't creep up and choke-hold her the way it did. She slid away from Mack, needing to create some physical distance to offset her wavering emotions.

Mack's dad crossed back towards them, keeping his eyes on the drink carrier, even when a spectacular, curvy brunette passed him with pasties, a neon orange handkerchief-turned-skirt, and a luscious smile.

"Here ya go." He handed them each their bubble tea, and they clicked their plastic cups in cheers. The refreshing blast of cold, sugary, creamed tea was a welcome reprieve from the summer heat.

"Good job keeping your eyes to yourself," Mack said to her dad while chewing on a tapioca ball.

"Your mom has the same outfit at home and wears it better."

Mack scrunched her nose. "How is it that I'm constantly both proud and disgusted with you?"

He tipped the rim of his hat with a smile.

Soon, they each pointed out their favorite costumes as a smolder of jealousy simmered in Charlie over Mack and her dad's obvious close connection. The only positive memories Charlie could conjure up of her father were a few random pancake mornings and a crabbing trip to Ocean Shores.

When a man in flamingo-pink paint and a yellow tutu passed them, Mack's dad nudged Mack with his arm. "Remember when Mom and I bought you that ballerina outfit for dance class when you were a kid?"

"Hmm. Maybe? Was I like five or six?"

"Charlie, you should've seen it." He leaned forward to catch Charlie's eyes. "Mack *refused* to wear it. Christ, those temper tantrums. Kicking at the floor. Screaming. Swear to God, I thought we were gonna get evicted. But after her mom bribed Mack with an obscene amount of candy, she finally put it on."

His smile was broad and contagious, and Charlie indulged in every nuance of his voice as he continued.

"So she storms out of the room with her little pink leotard thingy, and this huge, girly tutu, but she's wearing my mud-crusted work boots. And she. Is. *Pissed*."

He hopped up and stomped with an exaggerated growl, imitating a grumpy young Mack, his hands balled into fists as he swung his arms like he was wading through mud. "So me and my wife are all, *you're so cute, Mack. Do you love it? It's so pretty.* Then we asked her what's wrong. And she slams her hands on her hips and yells, *I. Hate. Pink!*"

The bench vibrated when he plopped back down and Charlie giggled.

Mack laughed. "You're so embarrassing."

"God, that's a great story," Charlie said, scratching the side of her neck where the wings tickled her. Along with it, she felt the all-too-familiar sensation of family relationships being a spectator sport. What would it be like to have a reliable parent? Just one to share stupid old stories about making forts in the living room or trying on your mom's old dresses and heels.

"Oh... look at that outfit." Mack wiggled her finger at a Black Widow costume. "I mean, Scarlett Johansson..."

"Right?" Charlie nodded in approval, her grin returning. "Iconic."

Mack stabbed at the ice cubes with her straw and took a final sip. "The tea was so good. There isn't a boba place near my apartment in Manhattan, so I never get one."

"But apparently, there's world-class bagels," Charlie cracked.

"Hey!"

Being with Mack shouldn't feel this good. She should leave but wanted to stay. Mack had a pull, something undefinable. An intoxicating mixture of fun and scary, and as much as Charlie wanted it to stop, she wanted it to continue.

Mack's dad slurped the last remnants of sweetness and stood. "Well, I'm gonna make like a baby and head out."

"Worst joke of all time," Mack groaned.

"I know." He clapped his hands together. "This'll give you girls the chance to walk around without me screwin' up your vibe."

"Oh, no. You don't have to do that." Charlie immediately regretted overstaying her welcome. She did not set out today to encroach on their family time. "You're probably having some great father-daughter quality time and didn't expect a chatty barista to hijack your conversation."

"Nah. I'll start getting on her nerves soon enough." He flicked his wrist to check his watch, then turned to Mack. "You good?"

"I'm good if Charlie is. Are you?" Mack's hopeful eyes directed towards Charlie.

Alone time with Mack? Outside of the coffee shop? Charlie nodded hesitantly.

"Yeah, thanks, Dad. I'll see you tonight."

Tonight? Charlie exhaled through her nose. *I can do this... I think.*

EIGHT

MACK'S DRINK SPECIAL: SUGAR-CRUSTED
BEGINNINGS BREVE

"We need to readjust our ranking, right? She's definitely the new number one." Mack flicked sugar remnants off her hand and held the bag of mini doughnuts in her palm for Charlie as they strolled through the Solstice Parade crowd.

"The Wonder Woman one?" Charlie popped the doughnut in her mouth and licked her index finger.

Mack tore her eyes away from the unintended sensual motion and stepped behind Charlie as a woman with unicorn pasties and denim overalls headed directly towards them on roller skates. "Yeah. That body paint was so detailed. I couldn't sit for that long. What do they do when they have to go to the bathroom?"

"I'll give you free coffee next week if you ask that woman over there." Charlie pointed to a woman covered head to toe in *Avatar* blue.

"Nope. No chance. I love my safe little mental place where I interact with as few humans as possible." Mack laughed when Charlie fake frowned. "Except you. You've been a beautiful distraction."

Oops. She hadn't meant to come on so heavily.

A few hours ago, she begrudgingly agreed to go to the parade with her whiny dad after he threatened to sing Lady Gaga while they were at Target. Festivals were noisy, crowded, and a cesspool of germs. But they were also a human-behavior science lab—perfect for character study. She didn't think she'd run into Charlie. Looking *freaking beautiful.* Like a human bag of Skittles with her rainbow fairy wings and sparkly dress that hugged every voluptuous curve, *just daring* people not to stare.

She needed to change her thought track to something neutral and nonsexual. She wouldn't typically hook up with women like Charlie—someone so sweet, kind, and generous with her smiles. Even if the thought crossed Mack's mind more than once, she wasn't going to screw up this opportunity.

Mack knew she had the intimacy intelligence of a pineapple. Sex would ruin their conversations. And she *needed* those conversations. Charlie was a golden muse. After spending every day the last two weeks at the coffee shop, she wrote nearly twenty thousand words. *In two flipping weeks.* No way would she give that up. No matter how enticing Charlie was.

"Do your parents live around here?" Mack twisted the cap to her water bottle and washed down the powdered sugar.

Charlie crinkled the doughnut bag and tossed it into the trash. "Not sure. Haven't spoken to my mom since I was a kid. And last I heard, my dad lives in the city."

Hmmm. Charlie rattled off that statement with the same emotion as if she recited what she ate for breakfast that morning. She didn't know where her parents lived? And hadn't spoken to her mom since she was a kid? As much as Mack's mom smothered her, she talked to her weekly.

"Wow, I'm sorry," Mack said quietly. "I didn't mean to touch on something so personal."

Charlie grinned and jutted her chin toward a wood jewelry

vendor. "It's just facts about where they live. Doesn't bother me at all to talk about their potential location."

Interesting.

The women searched through the various jewelry bins as hollow wooden wind chimes reverberated through the canopy. Mack's fingertips glided across the smooth bangle, and she slipped her hand through it. "So, Ben's your family?"

Charlie held up an oversized hoop earning to her ear and angled her face towards a mirror. "Yep. He's my person."

"What drew you to each other?"

"Probably equally terrible upbringings. We bonded over mochas and misery."

The level of disassociation in Charlie's voice, combined with the words she used, was a fascinating juxtaposition. Mack took out her phone and texted herself:

> disassociation and voice.

She stuffed the cell back in her pocket before Charlie could notice.

Mack followed Charlie as they left that booth in search of other vendors. She tiptoed closer to Charlie and leaned in more than once to discreetly inhale the hint of lavender that wafted off her.

"How did your parents end up in Seattle from New York?" Charlie asked.

"I was actually born here in Seattle. We lived with my grandparents until my parents turned eighteen." Mack shook her arm to soothe her twitching forearm muscle, an annoying but common nervous tic, then shoved it in her pocket to calm the spasms. "I asked my dad once why we didn't stay in Seattle. He basically said my grandpa was furious when he got my mom pregnant. So, as soon as he could, he packed us up. Thought there'd be more opportunities in New York."

"God, that'd be tough. Can you imagine being a teenager and moving your family across the country?" Charlie tugged Mack into the next booth to look at handcrafted, leather-bound journals with burned inscriptions and various pens. She traced her fingertips across the edge of a journal and glanced at Mack. "I want to admire your dad for sticking it out but also hate giving men credit for what women do all the time."

A beautiful, hand-painted ballpoint pen caught Mack's attention and she held it to the light. "So true."

"What do they do for a living? Seems like a hard place to try to 'make it' with a young family."

"Agreed. I think he wanted to get away from my grandpa 'cause he's kind of a dick. In New York, my dad was a maintenance person for an apartment building." Mack ran her palm over a velvety, leather-bound book and sniffed the binding. "The apartment was in a decent neighborhood. He worked in exchange for a two-bedroom apartment for us. And my mom was a waitress."

Charlie softly clanked an antique bell. "Maybe that's not a bad gig, getting free rent for your family. Why'd they come back?"

"My grandpa retired from his construction company and asked if my dad wanted to take it over. So that's what they do now. Dad's the muscle and Mom works on the contracts."

Charlie nodded but remained silent, her eyebrows furrowed as they moved a few spots to accessories. She dug through a cedar box filled with multi-colored agates and rolled one in her fingers. Her mouth opened and closed until she finally said, "I'm so curious about what it was like to be raised by teenagers."

Mack wasn't sure if it was a question or statement, almost as if Charlie kept it respectfully open-ended. No one had asked Mack that before. Raised by teenagers meant cereal for dinner. Her parents swinging right alongside her in the park. Game nights. Brutally loud screaming matches with her mom. Being old enough to remember her mom earning her GED at twenty-five.

"Honestly, I didn't know any different. When I got a little older, and other kids pointed out how young they looked or mistook them for my siblings, it got a little weird, I guess?" Mack stopped to swipe through a rack of silk scarves, tugging on the fabric to make them all hang evenly. "And they were so overprotective, especially when I went through a super rebellious phase when I was thirteen. It was like they took all the hopes and dreams they had for themselves and drowned me in it. And I had this... burden, I guess, to live up to these unattainable expectations. I think they worried I'd make the same mistake as them. Not that they'd call me a mistake, but you know what I mean."

Good God. Overshare much?

"I totally know what you mean." Charlie set the rock back down. "A fine balance between suffocating and overprotectiveness, right? I'm sure they tried their best."

"My parents have good intentions but can be so damn misguided. They always pushed me to hyper-hustle. My mom would say stuff like 'apply yourself more,' 'work harder,' and 'if you'd only tap into your potential.' I try not to let it get to me, but... it still stings sometimes."

Outside the tent, a welcomed breeze with perfumed oils and funnel cake whooshed around them. Mack twisted her body to avoid smacking into bystanders, thinking back to a time when a therapist mentioned that her parents had covered her in a pressure cooker blanket her entire life and she'd need some serious deprogramming to believe she was sufficient.

"My dad's kind of funny," Mack continued. "He used to put the fear of God into me about boys. When I came out at fourteen, he slapped his palm on his chest and said, 'Oh, thank God

67

my lectures worked!' Like he actually took credit for me being queer."

Charlie's chest lifted. "I love that. Everyone's coming-out story should include excited parents." She bit the side of her lip with a deep grin. "I thought you might have been part of the Rainbow Mafia, but I didn't want to assume."

"You mean my haircut didn't give it away?" Mack chuckled and brushed her hand against her undercut.

Mack never opened up like this, always preferring to be the bystander in conversations, observing from a quiet, dark spot away from the spotlight of discussion. But Charlie had this nonjudgmental aura about her, like Mack could say anything from she slept with the neighbor's wife to she has fifty cats and feeds them with baby bottles, and Charlie would give her a comforting nod and make her feel like it was the most natural thing in the world.

As the golden-hued afternoon faded into a fuchsia evening, Mack inched closer to Charlie and shared more than intended as a rush flowed through her from releasing tidbits of her past. As they turned the block to the food-vendor area, someone bumped into them and sent Charlie crashing into Mack.

"You good?" Mack gripped Charlie on her waist to keep her steady.

A smile flashed across Charlie's face, and a light spilled around her like a halo. A human firefly. *God, she's beautiful.*

"Yep. I'm good." She tugged on the bottom of her dress. "Tell me again why I thought platform heels were a good idea on a sidewalk full of naked intoxicated people?"

"I do love your typical hiking boots," Mack said with a grin. "But not sure it would've worked with the sequins."

The air turned dense with a smoky trail of fried onions and pork, and Mack swiveled to find the scent's origin.

"Seattle dogs! Have you ever had one?" Charlie pressed her hand into Mack's wrist.

The heated imprint made Mack's arm liquify. "A Seattle dog? What's the difference between regular hotdogs?"

"Only everything." Charlie rolled her eyes to the sky. "Seattle hotdogs are like heaven in your mouth. Hungry? My treat."

Hungry, no. The boba tea was as heavy as a meal. But hell if Mack would let this moment go, feeding off Charlie's enthusiasm as she explained how slathering cream cheese on the bun was the key to hotdog happiness, and a healthy portion of seasoned onions took the place of any other condiment.

"If you really want to class it up, some people put fried peppers on it," Charlie continued. "But I'm a traditionalist, so I stick with just the onions and cream cheese."

The meaty sizzle of searing hotdogs mixed with the low hum of crowd chatter surrounded them as they stood in line. Mack should pay more attention, listen to conversations, and observe through all senses what she was seeing, hearing, and smelling. Anything could spark an idea. But right now, all focus was on Charlie.

An oniony vapor rose when Charlie handed Mack the foil-wrapped dog and she sunk her teeth into the warm, salty food. "This has gotta be the best hotdog I've ever had."

"Right?" Charlie's bright voice matched her beaming face. She took another bite and held the hotdog away from her chest like she was worried the juice would fall on her. "All right, settle this once and for all. New York versus Seattle. Who has the best coffee and hotdogs?"

Even if Mack thought New York had better options, she'd never say it and risk removing Charlie's smile. "I'm for sure gonna lose my street cred, but Seattle wins. Especially the coffee."

A ridiculously cute blush swept Charlie's cheeks.

An unmistakable pull tugged Mack toward Charlie, but she had to knock this off. *Now.* Charlie popped with an energetic buzz Mack wanted to bottle up and aerosol spray around her. She had an innocence to her, like she danced ethereally in a technicolored world and blissfully ignored the boogie-man hiding under the bed. Refreshing and powerful, and Mack wanted to plug into that energy source. But Mack needed to high-wire walk that fine line. The more emotionally invested she became in Charlie, the more likely she'd lose her muse. Inspiration for her was always from afar. Too close and personal and the magic would disappear.

A potential scene erupted in her mind of Shelby taking her fairy-princess-clad daughter to a festival when she notices a local rival drug runner at the same festival with their child. Maybe a look could pass between them and a slow acknowledgment that, for the moment, they were just parents and not competitors. Mack's brain entered the fuzzy space of reality and dream, and she had to leave immediately and write this down before her mind lost the visual.

"Hey, I've gotta take off." Mack crumpled the foil and tossed it in the garbage. "Promised my mom we'd go downtown for dinner tonight." Making up an excuse felt gross, but she didn't want to dive into the mechanics of her creative space and how when inspiration hit, she needed to stop whatever she was doing, or the words would vanish.

"Totally get it."

Charlie's bright smile didn't fade, but the sparkle in her eyes that Mack loved so much dimmed briefly.

Charlie wiped her mouth with a napkin. "Thanks for letting me tag along this afternoon. It was great seeing you outside of the shop."

Normally, Mack would ask for her number after spending an afternoon together. Or, if it were someone else, take them home for a fun, yet empty, one-night stand so she could satisfy her needs and refocus on her manuscript. But this felt different.

Even though Mack wanted to do all these things, she also *didn't* want to, and her brain tripped over itself.

Leave.

Mack stood and put her arms out for a hug, drawing in the lavender-sage scent and swallowing the strong desire to grip those beautiful curves against her. "See you tomorrow?"

"Your drip and bagel will be waiting."

NINE

MACK'S DRINK SPECIAL: PRODDING PARENTS
PISTACHIO LATTE

Before the sun ascended, Mack's eyes flew open as images from yesterday's parade swirled like a neon kaleidoscope. She fished her laptop from her bag and dove into her fictional world. The keyboard popped like gratifying gunfire as the words burst out of her onto the page.

She'd fleshed out the backstory in the outline, but Charlie said something yesterday that Mack needed to record: *bonded over mocha and misery*. A decent line she could add to Shelby's thought process. *Bonded over coke, misery, and counterfeit cash*. She jotted this down in her note section and returned to the manuscript.

Her phone rattling against the counter barely drew her attention, but she glanced anyway.

> Mia: hey! Long time, huh? Saw on Insta that you're in Seattle.

> Mia: I'm visiting there next weekend from Vancouver. Wondering if you're up for drinks? Or coffee? Or...? ;-)

Crap. Mack really thought she was safe with this one. They met in a different country, for God's sake, when she spoke at a conference in Canada last fall. Viviane needed to stop telling the social media team Mack's location.

And Mack really needed to stop giving out her number to people.

She silenced her phone and returned to the manuscript.

Two hours later, a thunderous rap on the door caused her wrist to bang on the computer. "Yeah?"

An arm poked through the crack, holding up an *I Love NYC* mug. "Coffee?"

"Dear God, yes, please." Mack tossed her laptop to the side. "I've been up since five."

"Don't you ever sleep in?" Her mom shuffled towards her and handed over the mug.

Mack gripped the warmth between both palms. "Sometimes. But when inspiration hits, you gotta jump on that."

"Inspiration, huh? Oh... goodie. Tell me everything."

Mack pushed away her budding irritation and sipped. Coffee, fine. Conversation, not fine. She was powering through her word count and didn't want to stop for a chat. Besides, her mother knew her rules: No talking about the manuscript while in progress.

Her mom sipped from a mug. "Would this creative spark have anything to do with that smokin' hot redhead your dad met yesterday?"

Mack snapped her gaze at her mom. "It's really weird he'd say that. Did he use those words?"

Heavy booted footsteps stopped outside of the door. "Say what?" Her father poked his head into the room. "What did I do this time?"

Mack narrowed her eyes. "Did you call Charlie a smoking hot redhead?"

"No. She's the same age as my daughter. That'd be gross."

He nuzzled his head on her mom's shoulder. "But I might've said that you were candy-eyeing a cute redhead and ditched me for her."

"I did not ditch you! You left me."

"You're welcome." He smacked her mom on the butt before leaving the room.

Not like Mack actively thought about it, but her parents' obvious attraction after all these years was impressive. She'd been drawn to lots of women. Probably too many. If she burrowed deep enough to analyze her behaviors, she was most likely attempting to counterbalance her awkward, celibate high school phase by making it up for it now with soulless, yet efficient, one-night stands. But having sex with someone she loved? A whole new level of intrigue.

"So, this Charlie girl. Tell me about her."

She avoided her mother's probing gaze and scraped her thumbnail against the mug's logo. "I don't know her all that well."

Both true and untrue. Mack cracked up over Charlie's obnoxious customer stories and her refusal to relinquish her three-year-old Monopoly championship title by agreeing to a rematch with Ben. She gave Mack touching snippets about her favorite retired customers and told her about a rainforest up north where the earth spoke to her. But Charlie retold events with very few personal details sprinkled in. No talk about a family. No talk about friends. And the one time Mack fished for a tiny bit of information about her love life, saying, "The dating scene is brutal in New York. How about here?" Charlie made an excuse about needing to clean the storage room.

"Is that where you've been spending all your time?" Her mom's lopsided grin was one of her tells. She wanted intel. No way was she getting it.

Charlie was a magical entity. An auburn-haired, emerald-eyed genie who Mack needed to protect in her literary bottle.

Right now, Charlie's spirit was the only thing keeping Mack afloat. If she talked about her, she'd ruin the powers. "I wouldn't say *all* my time."

Mack's mom's lips drew into a straight line.

Oh no. Her mom's supersonic listening skills clearly heard the shift in Mack's tone.

"Are you in some kind of trouble?"

Yes.

But her mom didn't need to know that. Mack *had* to protect her mom this time.

When her parents called her three years ago and said, "Breast cancer," Mack transformed into hyper-research mode. She scoured article after article for medical treatments, naturopathy, a Shaman, miracles... literally anything that could help her mom.

But article after article focused on the cause. Genetics. Hormones. Environment. *Stress.*

Bingo.

Mack conjured up every occurrence of her terrible adolescent behavior. Holing up in libraries or coffee shops and ignoring everyone—including her frantic parents—for hours because she needed quiet like she needed air. Talking back. Sneaking out at night, solo, to see how the city slept. Screaming matches.

The fights gave Mack comfort. Because her mom loved Mack the hardest and challenged her the most, she was Mack's easiest target. She was Mack's *safest* target. And Mack couldn't bear to think of a world that didn't contain her.

Then her dad called her for help with decoding insurance and hospital bills. Her dad was the builder, not the contracts person, and there was just. So. Much. Paper. He tried to make sense of it all, and he tried to call different places, but things didn't add up. How did they owe *that much?* he had said. He had crap self-employed insurance, he knew, but he *did* have insurance.

Mack looked. After months and months of not doing jack for her mom, the opportunity arose. And the decision was easy.

"Mack. Are you in some kind of trouble?" her mother repeated.

"I'm *fine*."

Narrowed eyes zeroed in on Mack. The equivalent of an MMA fighter who shoved in their mouth guard, ready for the battle. "No. You're not."

Jesus. The tone slashed Mack's good mood. "Don't do this, Mom, please. Not now."

"Do what?"

Mack refused to respond. Right now, she didn't have her knuckles taped up. Her shoes were unlaced. And her coach vanished.

"Do. What. Mack?" Her mom's tiny frame turned rigid. "You're clearly holding something in. You're *always* holding something in. You don't visit, you stopped FaceTiming, and you give crappy one-word answers. I'm trying to pry any detail I can out of you to feel some actual connection. So tell me, what do you not want me to do?"

The words sputtered out, the verbal engine that was either going to roar or crash, and right now, Mack couldn't deal with either. What did her mom want to hear? That Mack was a selfish jerk who had abandoned her mom during her time of need after her mother sacrificed her entire life for her? That being around her vibrant, full-of-life, strong mom as she lost her hair at the same rate as her weight crushed her creative juices, and she chose to stay away and edit her first manuscript while her mom battled for her life? That when her mom got her double mastectomy, Mack didn't know where to look because her mom's body was a shell of what it used to be, and Mack going on submission and signing contracts was more important than holding her hand through reconstructive surgery?

So, no. Mack had nothing to say.

"I'm sorry, Ma. I'm just up against a deadline, you know. And I want to make sure I deliver." She forced a smile that she was sure her mom knew was fake, but her mom's jawline went lax a moment later.

Intermission. Thank God.

"So. Cute redhead, huh? When are you going to stop being single and actually settle down?"

Her mother. The master of the emotional grenade drop.

"I've never once heard you talk about anyone." Her mom blissfully ignored Mack's silence. "I'd like to think you're not wasting your prime years trapped in that tiny apartment by yourself."

Mack eased the empty cup to the edge of the nightstand and dangled her feet over the side of the bed. "I date all the time." Not *exactly* a lie. Dinner, conversation, and dessert in the bedroom. Maybe a few text messages so she didn't seem like a total asshole, and slowly fade into the background with one-word, delayed responses.

Her mother raised her eyebrows.

"After this manuscript is done, maybe I'll think about it." *Probably not.* Mack was not totally opposed to love, but she preferred the companionship of her words over human interaction. A disconnect occurred with anything three-dimensional, and she couldn't envision a nondigital future consisting of real-time dialogue and touch.

"You said that after your last one. And then said after the book tour was done. And now you're saying after this one."

"Jesus Christ, Mom. Really?"

How could Mack possibly focus on another human when she couldn't even focus on strengthening her current verb game? Or properly finishing a chapter. A partner would never understand her addiction to bury herself in a creative mental black hole for hours, maybe days, ignoring everything in the world, including them. They'd think she was a selfish jerk. *Because she was.* Look at how she treated her mom because she was uncomfortable, and preferred avoidance over confrontation. The relationship would be slaughtered before its inception.

"Sorry, sorry." Her mother patted her knee. "It's okay, honey. I just want you to be happy."

"I *am* happy." The words snapped like a whip as Mack recognized but failed to break the irrational irritation. She slid off the bed with a raging pulse and thudded to the closet. She shuffled each hanger three inches apart and flattened the fabric of the shirts between her forearms, so no shirt touched another. Soon, her heartbeat slowed.

Her mom didn't understand the suffocating pressure. She couldn't fathom the spotlight lurking behind the corner, begging to amplify her failures and expose her nightmare.

Her vibrating phone rattled against the side table.

"You have to get that?" her mom asked.

Mack sent it to voicemail. "No, it's Viv. I'll call her back."

Her mom moved to the window and cracked it open, the ambient sounds of the city street below piggybacking on the pine tree-scented air. Deliberate, short sips were taken from her mug. Her stiffened backbone was evident through her thin robe. "Mackey. We need to chat." Her mom faced her and set her mug down with a thud. "You're not happy. Something's going on with you."

Her mom had zero self-awareness that she should soften her body and tone when she made a loaded statement. Not stand there with straight lips, crossed arms, and Superwoman-style laser beams shooting from her eyeballs.

No way would Mack divulge what was really happening.

She would never put that kind of pressure on her mom, who'd for sure internalize everything and flail to fix it.

Under no circumstances could her mom know that a two-ton boulder had pressed down on Mack the second her first book sold one hundred thousand copies, and how each additional sale layered on a new brick. That demons whispered behind her that if she'd worked harder, she actually would've sold half a million. That having exactly zero to show for her dream advance, the one Viviane left maternity leave to secure, made her want to vomit. And every inspired minute on the screen was followed by five minutes of zoning out while words muddied in front of her.

"I'm good. Promise."

Her mother's cocked eyebrow verified she wouldn't drop the conversation.

"I'm feeling a little pressure to perform, you know? That's all. But it's under control."

Why did her mom need to stand there like that, all silent and glarey? Each expelled breath from her five-foot frame was like a critical, judgmental flame.

"It's not like senior year with how I acted with finals and college apps, and everything. I just need to get out of my head. And I need you to get out of this room so I can shower." Mack swooshed her mom to the door, who remained firm and unmoving.

"Mack."

"Get off my ass! Seriously."

Her mom didn't even flinch at Mack's icy tone.

Mack bit her tongue. "Please, Mom. I just need space."

Her mom's shoulders fell. Gripping the doorknob, she stared at Mack. "The pressure you put on yourself isn't good. You've got a lot to be proud of. Don't lose sight of that."

Mack swallowed as her mom shut the door. Maybe she'd tell her mom everything one day and brace herself for an hour-long, drawn-out spiel spiked with contradictory phrases like "just believe in yourself" and "why don't you try harder?"

Viviane's name flashing on her buzzing phone sent a sharp poke up her chest. She ripped a shirt off the hanger and stormed to the bathroom.

TEN

CHARLIE'S DRINK SPECIAL: CLOUDY COLD BREW WITH ONE PUMP FEAR SYRUP

Every time the shop bell jingled, Charlie's stomach dipped when it wasn't Mack. Four nights ago at the parade, when Charlie chickened out from asking Mack for her number, she sulked like a grumpy toddler for the evening. Maybe it was for the best, anyway. Charlie had as much game as a gangly eighth grader and would probably end up a blabbering mess if she succeeded in scoring her digits.

To divert her attention from sipping on the Mack lust latte last night, Charlie spent a stupid amount of time googling marketing plans. She read a gazillion articles about "building brand loyalty," "expanding your customer base," and "defining your target audience." By the end of the night, nothing made sense except that she had to hire a social media manager, website designer, and a freaking magenta unicorn to persuade people to buy some damn iced lattes.

So, she did what any other responsible adult business owner would do when they were a few short months away from bank-ruptcy. She shut off her phone, cuddled up with a bag of grape gummy bears, and rewatched two seasons of *Schitt's Creek*.

She hoisted the Kona coffee bean bag above her head to

refill the holding container. A few beans escaped and scattered across the wood floor. The echo wailed in the bare shop without a single person to absorb the sound. She lowered the bag and exhaled through her nose. She sent Ben home an hour ago after the shop had one visitor since noon.

One. Single. Customer.

At this point, she couldn't even afford to pay her damn self. She dragged herself to the storage room to grab lids when the bell jingled and she dashed to the front of the shop.

Mack sauntered in her with signature skinny jeans, white shirt, and that perfectly dimpled smile. And Charlie's heart flipped.

Be cool, be cool.

"Hey, you." Mack clutched the strap of her backpack and slid it off her arm. "Had to stop in before you close."

"I was thinking about you earlier and wondering if you'd come by."

"Thinking of me, huh? Have we moved to that level in our relationship?" Mack's tone was airy, but Charlie froze.

It's like she can read my face.

"Ha. No. Well, yes. I guess…" The coffee drink stopper in Charlie's hand became her new best friend as she focused on bowing it between her fingers. "I was gonna check if you were still emotionally damaged by the grandpa with the strategically placed amphibian sock from Saturday."

"Thanks for that. The memory started fading, but now it is front and center."

Charlie giggled and tossed the plastic in the recycling. "You want your usual?"

"Actually, a decaf." Mack's lips shifted to a disappointed side grin. "I know, I know. Caffeinated enthusiasts everywhere are shedding a tear into their double lattes. But I've had a crap-tastic couple nights' sleep and need to do everything possible to stay asleep tonight."

"Oh yeah? Got visions of purple pasties dancing in your head?" Charlie swiped Mack's credit card and moved to the espresso machine. She tried to breathe through the swarm of butterflies frolicking in her belly.

"I wish." Mack flopped on a chair and rested her elbows on the counter. "Nah. I just... I think I told you I have a book signing coming up, right?"

"Is that this week?" Charlie flattened her palm against the tamper to press the ground decaf, then dumped the shot glass of decaf espresso into a cup.

"Three days away," Mack said. "Stuff like that is the worst part of being a writer. I just want to write. I don't want to shake hands, autograph, and smile for six hours. I'm not trying to sound like an ass. For real. It's just exhausting."

Exhausting? Sounded like heaven. Like submerging yourself in a love jacuzzi.

Charlie set Mack's cup down before her and dragged the stool from under the till. Being this close to Mack was more difficult today than it had been before. The Solstice Parade cracked an invisible barrier between them, officially moving them from customer/barista to friends.

Charlie scooted back the chair to the comfortable zone. "I can understand that."

"Can you, though?" The words were harsh, but the tone was soft. "You talk and smile with people all day long. I do it for a few hours and dream of an ice bath to knock me back into alignment."

"I guess it's possible that I'm maybe more..."

"Friendly? Nice? Approachable?"

"I was going to say more extroverted than you." Charlie twisted open a water bottle. "I love being around people. Crowds, concerts, whatever. All their... shazam... gets sucked into this vitality vortex, and I plug into it and recharge. People make me feel good."

Silence tortured Charlie with memories. Like watching a movie with her dad, the familiar scent of whiskey trailing from his breath. Holding her raggedy doll while waiting for hours when he said he just had to run to the store. Paying two college guys with a six-pack of disgusting domestic beer to help her and Jess lug their Craigslist-purchased couch up four flights of stairs to their first apartment. Curling up on her bed, showerless and nauseated, trembling as she signed the divorce papers.

Mack popped a small piece of scone in her mouth. "But you understand how I feel?"

"Of course. I mean, maybe it is being around others that exhausts you. But to me, it sounds like the *performance* is tiring. Being someone you're not for that long would wear anyone down."

Mack's head tilted, and she nibbled on her bottom lip for a second before straightening her back. "Maybe I just don't like people?"

The bell snapped Charlie's focus to the door. Really? No customers for hours, and now one came in with... *what the heck?* She moved to the register and stared directly at nothing but the man's face. "Hey, there. What can I get for you?"

The man scratched at his chin and studied the menu. "Chocolate mocha with extra whipped."

Do. Not. Giggle. "Sure thing."

"This little guy here loves to lick the whipped cream." He patted the baby carrier strapped to his chest.

"I bet." Charlie used all her strength to avoid Mack's eyes. She reached for the milk as the water hissed over the beans.

"What a great little place you have here." The man paced the café and used his thick index finger to poke at the pictures, the plants, and the tables. "How long have you been in business?"

"Just had our six-month anniversary."

He moseyed back the counter. "I run a lot of executive meetings. Do you ever rent out the whole space?"

No chance this guy ran executive meetings.

Charlie layered the milk over the espresso and scooped the foam. "I haven't thought about it. Maybe bring in some of your partners next time, and we can discuss."

He tipped his head in thanks when she handed him his drink and waved as he sashayed out of the store.

Mack slo-mo twisted towards Charlie with her mouth opened. "Did I just see that right? Did he have a cat strapped to him like a baby?"

"*With* a bonnet." Charlie rinsed the milk pitcher and snatched a rag off the rack. "I'm seriously debating if that cat is the most loved animal on the planet or if I should call the authorities."

"I thought Browniegate was a good story, but this is a close second contender."

"I never told you about the guy who was jerking off in the drive-thru at the shop I worked at in high school."

Mack lifted the mug to her mouth. "What? No. Seriously?"

"There was a small part... small... that felt a little bad for him. I'm pretty sure he didn't realize we had cameras." Charlie crumpled a piece of abandoned wax paper in the display case and tossed it in the trash. "I put on latex gloves to hand him his drink."

"People are the worst." Mack clasped her fingers together and stretched her arms towards the ceiling, and her belly button peeked out.

Charlie flushed like she had just read an entry in Mack's diary, and for the second time in less than thirty minutes, she scolded her nerve endings that were staging a coup inside her body. She swiped the sanitizing bottle off the hanger, searching for phantom things to clean.

The haunting sounds of a Mumford & Sons song floated in

the air and mixed with the lingering scent of a fresh latte. Charlie whistled as she wiped down the prep station. Usually, the silent shop would vomit thought bubbles like an old Batman cartoon, but instead of "pow!" and "zam!" it was "bills!", "fore-closure!", and her favorite, "what the hell am I gonna do?" But today, the muted brainwaves were a gift.

Mack moved to the bookshelf, her long, delicate fingers traipsing across the books and games. "You have Battleship?"

"Yep. I loved that game growing up." Charlie gave up trying to find things to clean and surrendered the sanitizing bottle back on the hook. "Used to play it with my aunt all the time."

"My dad and I played super intense games when my mom worked." Mack's thumb tapped the box. "He's so competitive. Did not care for a second that I was a kid and never let me win. But I held my own."

What would've it been like to play Battleship or Candyland with her dad instead of taking off his tattered shoes when he passed out on the couch? Instead of sitting on the floor next to him and aimlessly flipping through TV channels because his breathing was so erratic and loud that she was sure if she went to her room, he'd stop breathing altogether.

Mack sucked in the side of her cheek. "Wanna play?"

Charlie's chest lifted. "Really? Don't you need to work on your writing?"

"Nah. I need a break." Mack tugged out the box.

And all friendly banter ceased.

Mack was her enemy. The only thing interfering with getting high off the nectar of victory. Charlie rubbed her palms together and contemplated her choice. It was risky, for sure. But she lined up each ship on the first and last letters, making a square around the perimeter. For thirty minutes, they eyeballed each other like godfathers in a sit-down.

Charlie opened her mouth to guess B7 when the sky

outside turned ashen, and her pulse slammed against her chest. "Whoa. Did it just get super dark."

It wasn't a question.

The metal chair shrieked against the hardwood floor, and she dashed to the window.

"It's just my soul leaving my body." Mack chuckled and joined her at the window, swaying to look beyond the trees. "Damn. It really did. I should probably take off."

"I'm totally cool with it if you want to stay."

Please stay.

Rain was a constant in Seattle. The pattering against roofs was a cozy, white noise embrace. But storms, especially unexpected ones, were a totally different beast.

"You sure?" Mack's eyebrows folded. "I know you have a business to run."

Charlie dipped her head with an exaggerated gaze at the empty shop. "Really?"

A thunder bullwhip cracked against the sky, and Charlie flinched.

"You okay?" Mack laid a warm hand on Charlie's forearm.

No. "Yep." Charlie half-assed a smile as branches slapped against the window. "I just get a little jumpy in storms."

Mack checked her watch. "You're almost closed for the day. Want to head upstairs?"

Rain bullets pelted the windows. The oppressive screeching of the furious wind amplified. Would the power go out? Where were her flashlights? Would the two vanilla candles on her kitchen table be enough? Charlie kicked herself that she never bought the generator that the contractor recommended.

The lights flickered as the ominous clouds hovered. Charlie's insides quivered while her feet were cemented to the floor. "I need to... close up shop." She cursed her shaky voice.

Mack clapped. "What do you need me to do?"

Charlie took a deep breath, breathed out her nerves, then

rapid-fire instructed. Baked goods were shoved in containers. The till counted down. Chairs thrown on top of tables. Mops saturated and pushed across the floor in record time. Charlie stuffed a few chocolate chip cookies, two bags of salt & vinegar chips, and some bottled water in a bag.

"You ready for this?" Charlie asked, cursing that the inside stairs were blocked off by product and they had to use the outside stairs.

Mack patted the front of her laptop bag strapped across her body. "This baby's waterproof. I'm good."

The furious wind ripped open the door and slammed it against the side of the house. The air smelled like a wet, moldy penny. Charlie's bell sleeves offered a sliver of protection for the pastries as she ran up the wooden stairs and attempted to shield her face from the rain razor slices. In the ninety seconds it took to lock the shop door and open her loft, her clothes clung to her skin, and drips fell from her hair.

She threw open the door, and Mack stumbled in behind her.

ELEVEN

MACK'S DRINK SPECIAL: STEAMED STORMY LATTE WITH A TOUCH OF SWEETNESS

Wet hair matted against Mack's forehead; she pushed it to the side. A saturated blend of lavender and vanilla traveled to her nose, and she'd be lying if she said it didn't do some sort of something tingly to her insides.

The loft was a stark contrast to her white-walled NYC apartment with its single couch, large bookshelf, and one hanging wooden clock. It looked exactly as she expected—like a fairy and a tornado joined forces. Twinkly white lights strung across the sage-green walls. Unfolded blankets on the couch, paperwork scattered across the desk, and stacked boxes filled the corner. Dozens of mismatched, randomly framed artworks with flowers, butterflies, city landscapes, and ocean scenes haphazardly hung across the wall.

Carefree and without rules.

Everything that Mack wasn't.

"A hammock in your living room. I have so many questions." Mack rested her laptop bag against the wall. She wrung her hands together and then stuffed them in her pocket.

Charlie toed off her shoes. "Sometimes I sleep there. I love feeling like I'm on a swinging cloud." A warm glow filled the space when she flipped on a few lamps.

A few hours ago, when Mack bolted from her parents' place, she didn't expect she'd wind up at Charlie's whimsical, fairy-dust-laden, messy-but-inviting place. The zings traveled figure-eight style from her gut to her head to her heart from being in Charlie's home.

A shiver spasmed up Mack's arm leaving an army of goose bumps.

"I'm gonna grab some towels," Charlie said, and returned with a stack of multi-colored towels. She slid a package out of the way with the side of her foot and hesitated. The heat of her eyes lowered to Mack's wet T-shirt for half a second before she shook her head and snapped her gaze to Mack's face, pink shooting to her cheeks.

Mack wanted to rip her shirt off as much as she wanted to grab a blanket and sink into the oversized couch. Air needed to funnel in, stat. A lust-relief IV to counteract the palpable energy.

They exhaled a collective breath.

"You're so wet." Mack rubbed the towel across her arms and shagged it through her hair.

"That's what she said."

"Oh no." Mack groaned but cracked up at Charlie's grin. "So bad. Such a truly terrible joke."

The wind howled outside, and a worry line cut across Charlie's forehead.

The fierce storm roused Mack, and she ached for her keyboard. *It was a dark and stormy night* was not just a cliché for cliché's sake. Having the lion's roar of the wind stirred some heavy, raw emotions, and if she could tap into that, she could typically write from that perspective.

Storms were romantic, maybe even sexy. The thunderous booms ricocheted under her feet. A club mix of pulsing rain.

Protected under the shield of environmental sounds, the wind drowned out nervous throat clearing.

Mack rubbed her thumbs against the soft terrycloth to stop her from touching Charlie, who had her arms wrapped around herself. She *wanted* to touch her and take away her anxiety. But she didn't trust herself to stop at a hug.

A chill ran up her spine, and she tried to mask the shiver.

"Hey, do you want me to throw your clothes in the dryer?" Charlie asked. "You can wear my robe, and I'll throw on my pjs."

"Nah, you don't have to do that."

The eye and lip choreography running through Charlie's face was a master class in human facial expression, and Mack committed the nuances to memory. Charlie's bit lip and hopeful eyes seemed to convey she was worried if Mack didn't take the robe, she'd leave. Mack wanted to dig for the origin of this fear.

"Actually, a robe sounds great."

Muffled footsteps pattered against the floor as Charlie hurried from the room and returned a moment later with a neon green robe with miniature unicorns because, *of course*.

"I have the identical one at home," Mack joked.

"No, you don't." A sheepish smile brushed across Charlie's lips when she handed the robe over. "Bathroom's down the hall to the right if you want to change."

Mack nodded and moved down the hall. The sheer amount of stuff in Charlie's bathroom was like Mack stepped into Ulta. Various shades of eyeshadow, mason jars of lipsticks, different pencils, and weird random tools speckled the counter. *How does someone even know how to use all these things?* Mack had unsteady hands, no vision of what looked good, and zero energy to do anything but wear her year-long, doesn't-matter-the-weather jeans-and-T-shirt combo. But Charlie always looked beautiful. And the way her red lipstick highlighted her plump, cupid-bow-shaped lips was not lost on Mack.

Oof. The robe was hideous. But seriously comfy. She scooped her clothes off the floor and inched towards the door when she brought the collar under her nose and sniffed. The soapy sage smell transported her to the Solstice Parade when she and Charlie hugged, and she closed her eyes to savor the moment.

What am I doing?

It'd only been a little over two weeks, but in that time Mack had said more words to Charlie than she had to most people in a year. She lost herself in the rhythm of Charlie's words when she spoke. Was hypnotized by her smile and deeply feminine movements. Mack wasn't wondering if something was on her face, if she sounded smart enough, or if she was speaking too slowly.

Charlie was a salty-sweet concoction of authenticity and joy. Mack wanted to get drunk off her laughter. Fist her hair. Suck on her lips.

Charlie was incredible. Kind. Smart. Driven.

And a perfect muse.

Mack had finished nearly twenty-five thousand words in about two weeks by observing Charlie.

Maybe Mack should tell her? Charlie contained layers that Mack had only started peeling. She wanted to know more. But was it for the book? Was it for her? Charlie was beautiful, for sure. The curves, the fullness, everything about her was soft, round, and feminine. Mack was probably a teenager the last time her belly cramped from laughing at a story. And Mack was a never-year-old the last time she thought of someone every night.

But diving in with Charlie would destroy everything she worked for. Until recently, writing was the only thing in her life she ever felt good about. The place where she was accepted, even *admired* at times. Considered an expert in her field, a master storyteller, although that was still hard to acknowledge. The only place where her brain relaxed and her soul fed.

She *could not* screw this up.

The warm glow of the strung lights, now accompanied by the crackling of the fireplace, invited Mack to the living room. Charlie stood over the fire with flannel pajama pants and a white tank top, looking unusually fragile outside her typical floor-length dresses. And Mack bit back the need to touch her.

Charlie twisted her index finger around the fabric of her shirt, a smile inching across her face. "I think you were born to wear unicorns."

Mack flipped the collar up. "I think this color works really well with my skin tone."

"Definitely." Charlie grabbed Mack's clothes from her arms and tossed them in the dryer. A rolling clap boomed outside and Charlie shrunk into the wall. The menacing clouds hovered, the sky a grim, murky blanket, making it seem much later than 6:00 p.m.

Mack wanted to rip Charlie's panic away and torch it in the fire. But she also wanted to know if Charlie's porcelain skin was as soft as it looked.

Dammit. Why couldn't it be both ways? But Mack already knew why. Sex would ruin the spell. Mack had never even once successfully met someone for lunch after sex. The idea of chatting over gyros the day after having part of their body in her mouth felt awkward as hell. *You have a magic tongue. Can you pass the mustard?*

No thanks.

Mack forced her hands to stay in her pocket. The seal needed to remain closed.

"Do you want some tea?" Charlie asked.

"Sure."

Careful not to trip over anything, Mack tugged the bathrobe tighter and swallowed the urge to tidy the space as she explored. Dozens of framed photos lined the fireplace mantel, and she skipped her finger across the edge.

"Is this you and Ben at prom?" The fire flickered against the silver frame holding a photo of Charlie in a teal ball gown, her arm looped through a tuxedoed Ben's arm.

"Yep," Charlie said as she pulled out mugs from the cupboard. "I still have the dress. I've worn it for Halloween a few times, but between you and me, I'd wear it on a random Tuesday if the tulle wasn't so itchy."

Prom. Yet another thing that Mack sacrificed during her adolescence in her quest for quiet. Regret pinpricked her. What would her life have looked like had she participated in these events? If she were social? A sliver of a void existed in her with her inability to connect with humans on a fundamental level. It made her fidget, touch her hair, scratch her skin, and she was always convinced she had food in her teeth.

Bottom line. Humans were too much effort. Being around others shrunk on the priority scale until it was nil.

"It's strange to see your bare skin from when you were younger." Mack placed the frame back on the mantel. When Charlie scrunched her face, Mack pointed to her forearm. "No ink."

"Ah." The kettle screeched. Charlie plopped in the tea bags, then handed Mack the *Merry effin' XXXmas* mug. "Gift from Ben last year. I don't even begin to pretend to understand the inner workings of his twisted brain."

Mack took a tentative sip of the steaming honey mint tea and leaned against the opposite counter from Charlie. The radiance from the lamps offset the darkness of the afternoon sky, and Mack's insides heated with the liquid.

"Tattoos are a bit of an obsession." Charlie rotated her arm. "Started at eighteen and never quit."

Mack examined the tattoos, a collage of colorful flowers and butterflies. "Why do you like them so much?"

Charlie stared at her fingers for several long moments. "I think it's because every piece captures something important in my life at that time. But… it's more than that. They make me strong. Or at least, they make me think I'm strong. With every tattoo, it's like I'm shielding myself." She blew into her cup and took a short sip. "I hate conflict. I have this idea if people see my… armor… they're less likely to mess with me. Tattoos are this, I guess, dichotomy. That's the word, right? It's like, *Look at me!* But also, *I'm covering myself up so you can't see all of me.*"

Charlie's face flashed pink and then turned white when she snapped her mouth shut. "That probably doesn't even make sense." She let out a deflecting chuckle.

Mack chewed on the information. She wrote a scene the other day about Shelby having a hidden dragon tattoo on her inner thigh. She'd focused on Shelby's physical strength to engrave herself in such a painful area, but she hadn't tapped into the emotional reasons behind the branding.

The craving for attention while covering yourself made perfect sense. Lots of people probably fought with those demons, the fear of being recognized coupled with the fear of being a no one. But why did Charlie specifically feel this way? She'd shared tidbits of her past, but it was like she was rattling off a Wikipedia page—impersonal and distant.

Mack needed more. But now it was less about the book, and more about a genuine curiosity. She cupped her hands around the mug, the heat transferring to her palms. "I know Seattle gets a lot of rain, but this is unusual, right?" she asked, even though she wanted to bombard her with questions: Why does she hide behind body art? Why does she smile when she looks like she wants to cry? Why do the flickering lights against her red hair make it seem like she's a fire goddess?

"Yeah, but normally it's just mist." Charlie hooked her finger around the curtain behind the sink and peeked outside. "I don't even own an umbrella."

Lightning cracked. Charlie turned pale and recoiled.

Mack was torn between wanting to scoop Charlie into her

arms and memorizing what she saw for her book: tense shoulders. White knuckles. A protruding neck vein. Eyebrows strung together like a drawbridge.

"Hey, it's okay." Mack put a reassuring hand on Charlie's shoulder, which seemed to soften from the touch. Mack couldn't remember ever being scared like this, minus when she was eleven and watched *The Exorcist* after her babysitter fell asleep. Charlie's face looked like something was about to possess her body and force out green demon projectile vomit.

"You know…" Mack jutted her head toward the middle of the room. "I've never actually been in a hammock before."

Charlie's eyebrows lifted. "Really? Never? You've never camped?"

"Nah. I feel like that's a Seattle thing. Or maybe a Pacific Northwest thing. In the city, there's not a lot of room to keep camping gear 'cause the apartments are so tiny."

"You gotta do it. Once you've properly shifted your weight, you'll feel like you're floating." Charlie placed her mug on the side table. She held out a hand to take Mack's mug, then motioned her to follow. "Sit your butt in the middle so it doesn't flip."

The hammock wobbled as Mack lowered herself. The fabric was unsteady and kind of awful until it wasn't. The moment her body hit the right spot, she sunk into the material.

"Wait until you get the full effect. It's pretty cool. One sec." The rain pelted against the window as Charlie dashed around the room and turned off the lights.

Charlie was not wrong. Mack was in the middle of a sparkling, warm, pixie-dusted house. Glowing stars filled the ceiling. White strung lights filled the room. Plants she had barely noticed before convinced her she was in a forest.

"Do you get dizzy?" Charlie placed her hands on the outside of the hammock.

"Like in general? No."

Charlie eased Mack into a swinging motion. *Heaven.* Everything in Mack's body faded. She wasn't a writer under a furious deadline. She wasn't battling imposter syndrome. She was just swinging, her eyes drooping, her muscles at ease.

A loud crack of thunder rattled the sky. Charlie dropped her hands from the hammock, ripped a pillow from the couch, and hugged it.

Mack's heart thumped.

This situation shouldn't be that stressful. They were friends, right? She never really had a friend besides Viviane. Although she was pretty sure friends didn't go to bed thinking of their friend's mouth on theirs. Or wondered what their friend's body pressed against them would feel like. Friends shouldn't be trying to recreate the smell and searching through Amazon for vanilla-scented lotion to rub against their pillow.

Mack cleared her throat. *Just do it.* Stop overthinking. Stop swallowing back a cough. This was a friendly gesture, nothing more. She patted the side of the hammock.

"I think you should join me."

TWELVE

CHARLIE'S DRINK SPECIAL: COZY COMFORT SPICED CHAI

Cozied up with Mack in the hammock sounded like a chicken soup comfort snuggle laced with glass shards. Lying in a hammock with another woman was *close*. Bodies-touching close. *Jess*-touching close.

The angry rain whipped against the windows. Its shrieking was like an air demon ready to drag her into the dark under-world. Charlie grabbed a blanket and climbed in.

"Whoa, holy sh—nope, I got this." Mack laughed and wiggled into the corner. "Yep, nope, definitely don't got this." The hammock twisted. Clunky arms and legs tangled and flailed until Mack planted her palm on the ground to steady the fabric.

Charlie's butt was in Mack's stomach. She scooted lower and was hyperaware of the intimate places that touched, and she debated how to defuse the seventh-grade-dance level of awkwardness. "We callin' dibs on who's little spoon or big spoon?"

To maintain some semblance of balance, Charlie firmed her core, flipped over, and shoved herself into the corner of the hammock. They mirrored each other, lying on their side with an arm underneath their cheek. Mint tea mixed with Mack's fruit and sea salt scent, and Charlie tried to ignore the dreamy scent.

"This okay?" Mack's voice was as gentle as her softened expression portrayed.

Charlie nodded and picked at her flannel pajamas. It shouldn't feel this good, this quick. It shouldn't remind her of the beginning when she and Jess promised to love each other forever. Or make her think of when they tattooed each other's zodiac signs and their wedding date on their backs during their honeymoon and cried as they admired their love branding.

Jess fed the soul of an orphaned child. She played the role of protector, confidant, lover, friend, and family. Charlie had given Jess her heart. And then she'd left. Just like her mom. Just like her dad. And now, lying here calmly with Mack—who Charlie had only known for two weeks—the comfortability was frightening. She couldn't, *she wouldn't*, fall into the seductive codependence trap. She'd never trust again like she had with Jess.

"It's so stupid, being scared of the storm like this." Damn her dad for leaving her so much as a kid. She hated that her deficient parental upbringing still affected her.

"It's not stupid at all. We all have fears."

A long time had passed since someone seemed genuinely interested in learning about *her*. Not the shop. Not which coffee region was the best. Not which tourist places people should check out. But her.

And Charlie kind of loved it.

"Even you? You seem so tough." Charlie grinned. "Like you'd kick a cabbie's ass if they inched over the crosswalk."

Mack angled her eyebrow. "Do I really give off that vibe?" A hint of defensiveness laced through Mack's tone. "I'm scared of a ton of things."

"Really, like what?"

Mack flicked her finger against her thigh. "Where do I start? Rats. Cockroaches. Birds. Wrinkles."

"Birds? Wrinkles?" Charlie asked. "Like you bathe in hydrating cream?"

"No. I like things crisp. I am a serial ironer, and I'll never apologize." She smiled and looked down as she raveled a hammock thread tourniquet around her index finger and released. So many seconds passed that Charlie wasn't sure if Mack was done speaking or just thinking.

Mack's chest inflated when she took in a breath. "I'm scared of failure."

Her voice was so quiet that Charlie wasn't sure if she heard her right until the weight of the words hung heavy in the air. A lot of people feared failure. Charlie did, too, at some level. Her desk drawer was weighted with unpaid bills. The coffee shop was going underwater, and no amount of manifesting and rubbing her favorite rock at night could change that. She broke inside thinking about not seeing the mother-daughter duo, Amanda and Erica. Or not having Ben there all day. Or fist-pumping regulars. She'd be alone again. Abandoned.

Failure was a byproduct.

The twinkling light above Mack's head held Charlie's gaze as her throat constricted. "When I was younger, I was left alone a lot." She usually kept her memories buried in a Death-Valley-level-of-deep grave. Her heart pounded with the admission. "One time, when I was eight or nine, my dad left to 'see his friends.' That's what he'd called it when he'd go out. He'd put on the TV, give me some gross microwave dinner, and I'd sit on the couch and stare out the window until I fell asleep. But this particular night, it stormed so hard. When lightning hit a tree in our yard, it rattled everything like an earthquake. I was so young. I didn't know if I should run out of the trailer or hide in the closet." Her heart broke thinking of her tiny self in her nightgown, gripping her ratty teddy bear, praying that her dad would come home.

Mack's forehead scrunched. "Oh God, I'm so sorry. You must've been so scared. What did you do?"

"I don't even remember. But the next morning, he gave me his unlimited pancake and syrup apology and took me to get my first 'coffee.' It was probably a mocha or something, but I remember it being a glorious cup of sweet and bitter, and I was hooked immediately." She didn't know if her love of coffee was born that day from the effects of the caffeine and sugar or if it was because she saw the remorse and love in her father's eyes during his blip of sobriety.

"Have you lived alone most of your life?" Mack's eyes, a dark, deep, brown haven she wanted to drown in, burrowed into her.

Charlie released a heavy breath. "No. When I was seventeen, I moved in with my now ex-wife."

Mack froze. "You were married?"

Charlie nodded.

A long pause passed as Mack flicked the thread from her finger. "Can I ask what happened?"

The wind eased up and her stomach slowly uncoiled, but her throat turned sticky. She wanted to reach for her tea but didn't want to disrupt the moment. The heat of Mack's body nearly matched the crackling fire behind them. Mack was too close. Charlie needed air that didn't smell like blackberries and salt and comfort.

But it felt so damn good.

"We just wanted two different things. In the beginning, we both loved to travel. Lived in the worst places to save money. For two years we rented a bedroom in a musty, old basement of a South Seattle house with robin-egg blue lead-filled paint chipping off the walls. It literally smelled like cat pee and botulism." She grin-groaned. "I thought we'd do this nomad lifestyle for like a year and then settle down. And I should've addressed it, but I was scared to talk to her about it. Scared that she'd leave me."

Mack looked at her so intently that Charlie was sure she was evaluating the colors in her irises. But Mack remained silent, her mouth parted like she didn't know what to say.

"Jess wanted to move to Europe, live in hostels, and see the world. I need, I guess, stability. Foundation. Roots. Without it, I feel... empty." Heat filled her chest, but she continued. "But it was unfair. I took everything I lacked in my childhood and placed that burden onto Jess. She's a good woman, you know? But she was a bird who couldn't be caged. She wanted to go to the Himalayas. Eat street food in Thailand. Have coffee in Italy. And I... wanted a family."

Was Charlie in a dream? Had she accidentally drunk truth serum tea? Shielded with the sky's darkness and flickering fireplace, her insides begged her to release. She never talked like this. Customers didn't want to hear about broken marriages. Ben offered some emotional support, sure, but he lost a friend when Jess left, and she withheld burdening him too much.

"Well, that was a lot of honesty. I'm usually more private about this type of stuff. Ben doesn't even know. Please don't ever tell anyone I told you this."

"Who would I tell?" Mack's face shifted from crimson to pale and back again, and she moved closer. "Thank you for sharing your past. It means a lot you'd open up like that."

The rain slowed and turned into tap dancing with the earth, making Charlie drowsy with sound. She studied Mack's face, her dark thick eyebrows, her sharp, yet full cheekbones. The wideness of her eyes, the deep plum of her lips.

Charlie cleared her throat. "What about you? Any exes?"

Mack shook her head. "None."

"None? Like none, none?"

"Yeah. None, none. Not high school, not college, not adulthood."

This tidbit marinated. Yes, Charlie was happy independent. It took a long time to get there. But the desire for human connection still pulled her, although the fear of getting hurt superseded her need for partnership. How did someone like Mack, a best-selling author at twenty-five, smoking hot, intelligent, and funny, not have an ex? It went against the laws of the universe.

Or was it a red flag?

"You're a super attractive, intelligent woman. Who lives in New York. Gays grow on trees out there, just like here. It's not like you live in a small Minnesota town or something. Why none?"

Mack's eyes focused on a hammock rope knot. The rope squished between her fingertips, and she exhaled. "I think I keep waiting. I always feel like I have one more thing I need to complete first, you know?"

"Where do you think this drive comes from?"

"My parents," Mack answered without hesitation. "Growing up, I didn't know we didn't have much money. My parents hustled, worked so many hours, and made sure one of them was almost always home with me. I think their life's mission was to make sure I succeeded, so they pushed me. Hard.'"

But Mack had a best-selling book. Was more accomplished than most of the human population, much less people their age. Something wasn't adding up. "Do you feel like you're wasting the best years of your life?"

"Do you?"

Charlie was struck silent. "That's fair. But I've already tried. Didn't work out." Did she really want to dive into what happened when her heart shattered and splintered after the person she loved betrayed her and left? That the broken heart carnage left her shaking and terrified of ever trusting again?

Silence hung in the air, along with the scented candle. Charlie lowered her eyes to Mack's mouth. Charlie wanted to talk more. She wanted to stop. She wanted Mack not to have the tiny curve in the corner of her lips like it was a dimple hideaway, and if she said something clever, it would peek out.

"You're so easy to talk to." Charlie's voice was barely above a whisper.

Mack shook her head. "*You're* super easy to talk to. You say you don't normally talk like this? I normally don't talk. At all. Sometimes it'll be days before I've realized the only words I've spoken out loud is when I ordered my coffee."

Thoughts, smells, flickering lights, and words surrounded her like a dusty haze. The electricity bounced between their skin. The softness of the rain, now a light dance against the earth, combined with the fireplace's heat and the glow of Mack's skin, made Charlie's heart palpitate.

What are we doing?

Mack lightly trailed a finger on Charlie's arm, outlining the butterfly ink.

The surprising touch shot tingles to her toes.

"This is really pretty." Mack's thick honey tone slid into Charlie's ears. "So many of your tattoos have wings. Butterfly wings, fairy wings..."

"Angels on my back. Apparently, I'm trying to take flight." She meant to say it like a joke, but her voice constricted. "I love everything about wings. The airiness. The freedom. This feeling of safety like they'd wrap themselves around me and fly me away if needed."

The space was too small. Charlie didn't care that there wasn't enough air for them to breathe. A warm, buttery sensation traveled up her as Mack traced Charlie's tattoo with her fingertips. Charlie twisted her arm, and when the pads of Mack's fingers grazed her inner wrist, her breath hitched.

"This one... is a favorite..." Heat blushed across Charlie's cheek, and her heart pounded in her ears. Mack stopped when she reached the top of her arm and removed her touch. Charlie ached for it to return. A finger, hand, mouth, breath, *anything*. She wanted to feel Mack against her.

Her heartbeat pulsed everywhere, and Charlie was sure Mack could hear it over the melody of increased breathing. Mack inched a little closer and hovered her fingers over Charlie's chest, avoiding the contact that Charlie's body craved. She wanted to be touched but was scared.

"What about these?" Mack's gentle hand swept the air in front of the roses and vines ink draped across her chest.

Charlie stopped breathing. Mack looked at her so intently that she was sure she could read into her soul.

"Tell me about these tattoos."

"These... I thought were sexy," Charlie said, even quieter.

"They're very sexy." Mack's voice was husky now, her rasp layered like sugared cream.

Touch me.

Several excruciating moments passed. Charlie interpreted every heartbeat, the sighs' decibels, and the rising chest frequency. They spoke no words but delivered messages. Charlie's cells fired from the top of her scalp to the tips of her toes. Reaching up, she took Mack's silky-smooth hand and gently guided her finger across her neck and chest to continue outlining.

Mack dropped her hand to the back of Charlie's neck and pulled her in. The plushness of Mack's lips pressed into Charlie's, and she savored the minty honey taste. Mack moved her mouth, owning every bit of Charlie's lips, and Charlie melted.

"Is this okay?" Mack whispered, pulled back, and darted her eyes between Charlie's.

"Yes... is it okay for you?" Barely formulated words left her mouth.

Charlie cupped the side of Mack's face and drew her closer, pushing her lips onto Mack's. Everything burst. Was this a dream? The kisses, the moment, were surreal and beautiful, and she didn't want the magic to disappear.

She opened her mouth and accepted Mack's velvet tongue against hers. Their breaths intertwined. Gentle but firm hands glided down Charlie, and she drank in the sensation of skin on hers. Lingered touches left a path of tingles. Her goose bumps flattened against the warmth of Mack's hand.

"Still okay?" Mack asked again, and Charlie mumbled out an affirmative.

Mack's lips were everything Charlie thought they would be. Strong, firm kisses, brimming with purpose and desire. Mack captured Charlie's mouth deeper, and Charlie liquefied. Her limbs turned to jelly, her brain to mush. Mack's hand rested above Charlie's neck, but her hand didn't move any lower, and Charlie's insides curled with longing.

Lips pressed against Charlie's neck. A tongue swept across her collarbone, her earlobe, and back down. Mack murmured adorations. She was so close to Charlie's heart, so close to satisfying the urge to be touched. She wanted Mack's mouth on her. Everywhere. Her belly tightened with pressure, and her aching increased.

Charlie slid her arm under her head to reach for Mack.

And almost knocked them over.

"Oh no!" they both yelled in unison, and Charlie tumbled on top of Mack, who slammed her hand against the floor, forearm muscles protruding to keep them from falling out. The hammock swung bulky and twisted, and they each gripped the edge.

"Buzzkill." Charlie laughed as they steadied.

"Got it? You good?" Mack asked, her cheeks pink and lips red. "I'm going to slide out."

Charlie balanced herself as Mack slipped out, and Charlie rolled over. No sexy or graceful way existed to exit a hammock. She giggled as she plopped onto her knees to escape the twisted net right as the drier beeped.

"Oh, uh, here, let me grab your clothes for you." Charlie shuffled to the drier with trembling hands and breathed through her nose to calm her screaming heart. She needed to settle down before she hyperventilated. Her skin was prickled and sensitive. She swiped a fingertip across her pulsating lips, feeling dizzy and dreamy. And terrified.

I can't believe that happened.

The warmed clothes soothed her shakes, and she tumbled out of the hallway and shoved them into Mack's arms.

"Here you go! All warm and roasty and toasty."

What the hell am I even saying?

"Now that the rain is all done, I think I'm free to fly solo again." Charlie giggled, or at least she tried to giggle, but more of a high-pitched, record-scratching squeal was released. "Thanks for being such a great escort. Do I owe you for babysitting fees?"

Seriously, shut up.

She said so many things to Mack. *And they kissed!* She was just barely over Jess. *Finally.* Healed and whole, and she wanted to screw it up? Open herself up again? What was she thinking? So dumb. Irresponsible. Her heart hated her right now, and pleaded for her to protect it.

Flames crawled up Charlie's face when Mack grabbed the clothes, stared at her for too long, and said, "Funny."

Just... funny.

Not, *are you as nervous as me?* Or, *are you thinking the same scattered thoughts?* How about, *did that just effing happen?*

As Mack got dressed, Charlie scooped the mugs and

brought them into the kitchen. The click of the bathroom door opening was like a sonic boom, and Charlie jumped.

Standing against the wall, Mack tied her shoes. Time ticked by at the speed of a glacier as Charlie avoided eye contact.

"Are we good?" Mack finally said after a hundred trillion moments of awkwardness passed. "Sorry, is this weird?"

Her cheeks flamed. "No, I'm weird. I'm so weird right now and don't know how not to be. It's me, not you."

Regret seeped into Charlie. But regret for what? What was happening here? They were single. They shared a kiss. Okay, a knee-buckling, earth-moving, heart-attack-inducing kiss. But they were friends. Attraction was fine, right? Normal, even.

No. Yes. *Gah!*

"Can I get your number?" The words flew out of Charlie's mouth before she could pull them by the tails and stuff them back in. She just asked for a woman's number. She was heavy and light, and her belly was doing Olympic-size somersaults.

"I thought you'd never ask." Mack's eyes twinkled along with her voice, and Charlie flushed.

They swapped phones, and a call popped up on the screen when Charlie put in her number. With a flame icon as the name. *Odd. And none of my business. One kiss does not give me all rights to Mack's private life.* Charlie handed the phone back to Mack like it was burning. "Do you need to take this?"

Mack looked at it with a frown and hit decline. "Nah, I'll call her back."

An instant ping of jealousy pounced through Charlie. *This* was why she didn't make out with random people. For all she knew, flame icon could be her hairdresser, and she shouldn't have this level of fire in her belly.

Nope. She was not doing this. Tonight was fun and satisfied the itch of needing to know what Mack's mouth tasted like.

But now Charlie could let it go and resolve to be friends.

THIRTEEN

MACK'S DRINK SPECIAL: LINGERING LOTUS LATTE

Mack slid into her bed and licked her lips to taste the remnants of Charlie's lipstick and honey tea. The sensation of Charlie's mouth locked with hers lingered, and her body burned from the kiss. Her arms were vacant, almost sore. They wanted to touch Charlie, hold her, and tell her she was safe. Mack closed her eyes, slid her hand across her chest and down, and rested it on her lower belly to relive the sensation of Charlie's body on hers before it ghosted.

Ten minutes later, she grabbed her laptop.

Her strawberry gloss fills me, burns down to my toes. I want to feel her, to touch her, to taste her. As if drawn together by an intoxicated force, I stumble towards her. My body aches to connect with hers, steal me away, and make me forget the demons inside. Tonight, there is no internal hell. Only the scent of her vanilla skin.

Mack hadn't planned on a sex scene. She hadn't even planned on addressing the sexuality of her characters. But emotions were high, and her mouth and fingers were heavy with want. She pounded against the keyboard, rejected her parents' offer for food, and continued to translate her developing feeling for Charlie onto her character for the next two hours.

She interlaced her fingers and stretched her arms above her head. She paced the room, sipped water, and stepped onto the patio. The city hummed fourteen stories below, and the night sky covered the view of mountains. After bringing in a deep breath, she exhaled and pictured Charlie snuggled in her bed. Did she fall asleep? Was she worried about the storm starting again?

How horrible would it have been to be a child, waiting at the window for a dad who may not get home. Did the windows fog? Did she draw pictures on the pane to pass time?

Wait a second... *windows fogging.* She flew back into the room and flipped open her outline. She'd written a scene where Shelby had to leave her daughter to go on a drug run, and struggled with the guilt of leaving her with the adrenaline of a potentially large score. What if it were raining? What if the babysitter left early? Mack returned to document.

She blows onto the window, the palette she needs to draw. Her tiny fingers swipe against the moistened pane. Stick figures take shape. "One for Mommy, one for me." Why wasn't she home yet? The thunder slams into the house, the stick figure shakes. She grips her frayed teddy bear, the one with the missing eye and purple marker drawing on the arm, the one that her mommy tried to replace so many times with newer ones, but she doesn't like the newer ones. She likes this one.

Another hour flew by before she rested her laptop to the side and picked up her phone. *Crap.* The flame icon flashed on the screen.

> : Hey you! Been trying to reach you. I'm going to be in NYC next week for business. Checking to see if you're up for a visitor ;-)

> Mack: Hey, I know it's not cool to do this via text, but I don't think we should contact each other anymore. I'm seeing someone and want to be respectful.

Mack: Wishing you the best.

A crappy greeting card send-off, for sure. But they'd only hooked up once, a month or two before the great escape to Seattle, and exchanged a couple of half-assed, obligatory messages since then. Flame icon would be fine.

A slow grin crept while reading *I'm seeing someone*. Didn't matter that the statement wasn't true. Just because she and Charlie shared a kiss—a hell of a kiss—didn't mean they were seeing each other. But her insides still danced at the words.

The dating world was a foreign concept. She wasn't an idiot. She had a general idea of what it entailed. But wanting sex, snuggles, dessert, *and* to play a wicked game of Battleship with the same person was incomprehensible. Until Charlie.

She sprang off the bed with a squeak and reached for the iron. The fabric of her shirt stretched across the board, and the methodical swipes of the hot tool allowed her brain to slow.

Maybe Charlie wouldn't mind that she'd inspired parts of the book. She'd whispered in Mack's ear, "Please don't ever tell anyone I told you this..." But that was different from being a muse, right? Most people would be flattered to be considered an inspiration. And even though Shelby dealt drugs and had a violent streak, she had a lot of good, too. Mack would simply explain the concept of morally gray protagonists and zero in on the character's integrity.

Okay, settled. She'd tell Charlie.

Probably.

But what if Charlie said no? Clammed up and wouldn't let her back into the coffee shop? Not spending time with Charlie would be equally as bad for her as for her manuscript. She liked Charlie. A lot. More than what seemed normal or fathomable at this stage. Genuinely more than anyone she'd ever met besides her family and Viviane.

Without Charlie, her two-week winning word count streak

would dry up, and her career would shrivel up and die. Who knows what would happen with the advance that Mack already spent? What she used it for couldn't be returned.

Her phone rang, and her heart sprang. *Charlie?* She snatched it off the desk and her chest dropped.

"Viv."

"Hello to you, too, princess."

Mack looked at her watch. "It's like one thirty in the morning for you."

"I know, but Caleb had an ear infection, and urgent care was backed up, and Anthony didn't get home until late, and well, now's the first chance I've had. And I know you keep vampire hours." The sound of zippers and rummaging in the background funneled through the phone. "Status check. How's things?"

"Like chipping at an iceberg with a baby spoon."

The rustling stopped. "You serious? I thought it was getting better."

"I'm kidding. The manuscript's coming along. Up to fifty-five thousand."

"Good. Keep me posted," Viviane said. "All right, I'm flying in tomorrow, late. Too long of a story to tell this late at night, but I had daycare issues."

"Damn kids ruin everything, huh?"

"Ha. True. Anyway, I had to change the flight, so I won't land until close to midnight. On Friday, you'll meet me at eight a.m. sharp at the hotel lobby, we'll walk to the conference area together, then head downtown for the book signing."

Mack eased into the corner chair and put her socked feet against the wall. "I thought we were meeting at nine?"

"You'd know it moved up an hour if you answered your damn phone or emails." Viviane released a deep breath. "Confirming you haven't developed an escape plan or decided to fake a cracked collarbone to get out of your obligations?"

"Jerk."

"Good. Look, I know you don't like these things, but they're important, and well, they paid for your trip out there and then some."

Not liking these things was the understatement of the century. Conferences, book signings, and mundane conversations with strangers nearly brought her to her knees. She'd always subtly lift her arms to see if she smelled, run her tongue across her teeth to confirm food wasn't stuck, and by the end of the night, her mouth burned from chewing through a tin of Altoids.

"And you're all prepared for your workshop?"

No. "Yeah."

The material was her conference class go-to, and she'd taught the course at least a half dozen times last year but needed to refresh herself on the content. In the past, she would've been more nervous and more prepared. But her mind parallel pathed on exactly two focuses right now: her manuscript and Charlie.

"Mack, is everything okay? Besides, you know, the book."

Words verged on the tip of her tongue, but no way would she burden Viviane, who'd for sure want to fix it. What would she say anyway? That she was falling for Charlie. Struggling with what that even meant. New feelings and sensations, and her heart couldn't reconcile it all. Using Charlie for content. Just weathered a Seattle storm, had a make-out session of a lifetime, and tripped on her ego after getting thrown out. Everything was just peachy.

"Yeah, I'm good. Just feeling the pressure." The heaviness in her chest shattered when her phone beeped with a text from Charlie. "Hey, gotta run. See you in a few days."

She couldn't hang up fast enough.

Charlie: Hey, it's Charlie.

Just *it's Charlie.* The full extent of the message with no bubbles to indicate she was still writing. Mack warmed at how much courage it must've taken for her even to send that message.

> Mack: Not Kitten.

> Charlie: ha. Yep

> Charlie: um, can I call you?

Mack dialed.

"Sorry I got so weird tonight," Charlie blurted. "It's just been a long time, you know? And I'm all super extra and odd, and, well, I'd hate to lose a customer."

"We wouldn't want that. I promise I'll still come in for coffee." *And to see you. And to look at your lips. And to listen to your laugh.* "Sorry I almost flipped over your hammock. No idea my core needed that much work."

Charlie sounded like she was swinging in that very hammock. "What are you up to?"

Writing about you. Mack moved to the bed and propped the pillows behind her. "Just about to revisit a lesson for a class I'm teaching on Friday."

"Oh yeah? What kind of class?"

"The seminar's called *Loving the Unlovable: Rooting for the Villain.* The class is for writers who need to humanize people who do bad things."

Charlie was quiet for a moment. "How do you make someone like a bad person?"

"There are ways. But I think it also depends on your definition of a villain." She flipped to her side and put the phone on speaker. "What do you think makes someone a villain?"

A few moments passed, and Mack closed her eyes. Did

Charlie have the same blanket wrapped around her from earlier? Was she cradling a pillow?

"I think a villain deceives and lies." Charlie paused. "Shows people one side of them while hiding the other. Because if the villain showed their true colors right away, there'd be no way people would root for them."

Well, shit.

"So, how do you make a villain likable?" Charlie's voice calmed from earlier, and the faintest squeaking sound of the hammock rope moving against the metal hook funneled through the phone.

Mack thought for a moment about her class material. "First, you gotta have them do something redeemable. Rescue a puppy. Help someone cross the street. Fix a stranger's flat tire. Some action that shows they're not a complete asshole." Have them come into a coffee shop with smiles and big tips. "Second, you have to show a purpose behind their actions. Unless they're a sociopath—which I don't write—some justification exists that the reader empathizes with. A reason behind the action."

"The method behind the madness."

"Exactly."

The following silence was more comforting than awkward. Soft breaths filtered through the phone. Was she still wearing her flannel pajamas? Or twirling her hair around her fingers?

"Do you like teaching?" Charlie's voice teetered on drowsy.

"Teaching's my favorite part of the conference. The meet and greet stuff, the book signing event, slowly kills my soul. I'll be okay, though. My agent's coming into town, so I have my wingwoman to help me out of uncomfortable conversations." Mack's chest tightened. "I'd rather be spending the time with you."

The room got hot, fast.

Charlie was quiet. Too quiet.

Now her throat was all tacky and gross, and she fanned her shirt.

"Thanks again for tonight," Charlie said after a painful amount of moments passed. "See you tomorrow?"

"Absolutely."

FOURTEEN

MACK'S DRINK SPECIAL: MANUAL LABOR
MACCHIATO WITH SORE MUSCLE SYRUP

Mack slept late for the first time in forever, not wanting to wake up from some gloriously sexy dreams. Her hands circled and explored what she wished Charlie would have the night before. After her shower, the writing resumed. She needed to get some words in, but every time her fingertips touched the keys, Charlie's lips haunted her.

"Knock, knock." Her mom's voice accompanied her knuckles against the door. She poked her head in, wearing a black business suit.

"Whoa, who died?"

"You're such a poop." Her mom grinned as she flipped open the blinds. "The room's so dark. How do you even see anything?"

"It's only dark to you. I'm still in my twenties."

"Now you're just being mean." Her mom tapped Mack's leg to scooch over. "I'll have you know I'm meeting with an important client today. Bidding on a contract to renovate office spaces, which would be ah-mazing."

Mack folded herself into her mom. She breathed in the

comfort of her apple-scented hair and squeezed harder than she had in years.

"What's that for?" her mom asked while patting her back.

Mack pulled back and shrugged.

She should've never waited a year to visit her parents. When her mom was sick, Mack worried she'd die. So, what did Mack do? Ran like a scared toddler. Delayed visits and trips. Called her dad late at night when she knew her mom would be asleep. Maintained a delusion that somehow her avoidance would all make things easier if something terrible happened to her mom.

But now, being back, seeing how far they'd come, warmed Mack. Gone were the days of her exhausted, overworked mom sinking into the couch while her father massaged her feet and fed her boxed mac 'n' cheese made with government milk. Replaced by her confident mom standing in her beautiful condo with Jimmy Choo shoes and a Coach bag.

Mack swatted at her mom, who tousled her hair. "Really?"

Her mom stood and leaned against the door frame, leveling a stare at Mack. "I worry about you."

"I know."

"You seem better than when you first arrived. Thank sweet baby Jesus." She clapped her hands together and looked at the ceiling. "But you're still hiding something."

Her mom didn't pry any deeper. But she didn't leave, either.

How could Mack possibly deduce and articulate everything happening in her world? All these unsettling but warm feelings gave her a fierce, slightly addictive lust buzz. She used Charlie. She missed Charlie. She wanted to kiss, hug, and run away from Charlie. "Do you ever sometimes... just not know what to do?"

Her mother's chest lifted with a sharp inhale. Unclear if her reaction was relief or surprise that Mack opened up. Her pumps clicked across the floor, and she sat down at the edge of the bed. She fiddled with her watch and looked out the window for several long moments. "When I first got sick, I wasn't even scared. I just kept thinking, nah, they're wrong. I'm only thirty-nine. Cancer happens to old people. I was numb for days after getting the news. Until I wasn't numb anymore." She crossed her legs. "And then I was scared. So scared. I hid it from your dad, hid it from you. But you were scared, too. It wasn't like I didn't realize you stopped visiting."

Flames flew up Mack's cheeks. "Mom, I'm so sorry—"

She put her hand up. "Stop. I understood why you stopped visiting. And honestly, I was grateful because I was ashamed at first. Like, who gets ashamed about having breast cancer? But I kept thinking back to when I made dinner in the microwave, the crappy fast food I fed us, or when I was younger and smoked weed."

Mack looked down at her hands. "You think food or pot gave you cancer?"

"I didn't know what did, but I needed to blame it on something. After the hospitalizations and surgeries, I heard your dad panicking with the insurance company." Her mom grabbed a pillow next to Mack and laid it on her lap. "But I was so tired. I couldn't do anything. I only looked at the bills once and completely lost it. So much money, Mack. And so much paperwork. He had stuff everywhere. Business cards, bills, random numbers covered our fridge. And you know your father... I manage all our finances for a reason. But he told me to trust him, and he'd figure it out."

The heat in Mack's chest burned down to her core. She kept her eyes on her hands.

"And you know what happened? For the first time, I let it go. I focused on getting better, he focused on working his ass off, and everything worked out."

"What happened with all the bills?" Mack knew. But she needed confirmation that her story aligned with her mom's beliefs.

"I thought the bills would ruin us and drive your father to an early grave. Truly. Turns out all that stress and worry was a billing error. Everything was taken care of like that." She snapped her fingers.

And Mack exhaled.

Her mom stood and tossed the pillow next to Mack. "And look at us now. We live in a baller condo—"

"No one says that."

"Killer condo? A condo with ice in its veins? The condo caught a vibe?"

"Make it stop."

"Oh, and I got a fabulous new set of tits."

"Mom!"

"What? True story." She squeezed Mack on the shoulder and walked to the door. "Point is, Mackey, sometimes you gotta trust things will work for the best. Have a little faith."

Mack smiled and scooted up higher on the bed. "Thanks, Mom."

"Forgot to mention I grabbed a new creamer from the store. A sugar-free extra spiced pumpkin and nutmeg flavor. You don't even need to refrigerate it!"

"Let's not ruin this nice moment, 'kay?"

Her mom laughed and shut the door.

Once she was alone, Mack's thoughts trailed back to Charlie and how she spent her morning. Did she hug the retired couple today that came in every day? Did her mom/daughter team stop by? Did she sleep okay after the storm?

She glanced down at her word count and frowned. Two hours into messy, disorganized writing, she shut the laptop. If she was going to be distracted by thoughts of Charlie, she might as well go to her shop and see her in person. Maybe then she could get some writing done.

. . .

The wet streets sloshed under Mack's tires. Pockets of giant puddles and downed branches strewed the roads. Several people picked up yard debris, surrounded by green garbage bags and rakes. Everyone knew Seattle got a ton of rain, but last night's storm must've been out of the norm.

Her belly flip-flopped. Something had shifted between her and Charlie last night. After slowly growing closer, they took a sharp turn and accelerated. Yeah, they kissed. But Mack's heart screamed that it was more than a kiss. And sure, the feelings intertwined with the kiss scared the hell out of her. But she still wanted to do it again.

She slammed the car door and skipped over a puddle on the sidewalk. The bright sun was in sharp contrast from yesterday's gray. The air was unusually soggy and sticky, the heat mixing with storm remnants, but the copper scent clouding the air last night reverted to a pine scent. She rounded the corner and stopped.

What the...? Sugar Mugs's lights were on, but blinds covered the windows, and the closed sign faced the street. Maybe Charlie forgot to flip the sign to *Open*? But that wouldn't explain the blinds covering the windows. She turned the knob. Locked.

She didn't want to be a super creeper, but everything about this was odd. Her shoes squished into the earth as she tiptoed to the side of the house and peeked through the window.

Oh no.

Charlie frenzy mopped with a deep frown, flushed face, and a lopsided, unkempt ponytail. Leggings and a T-shirt in place of her typical flowy dress garb. Whatever happened, it wasn't good.

Mack's knuckles rapped on the windowpane.

Charlie whipped up her head. No smile, no soft wave. Charlie shoved the mop in the bucket and pointed to the front door.

With her stomach sinking, Mack jogged to the entrance and stepped inside.

"Are you okay?" Mack asked. "What's going on?"

Chaos covered the shop. A paper-towel-and-rags bomb had exploded. Water piled on the floor. A bucket propped open the back door. Chairs topped tables. Like trying to boil the ocean, a human-size puddle had one pathetic fan aimed at it.

"The shop flooded... last night... I don't know what to do." Charlie's breathless and shaky words flew from her mouth. She released her hair from the ponytail elastic and regathered it on top of her head. "And Ben's out of town. He couldn't come, and I... ugh!"

"God, I'm so sorry. I can't believe all of this happened from the storm." Mack reached out to hug Charlie but dropped her arms. After last night, physical contact rules changed. With how abruptly everything ended after the kiss, no way would she make Charlie feel uncomfortable again.

"The storm messed everything up... I don't even know how much damage happened." Charlie swiped her wrist across her forehead and fanned her shirt.

"Let me help." Mack rested her laptop bag on the counter as Charlie slapped the mop across the floor.

"I can't ask you to do this." Those were her words. But her eyes said, "Please help me."

"You didn't ask me to." Mack dashed a glance around the room. "What happened?"

The top of the mop offered a resting place for Charlie's chin. She inhaled and pushed a few escaped strands behind her ear. "Apparently, this place is sloped because the rain collected here." She pointed to a several-foot-wide shallow puddle near the storage room. "I bucketed the corner, too, but I can hear it under my feet. The floors are supposed to be waterproof, but... I think it seeped in."

"Do you have more towels?"

She nodded and walked toward the storage area. When she returned, she threw an apron at Mack and chucked a stack of towels on a table.

The next hour, they barely spoke. Area rugs were scooped up and hung against the iron railing in the sun. Dirty towels tossed in the washing machine. Water squeegeed and dumped outside.

Mack accepted the water bottle Charlie handed to her and toed different areas of the wood floor until water oozed out. She squatted down and pushed on the seams. "I think you'll need to rip up the flooring."

Charlie vigorously shook her head. "I can't!"

A flood would be stressful for anyone. But Charlie looked like she was on the verge of an actual breakdown. And Mack's heart verged on breaking by looking at her. She planted her arms firmly at her sides to avoid scooping Charlie into her arms. "Hey, it's okay. Tearing out the floor sucks, but you have insurance, right?"

Charlie swiped her forearm across her upper lip. "I had to take out the highest deductible 'cause I couldn't afford the premium. But I don't have enough for the deductible." Her voice cracked.

Mack's gut turned. "I'm no expert, but maybe the contractor screwed something up and it'd be on them to fix. Do you have their number?"

The wooden mop hit the floor with a resounding thud, and Mack flinched. She took a tentative step towards Charlie, who dropped her head in her hands. Her shoulders shook and a wail escaped her lips.

Hug or not? Charlie pushed her away last night. Mack didn't want her to think she was using this moment as an excuse to touch her. But the sobbing was so raw that Mack's skin prickled. She gnawed on the inside of her cheek and placed a gentle hand on Charlie's shoulder.

"I know this is super stressful, but I can help." Mack kept her voice calm. "Do you not have their number anymore?"

Charlie leaned into the wall and slid down on the wet ground. She pulled her knees up to her chest and wiped her eyes on her sleeve. "I know where the numbers are, but no way in shit am I gonna call them."

Whoa.

"Why not? Your place is great. Everyone loves it here, but the construction maybe isn't the best. No way should the seams be like that."

God, she hoped the truth wasn't insulting. Charlie obviously spent a ton of time decorating, each detail perfect and beautiful, but Mack had noticed some odd woodwork and door-frames that didn't line up on day one.

"I can't."

Mack slid down next to her. "Talk to me."

Charlie exhaled a sad, defeated breath and pinched her nose's bridge. "I'm so behind on bills. I owe them money, and I owe the vendor money, and I owe everyone money, and I'm totally failing."

The tears returned.

Screw it. Mack scooped Charlie into her arms and held her tight as her neck turned sticky from Charlie's tears. Her rigid body shook in Mack's arms, and Mack firmed her grip until Charlie's body softened and collapsed. Mack whispered everything would be okay while she rubbed Charlie's upper back.

"You're not failing." Mack maintained a soft and gentle voice. "You're killing it. You're a female entrepreneur who turned a home into a beautiful, welcoming coffee shop."

When Charlie's breath slowed and the shakes slackened, Mack released.

"Want to tell me about it?" Mack asked. "Maybe there's something I can do, or talk to someone, or... I don't know, look at the bills or something?"

Charlie shook her head. "No. No thanks. I just need to figure this out myself."

"Really, it's no problem at all. Sometimes having a fresh set of eyes on something—"

"No." Charlie unraveled herself from the floor and swiped her hands down her sweaty, muddy shirt. "Drink? I really need a vanilla latte."

Message received. Mack exhaled. "I don't think I've seen you drink a latte before." Mack pulled one of the stools off the counter.

"Lattes are the yoga pants of drinks. Easy and comforting." Charlie seeped the espresso, then layered the oat milk. She slid the drink to Mack and fell back on a chair.

The creamy sweetness hit her tongue. Charlie was right—this drink *was* like yoga pants.

After several moments of silence, Charlie inhaled a shaky breath. "I don't know what I'm gonna do."

Mack's insides lifted that Charlie was opening up. "Have you talked to Ben about this?"

"God love Ben, but he's no help whatsoever."

"Who helped you set up this shop in the first place?"

Charlie took another short sip and fiddled with the cardboard holder. "What do you mean? Like which vendors?"

"No. Like who guided the business decision? Found your contractor?" Mack stirred the foam on top with a stick. "Who helped make sure you had the right permits and licenses, and all the things that go along with opening up a business."

"Me."

"You? All alone?"

Charlie nodded.

"Are you serious? You're incredible." How did Charlie navigate construction and opening a business solo? When Mack received multiple agent offers, she must've called her parents ten times to help her with the decision. She'd paced for a week, scribbled a pros-and-cons spreadsheet, got overwhelmed and anxious, and finally decided to go with Viviane because they meshed the best.

Charlie pushed back a fallen red stray from her bun just as the sun dipped through the blinds. And now Mack wanted to kiss Charlie. Really, *really* bad. But she forced herself to retreat. Charlie's reaction last night and today's stress turned this moment into the all-time worst occasion to try anything physical.

Charlie wiped her hands off on a towel. "Not sure I deserve that praise. I clearly didn't budget correctly. I thought I did, but when they came in to remodel this place, the charges and time-lines kept fluctuating, and I couldn't keep up with everything. The remodel ended up costing double the bid."

"Double?" That figure sounded suspicious, but Mack didn't know the inner financial workings of a remodel. "Hey, I'll be right back. Gonna make a quick phone call."

The bell jingled above the door when Mack stepped outside. The warm air and sun enveloped her, and she tugged her shirt collar up to wipe her face. She skipped over a puddle and made her way out of Charlie's earshot.

Mack picked up her phone and hit dial.

FIFTEEN

CHARLIE'S DRINK SPECIAL: DEVASTATION DRIP WITH A SHORT SHOT OF OPTIMISM

Charlie slumped down on the stool, her shoulders weighing a million pounds. What the hell was she going to do? Every second her shop stayed closed, she lost a sale. And every sale lost dug her debt grave deeper. One step forward, two steps back. After additional thought, she came to a gut-wrenching conclusion: The universe sent the storm to give her the push needed to close.

The trembles started again. Slow in her chin this time, then her arms. Stress tears threatened to spill. She should give up. Maybe go to college. Maybe work at an office somewhere. Maybe buck any sort of civilization, run away, and live on an island with some sea turtles.

But her coffee shop was more than a house. Her place captured her only good childhood memories from her time with Rosie. No matter how enticing Barbados or Fiji sounded, she'd never leave this place.

The counter was cool against her forehead as she rested against it. She pulled herself up and peeked out the window at Mack pacing up and down the sidewalk on the phone.

Mack. Twelve hours earlier, she had Mack's tongue in her

mouth. And if she thought she was conflicted before, her confusion doubled down. Besides Ben, she couldn't remember the last time someone helped her out just because. Sexy, intelligent, and now helpful? What was she supposed to do with that? Her body tugged her in the same direction as her heart, but her brain yanked her back to reality.

Mack returned with a sheepish grin. She wrung her hands together before scooting a chair near Charlie. "Hey, um, I called my dad. I hope I'm not overstepping here, but he's happy to help."

"Your dad? George Clooney?"

Ben would help if he were in town, but even though he could bring muscle, he couldn't advise.

"Mack, I barely know you."

Mack winced. "Do you really think that? We only met a few weeks ago, but I feel like we're friends, right?"

Friends. Mack said the word hesitantly, almost like she wasn't sure what constituted friendship.

Sure, they were friends, but Charlie's mouth watered when she looked at her. Their lips touched. Charlie thought about her every night. Her heart skipped when Mack walked through the door. In the morning, she added an extra spritz of perfume just in case Mack visited. She'd never done any of this before with a *friend*. The only time she'd done this was with Jess.

"Yep, of course, we're friends." She tossed her cup in the trash and scanned the room.

A cyclone and earthquake had a devil baby and it ransacked her place. A nerve in her shoulder death-pinched her, and she pressed her thumbs against it. She needed a shower and a massage. And a really, really long vacation. But hopelessness faded for the first time in seven hours since she stepped into the shop and saw the damage.

An hour later, Charlie swallowed the last bite of a turkey on brioche sandwich, Mack tossed her banana peel into the garbage, the floor had dried, and Charlie popped an aspirin.

The front door chimed, and Mack's dad strutted in with a toolbox and a smile. "Hey there, Charlie. Helluva night, huh?"

"You could say that," Charlie said with a weak grin.

"Hey, kiddo," he said to Mack before shifting his eyes to Charlie. "Mackey said you might have some water damage, but looks like you two cleaned up everything pretty good. Wanna point me where I should look?"

Charlie pulled her shoulders back. She wanted to tell him that she confirmed the material was waterproof, sturdy, and eco-conscious before installation. And that she took three days to review their contract and ensure everything fit in the budget. Instead, she opened her mouth, closed it, and hung her head. "I don't know what happened. I think there was too much rain."

He smiled. Warmly. Kindly. *Fatherly*. He took deliberate steps and pushed into the floor with the tips of his shoes. Mack gave her hand a reassuring squeeze, and her touch provided everything Charlie needed not to feel alone. Without thinking, she rested her head on Mack's shoulder.

"What do you think, Dad? Fixable?" Mack asked.

He snugged his jeans up and crouched down. His eyes narrowed as he pushed his palms into the floor. "The joints weren't installed properly. We have to rip them out."

His casual tone didn't reduce the weight of his words.

Charlie's knees verged on buckling. To keep from crying, she clamped her teeth on the inside of her cheek. "I... uh, can't afford to replace them."

As his eyes dashed between her and Mack, he softened his stiffened shoulders. His slow nod and compassionate smile made her want to grip him around the waist, lean her head on his chest, and have him confirm everything was okay.

"Listen. If you can do the labor, we have some surplus at the warehouse that matches pretty close. Cover the area with a rug, and no one will notice the difference." He paused. "Think you can handle the labor?"

The thousand-pound weight she'd been carrying around since 5:00 a.m. started to vanish.

"Absolutely." She had no idea what to do. But she had YouTube, Google, and a library card. "I mean, I think I can handle the labor."

He placed a hand on her shoulder. "I *know* you can."

His confidence held a magic thread that straightened her back. She glanced at Mack, who grinned at her father.

"Installation's probably a two-person job," he said. "I can show you how to tear it out and install it, but then I need to leave."

"I'll help." Mack raised her hand.

Her dad angled his head. "You sure, Mackey? I don't think you've ever even hung a painting."

"Seriously?" She groaned. "I can absolutely help."

He lifted an eyebrow and treaded around the shop. He ran his hands over the walls. Was there something in the drywall that he could feel? Heat? Cold? Moisture? He tugged on door-frames, opened and shut doors, leaned his ear towards the wall, and knocked. Later, she'd try the same and check if the echo differed depending on where she hit. He stretched on his toes and pushed his fingertips into the ceiling beams as his eyes narrowed.

"Charlie, who did your remodeling job?"

Several different names flashed through her mind, and she thought for a moment. "I had two different companies. One did the floors and knocked out the walls, and one built the bar and bathroom."

He dropped his arms from the beam. "Who's the one that did the floor, frames, and walls?"

"Freddie's Remodeling."

His mouth twisted.

She didn't know him well enough to interpret his thoughts, but he didn't look pleased.

The metal clank of the toolbox clasp banged against the side, and he dug out a few tools. He shoved the crowbar into the floor and hit it on the top with a mallet. A chunk of flooring popped out with a crunch. After months of remodeling, spending everything she had, and borrowing against everything she didn't, he ripped the plank out like an infected sliver.

"The water probably only seeped through about six feet, but we're going to double that and remove a twelve by twelve section." He pulled the tape measure out and marked the area with a Sharpie. "If you see it's still wet after doing a six by six space, we might have to rip more. Mold's tough to get rid of once it grows."

She swallowed and contemplated running upstairs to light some incense.

"All right, show me your crawl space. I want to do a quick sweep." As they passed Mack, who was sweeping in the corner, he tipped his chin up and smiled.

Even though Charlie was sweaty and disgusting, the sun felt good against her back. She pointed out the crawl space and cringed at the sheer amount of dangling spiderwebs waiting to attack him as he climbed down.

"You okay down there?" Her hollowed voice boomed.

"Yep, good." A few minutes later, he ascended and dusted off his jeans. "Good news. I didn't see anything dripping." He tapped the back of his hand on the gutters. "I think the flooding came from the gutters. They need to be rerouted."

"Is rerouting hard?" *Expensive?*

"No, it's pretty easy." He slid his baseball cap backward. "I'll go back to the office and grab some flooring. And I'll send one of my guys here tomorrow to do the gutters."

The riptide that rushed through Charlie was overwhelming in the best way possible. She didn't mean to, but she wrapped her arms around his waist. He gave her a firm shoulder squeeze, and she stepped back. The back of her eyes burned, but she refused to cry in front of him. "I can't even thank you enough... I don't know what to say."

He swooshed his arm. "Happy to help."

She crumbled under his sincere tone and opened the door to the shop. "Can I send you off with some coffee? Snacks? A golden retriever?"

He paused for a moment. "You know, I'd love an Americano and one of those blackberry scones."

Mack attached the pan to the broom and glanced up. "Get it all figured out?"

"Yep, I think everything's gonna be okay," Charlie said as she stuffed a bag with scones and cookies and handed it to him with the drink.

He thanked her, whispered something to Mack—who beamed at her dad—and left.

"All right, let's do this." Mack clapped and retied the apron around her.

Charlie wrapped her arms around Mack, who clasped her tight like a winter scarf shielding her from a blizzard. Salty skin, spring soap, and berry scent permeated Charlie, and she buried her nose into the crook of Mack's neck.

Her chest heaved as she breathed in. "Why are you helping me?" Charlie whispered.

"Why not?" Mack whispered back.

Charlie never wanted to let go. For the first time in her life besides Ben, she had backup. Kind, warm, altruistic backup.

They spent the next hour popping in the crowbar and ripping out planks. Adrenaline torpedoed Charlie to save her drowning baby. And Mack stayed solidly at her side, working equally as hard on the rescue mission.

The air-conditioning couldn't keep up with the labor-intensive work, and sweat gathered and dripped down her back and chest. She smiled at Mack's crumpled, dirty shirt. Mack never mentioned it, but Charlie bet good money Mack was dreaming of a bleach bath.

Fatigue tingles shot through Charlie's fingers, and she shook them out. She'd keep shaking her arms until they fell off if that was what it took. Mack stretched her hips, rubbed her neck, and returned to pounding the mallet against the bar. And, *dear God*, her strained forearms and glistening skin were the performance-enhancing drug Charlie needed to push through the pain.

Almost two hours later, her limbs were totally shot. Arm muscles twitched, her tacky and dehydrated mouth begged for liquid, her fingers were raw.

Mack picked up the crowbar and it slipped through her hand like it was coated in oil. "I literally can't even grip it."

They both gripped the final piece of flooring and tugged. The plank landed in a corner behind them and they collapsed.

"I'm. So. Tired." She deadweight propped herself against the wall, and Mack crawled to join her.

"Same." Mack leaned her head on Charlie's shoulder, and Charlie rested back on her.

How the heck did Mack's dad do this kind of stuff day in and day out? Even her eyelids hurt. Time passed, she wasn't even sure how long, before she took a solid look at the shop. If Sugar Mugs was destroyed earlier, a trifecta of natural disasters hit it now. The place was a shipwreck meets earthquake meets frat-house weekend bender.

But her home was fixable. And gratitude overflowed.

A stomach growled. "Was that me or you?" Mack chuckled.

"No idea." Charlie dragged herself to her feet and grabbed two plates from the counter. "Coffee cake?"

Mack nodded and flung herself face down on the couch. She rolled over and propped herself on her elbows when Charlie handed her the cake.

"Can I ask you something?" Charlie closed her eyes as the cinnamon-and-brown-sugar relief swirled on her tongue.

"Of course."

"What do you get out of helping me?"

Mack set the fork down. "Are you serious?"

"I don't mean to sound accusatory. I appreciate you so much right now. But people don't normally just help others like this, you know?"

Mack softened and reached for her fork again. "Has that been your experience?"

"I'm just used to doing things on my own." She learned how to do laundry at six years old so she wouldn't wear dirty clothes to kindergarten. Took her dad's shoes off when he passed out on the couch because it was easier on his feet the next day if she did. Left a glass of water on the coffee table because he always woke up thirsty. "I feel like I have to pay you or something."

"Oh God, stop." Mack twisted the cap open on a water. "I've used your shop as an office the last few weeks. I should be paying you rent. So, we're even, okay?"

They were both disgusting right now. Dirty, stinky, and sweaty. And Charlie was pretty sure she'd never been as deeply attracted to anyone as she was at this moment.

The door opened, and work boots stomped across the floor. "All right, ladies, come grab a few boxes."

"I... can't... move..." Mack said, and Charlie hoisted her to her feet. They shuffled outside as Mack's dad lugged the boxes toward the opening of the truck's cab.

"Dang, these are heavy," Mack said as Charlie held the end of the box and walked backward into the house. After unloading and stacking the boxes in the corner, Mack's dad summoned them back to the floor.

"I'm gonna show you two how to do this. I'll come back later to check the joints and make sure everything is sealed properly, so we don't have this issue again." He lined up the planks and snapped the adjoining piece. "Installing is a helluva lot easier than pulling them out."

Thank God.

Mack's dad brought in extra towels and told the women he'd be back in a few hours. Charlie and Mack stuffed the towels underneath their knees and got to work.

He was right. The work was more manageable. They connected the pieces in under an hour, hauled the floor chunks and paper towels to the dumpster, and swept and mopped.

And then crumpled onto the couch.

"I can't even think." Charlie wiped her forehead on her arm. "Don't ask me my name, or zodiac sign, or favorite color. All I can think about is a hot AF bath and my bed."

"A bath." Mack flung her arm over her head and slouched down. "With lavender bubbles. And a vanilla candle. Followed by a massage and a Netflix marathon."

"Okay, now you're just flirting." Charlie grinned. "Pizza?"

Mack yawned. "Yes, please."

Charlie reached for her cell. "Let me guess. Thin crust. A respectable New Yorker wouldn't have it any other way."

"I'm starting to think you know me."

The sky shifted to a darker hue, and few words were spoken as the women devoured pepperoni, black olive, and jalapeño pizza. Between yawns, stretches, and four additional water bottles scattered across the floor, Charlie was officially done.

She reclined on the couch and stared out the window. "Your dad's a rock star."

"He's pretty great." Mack burrowed into the side of the couch. "Sometimes, I take him for granted. I get so wrapped up in my writing world that my parents fall off the priority list."

Charlie didn't say anything. If she were born into a family like this, would she take her parents for granted, too? Seemed unfathomable. Right now, Mack's dad was on par with Superman.

"Can you believe this is the first time I visited them in a year?" Mack asked.

She couldn't. Sure, she and her own dad sometimes went a year without seeing each other, even though they lived in the same state. But her dad was, well, her dad. Not a man like Andrew. "Why did you wait so long?"

Mack's face fell. A myriad of expressions bounced through her eyes. Sadness, maybe? Sheepishness?

"Long story." Mack stood and tossed the pizza box in the compost. "So... um... I really don't want to make this weird or overstep, but my dad texted. He's wondering if he could look at the contract for the remodel."

Charlie's face heated. "Why?"

"He's just offering to see if they're liable for the installation," Mack said. "He wants to show it to my mom. She can be a bulldog with these types of things."

The paperwork contained a ton of private information, namely her complete incompetence in paying the bills. Fire spread in her chest picturing Andrew reviewing her paperwork with a disappointed frown. "I had so many dreams for this place. I kept thinking if I created a space that felt like a home, people would magically come."

When she drafted the remodel plan, she studied every article she could and designed it herself before bringing it to the contractor. Every thought, every detail, surrounded making her coffee shop as homey as possible. The coffee stand in the middle like a kitchen island. The bookshelf and couches like a living room. She filled her Jess void for a year with blueprints, wood furniture, and books, and found a purpose.

Mack wiped her mouth with a napkin and balled it in her hand. "I love the space you created. The second I stepped in, I immediately noticed the warm feeling."

Her eyes dropped to Charlie's lips, and she pulled back up. The zing from that look reached Charlie's toes.

"And then I saw you." A blush swept Mack's cheeks. "And you were the only thing I noticed."

Charlie was a certified hot, stinky mess, but every cell in her body wanted to pull Mack into her lap and taste her mouth again. Her legs tightened, and her neck grew warm. She wanted this. She didn't want this. She couldn't think and needed to think and didn't want to think.

Dammit.

Stop. Too soon. Too much. Too scary. Two years passed before she got over Jess. Did she really want to throw all that healing away? She leaped off the floor. "We should have Italian sodas. Cherry?" She didn't wait for an answer.

Mack slumped back into the couch as Charlie dug out the supplies.

The ice rattled against the plastic as Charlie mixed the club soda, cream, and cherry syrup. "I don't want to lose this place. My shop is my heart, you know? I genuinely thought that when people walked in, they'd love it as much as me, and I'd have to set up outdoor seating to accommodate. But... I need more customers."

Mack moved to the counter and leaned her cheek into her hands. "What's your social media presence like?"

"Next to none."

Charlie slid the soda to her. The way Mack's spectacular deep pink lips wrapped around the straw made Charlie crumble. Needing a safe space between them, she dragged her chair out from under the till. Everything from gratitude to Mack's honey mouth tiptoed the emotional highwire, and she didn't trust herself. "I'm not great with social media, and I totally overthink my posts."

"I get that. We have a social media team that takes care of all the posts 'cause I hate it, too. I like prose. Short snappy words are not my thing." Mack took the straw out and licked the cream from the bottom.

Charlie nearly lost her cool watching the motion. Her fingers itched to reach out and slide across Mack's silky skin.

She had to shift focus. She and Mack were nothing but friends. Friends who kissed. But the fiery burn in her belly persisted. An uneasy combination of potential rejection, lust, wanting to be held, and disappointment in herself for feeling those things all left her restless.

Mack's phone rang. "I'll be right back."

Charlie wiped down the syrup bottles and spoon when Mack returned.

"Hey, I need to get going."

Charlie's chest deflated. Of course Mack had to leave. She'd been here all damn day. Did she think that Mack would join her in a bath? Okay, *perhaps* that crossed her mind. She held a plastered smile. "For sure. I can't believe... you've been here all day. You probably have people to see and—"

"No, it's not like that. I need to Zoom with my agent and I really need to shower. Not that she hasn't seen me look like hell before, but I just..." She flashed her arms across her dirt-covered chest. "I have to get ready for the conference and book signing tomorrow."

Charlie smacked her hand against her forehead. "I'm ridiculously selfish. I literally didn't even think of that."

Mack wrapped up the apron and tossed it on the counter. "Don't make me go."

"That bad, huh?"

"Writing sometimes feels like my side chick. Horrible term, I know, but follow me along on this little misogynistic analogy train ride." She threw her laptop bag across her shoulders. "I love it. I'm seduced by it. But sometimes, I feel like it's going to strip my sanity. Book signings feel like I sold my soul to Satan's bride."

"I wish I could do something to make it easier for you."

"Unless you can sit by me feeding me scones and Americanos, sadly, no." She grinned and reached for her keys. "My dad said he'd come by in the morning and double-check the flooring."

How did she win the jackpot with Mack and her dad? "I didn't thank you enough for this. I don't know how to repay you."

"Go out with me Saturday night for dinner?" Mack stepped back like she saw a ghost. "Oh my God, not that you need to repay me by going out with me."

I shouldn't. I can't. "I'd love to."

Mack waved her wrists. "Nope, I just made it super awkward. Now I'll never know if you would've accepted no matter what or if my intensely superhuman manual-labor skills made you feel obligated."

"Stop." Charlie smiled. "I feel like I should be taking you out for dinner."

"No, we're even, remember? New slate." Mack tapped her palm against her bag. "So... dinner on Saturday?"

A date? Shouldn't she keep Mack in the friend zone? She'd barely healed from her divorce. Mack wasn't even from Seattle.

Her insides scrunched, twisted, and turned.

Screw it. I deserve some fun.

"Saturday sounds perfect."

SIXTEEN

MACK'S DRINK SPECIAL: OVERSTIMULATED
CHAI TEA WITH WHIPPED CREAM RELIEF

The buzzing alarm cut through the darkness. Mack slapped the nightstand in search of it and eased one eye open. 5:00 a.m. Yuck. Graveyard shift. She counted backward from ten and tumbled off the bed. The heated, high-pressure shower soothed her aching muscles. No wonder her dad was so fit. One day of manual labor work and body parts burned she didn't even know existed.

Twenty minutes later, she pulled and tucked the sheets until she achieved proper hospital corners, then reached for her comfort board. With every methodical swipe, the iron dissipated her nerves. A mere twelve hours from now, she'd be done schmoozing with humans and could hide under the covers in a dark room until the jolts faded.

Beep. Her heart skipped at Charlie's name.

"What the..." She tapped on the message to enlarge it. A picture of a scone with a butcher knife filled the screen.

> Charlie: if you ever want to see your scone alive again, you'll meet me on the corner of Pike and Pine wearing a Macklemore t-shirt, converse sneakers, and carrying a gallon of oat milk.

> Mack: did you send me a scone hostage photo?

> Mack: I'm impressed. But also calling the gluten authorities

Charlie: ;-) I just want to say good luck today

> Mack: I told my agent I was sick, but she called bull

Charlie: You're going to be great. If you want to chat after, you can call me.

Mack didn't want to chat after the signing. She wanted to swing by and recreate the hammock moment.

> Mack: if you'd sit by me during the book signing, I'd feel so much better

Charlie: You're funny

> Mack: I'm not joking!

> Mack: Hate this, but I've gotta run.

Charlie: all good. See you tomorrow 😊

Tomorrow. A real live, adult, proper date. Yesterday, when she asked Charlie out, the words slipped from her lips before she could reel them back in. God bless fatigue, flooded floors, and Italian soda for giving her a swift kick in the ass to take the leap.

The giddiness of spending time with Charlie outside the shop counteracted the pending nerves from chatting with a hundred million people today. Everything about Charlie was warm and gooey, and Mack wanted to swallow it whole and let it swim in her belly. Charlie's kindness, sharp tongue, laughter. Her hair... those lips. *Damn.* Mack had never felt a connection before. Not like this anyway. Wanting to sleep with the same person she wanted to talk to for hours was a new sensation. And more than a tad terrifying.

Also new? Flutters in her chest. The yearning to hear someone's laugh. Wanting to know someone's favorite ice cream, favorite movie, *and* favorite position.

Mack clasped on a multi-layered necklace, double-checked her hair in the mirror, and read through all of her and Charlie's text exchanges, *again*, gorging on the buzz. How did simply reading texts cause this much of a physiological reaction? She was a writer. These were words. And yet... all unholy places stirred.

"Bring it in." Viviane's bangles clanged like a symphony when she opened her arms wide for a hug.

The assaulting bright lights of the hotel lobby lessened as Mack closed her eyes and inhaled Viviane's comforting signature coconut scent. "What time did you land?" She wrapped a conference badge Viviane handed her around her neck.

Viviane tugged the bottom of her satin gold shirt. "Didn't get to the hotel until almost two in the morning."

"I don't understand how you still look beautiful jet-lagged."

"Oh, Mack. Go on." She swept her long braids over her shoulder with a grin. "Let's get out of the lobby before any groupies spot you."

She rolled her eyes, but Viviane wasn't wrong. Growing up a certified book nerd, Mack had *no* idea the type of action she'd get offered at conferences and book signings. The number of people who slipped their contact info into her hand or asked to buy her a drink probably matched what bartenders at a swanky nightclub received. She shouldn't indulge as much as she did, but it was *so easy*. Every few months after maintaining a self-inflicted dry spell, she got laid to help her focus. Maybe hooking up with no intention of a relationship wasn't cool, but a nonverbalized agreement of a mutually beneficial encounter always seemed present. She satisfied her physical needs and got her creative juices flowing, and they gained the notoriety of sleeping with one of their favorite authors. Dinner or breakfast was never part of the equation. And cuddling was out of the question. Doing rugged, messy, dirty things, then snuggling after, always felt a little gross.

"Let's grab some coffee and snacks from the prep room." Viviane simultaneously walked, talked, and texted like a champ. Her phone pinged so much it became like crickets chirping in the background. The beauty of having an agent to coordinate, talk, and sell meant Mack's phone remained perfectly quiet.

"Mack Ryder. So excited to have you with us," the blue-haired conference coordinator said as she approached with her hand outstretched. "I loved *The Edge of the Shadow*. Personal top five of all time."

Less than twenty words spoken to someone outside her bubble, and already beads of sweat brewed beneath the surface. "Nice of you to say. Thank you." *Nice?* She had a thesaurus in her brain and came up with "nice."

"If your ears have been burning, it's all the buzz about you from the attendees. People are really excited to learn from you today. You may have broken the record for the quickest time filling a class."

Probably not true. But Mack smiled anyway. God, she wished she could take a compliment and move on. Now she was even more nervous, and her imposter syndrome demon sat upright on her shoulder, ready for battle.

The coordinator led them to the conference room. Without breathing, she rattled off the classroom's technical capabilities, gave her the name of the moderator who'd be fielding questions from the virtual audience, and asked for the third time if Mack needed a snack. An assistant knocked on the door juggling five bottles of water—per Mack's strict request—and lined them up on the desk. *Perfect.* Now Mack was prepared for a coughing attack while presenting.

After the coordinator left, Mack paced the room's perimeter, her pre-speech ritual.

"Woman." Viviane's clipped voice echoed in the open space. "The PowerPoint presentation is confirmed working, your microphone tested, and your obscene amount of water is here in case you need to take a bath."

Mack tossed up her hands. "Yeah?"

"So why are you still pacing? You've already done your standard two times."

Mack shrugged. Now was not the time to have a heart-to-heart or ask for love advice.

Viviane set her phone upside down on the podium.

Never a good sign.

"You know I have to ask." Viviane's deep brown eyes locked with Mack's.

She squirmed under the weight of the look. "It's good."

Viviane lifted an eyebrow and remained silent.

"Do you use this tactic on your kids? Death-glare and silence until they speak?"

"Yes." Viviane squeezed Mack's forearm. "Come on, give me something."

Hmmm. Found a muse. But she was innocent and sweet and completely unsuspecting that Mack exploited her trauma and mannerisms to build a murderer's profile for her stories. And she deserved so much more, and the guilt slathered on thick, but she couldn't stop because the content was too damn good and would elevate the manuscript. And she was falling for her, *so hard*, and didn't know what to do.

"Going way better than it was a few weeks ago. Thank you,

literary gods." Mack finally offered after succumbing to the Viviane Pressure Cooker Gaze. "And I'm not leaving Seattle anytime soon."

"Oh yeah?"

"I might stay until I finish the book."

"Really?" Viviane angled her head. "Tell me more."

Spilling the details about Charlie was the last thing Mack wanted to do right now. Viviane was Mack's closest—only—friend, but she'd dig for details until Mack folded. "I'm taking the story in a bit of a different direction from the outline. More interiority."

Viviane crossed her arms and leaned a hip into the podium. "Too much interiority's dangerous to do with a thriller, Mack. People like to be kept on their toes and don't care as much about feelings."

"I know that, *thank you*." She didn't hide the sarcasm in her voice. "But I need to humanize Shelby a little more. I want everyone to love her as much as I love her. To see the reasons behind what she does. I know it's a balance, but I think I'm nailing it."

"What's your word count?"

"Fifty-eight thousand as of yesterday."

Viviane nodded. "Still behind schedule."

Viviane never minced words. Her directness and no-BS nature drew Mack to her in the first place. But anything except Viviane's undying love and approval always created heartburn.

"Mack. I'm just saying truths here." She gripped her hand. "You know this, right? You got this."

Mack's chest tightened, and she tried to take a breath. With a little over a month until the deadline, she should be in her final stages of editing—not staring at a half-written book, praying it would finish itself. The amount given to her for the advance flashed in her mind, and she blinked the image away.

Those funds were gone—and without a finished manuscript, she had no way of paying it back.

Someone knocked on the door, and a woman with headphones and a clipboard peeked through the cracked door. "Ms. Ryder?"

"Please call me Mack."

"We'll be ready for final testing in fifteen."

Mack reached for the water. She grabbed a notebook on the table and fanned her face, then darted to the mirror to confirm her shirt hadn't creased. Breathing out even, slow breaths finally slowed her pounding heart.

"Something else is up with you." Viviane rolled a chair closer to Mack. "You wanna tell me why you seem different than the last time I saw you?"

"Huh? Nothing's different."

Viviane cracked a smile. "Did you meet someone?"

The warmth now extended past Mack's chest and blasted directly to her neck and cheeks.

"Mackenzie Ryder... whaaaaa? I've known you almost four years and have never heard you talk about someone. Wow. She must be a special one."

Damn Viviane and her super sleuth superpower. Mack couldn't help but smile.

Viviane smoothed out her shirt and effectively dropped the conversation, probably knowing that Mack was on the cusp of a breakdown from the day's activities. But she patted Mack's hand a little longer than usual. "I'm heading to the ladies' room, then over to the pitch area. Wanna text me when you're done, and we'll meet up?"

"Hey, maybe we can cancel—"

"Nope." She waved from behind her head as she exited. "See you in a few hours."

Mack shook out her spasming arms, finished one more lap, and waited.

The class filed in, pulling an opposite of high school, where the first rows filled up the quickest. Mack quietly exhaled and straightened her shoulders.

"Good morning, everyone." She smiled at the crowd before pulling up her presentation. One more unsteady breath exhaled, she wiggled her toes to keep the blood flowing and clasped her fingers together. "Who's ready to learn how to make people love the unlovable?"

Three hours later, Mack completed the class and follow-up Q and A session without technical issues. She threw back a salad, chatted with a couple of fellow authors, and another hour later, she popped a Tylenol in the Uber as she and Viviane made their way downtown.

Viviane caught Mack's gaze. "Headache?"

"Preventative measures." Mack snapped the cap back on and tossed the bottle in her bag. "And I messed up my shoulder a little yesterday helping a friend."

"Helping a friend. In Seattle. Uh-huh." Viviane's fingers tapped her crossed arms. "Is this who you blushed about earlier?"

Viviane was Mack's closest person in the world besides her parents. Why was she keeping Charlie so close, like a mystical ancient scroll? Maybe it was less about Charlie the person and more about the feelings that stirred with any thought of Charlie. The newness of everything left her squirmy, and she barely had time to process things.

"Yeah." Mack exhaled. "She owns the coffee shop I've been working out of 'cause if I spend too much time around my mom, I'll go crazy. But she had a water issue at her place, and I helped her out."

"Interesting." Viviane's mouth twisted, and her face softened. "How's your mom?"

"Annoying."

"Excellent. Annoying moms are good. Means she got her spunk back, huh?"

"She's up my ass all the time, but I kind of like it." Mack drummed her fingers against the window ledge. "But I'll never tell her that, and if you do, I'll write a terrible children's horror book and tell the literary world you made me do it."

"Dammmmn. Tough words." Viviane's neck stretched as she peeked out the window. "Well, sister, we got a pretty healthy line already. You good?"

Oof. The crowd wrapped around the block, and at least two dozen other people trudged up the sidewalk with bags or books tucked under their arms. Mack cracked the window and yanked off her necklace that dug into her skin and constricted the last of her air. *Inhale, four. Hold, four. Exhale, four. Hold, four.*

"No." She slammed back the rest of the water and swiped her hand across her upper lip. "It's too much. Why didn't we schedule this on a different day?"

"Because you like to knock it all out at once." She directed the driver to the alley. "Come on, all these people bought your books and are here to see you."

"I know, I know. I sound like I don't appreciate them, and I do. I'm just over being around people."

Viviane wrapped her warm fingers over Mack's, her multiple stacked rings settling on Mack's knuckles. "I know you think you have to put on some façade in public, but you don't. I'm gonna let you in on a little secret. You're pretty amazing, just as you are. Got it?"

Mack rested her head on Viviane's shoulder and prayed, through the power of osmosis, she could soak in some of Viviane's kindness and strength.

Mack dragged her hands down her face. She'd give anything to be sitting at Sugar Mugs, listening to Charlie's candy-sweet voice and indulging in the whisper of vanilla that fluttered to her nose whenever Charlie stood close. Charlie was a circumference of joy and light that somehow beamed energy into Mack, rather than taking it away. Then maybe she'd have enough oomph to deal with the crowd.

Viviane exited the car and held a hand out for Mack. "Come on. We got this."

Needing any support she could get to leave the car, Mack accepted her hand but groaned as Viviane tugged her to the alley entrance door.

"Welcome!" The overly chipper owner with a name tag that said *Ken* wiped his hand on his thigh before shaking Mack's hand, and escorted her into the multilevel bookstore with brick walls, cedar bookshelves, and creaky hardwood floors. "Happy to have the talented M. Ryder in our midst."

She discreetly dragged her thumb across her itchy stomach, and in T minus three minutes, her back would be tacky with sweat. But the need to put him at ease superseded her need to hide, so she smiled. "Happy to be here. Your store's beautiful. How long have you owned this?"

"My grandfather opened it over fifty years ago." Ken motioned her to an oversized sitting chair. "I expanded about ten years back."

"Incredible. Really lovely."

He checked his watch as his foot tapped against the floor. "We've got water, coffee, snacks, and all the pens you may need. The office assistants will keep the line moving and have strict instructions to allow thirty seconds for every interaction."

She peeked up at Viviane. "We changed that from sixty?"

Viviane nodded. "We don't want a situation like we had in Brooklyn in the spring."

Timing the interactions sucked, but it'd be unfair if she burnt out by depleting her energy on the people in the front, which happened in Brooklyn after the crowd doubled from the anticipated size.

The buzz of the people murmuring behind the thick velvet

curtain triggered her hands to sweat. She shoved them under her arms. Viviane nudged her, her indication to take a more welcoming stance. Apparently, her need to self-soothe reflected she was a snob. She rolled her eyes with a quick grin and picked up a pen to twirl instead.

Viviane held open the curtain, and Mack tiptoed through. An uncomfortable gentle chorus of claps erupted, and she waved. The audience wasn't like a rock show. No thunderous applause or screams bellowed from the room. But all eyes burrowed into her as she settled.

She gulped down a quarter bottle of water and slid over to make room for Viviane. A notepad lay in front of her, and she scribbled to confirm the ink worked. She scooted back and forth on the chair until she got comfortable, every movement seeming to echo in the engulfing open space.

The crowd moved clunkily at first as she got her bearings straight. A solid twenty minutes into signing, a beautiful woman with a shaved head and black chipped nail polish rested a book on the table.

"Hi there." Mack smiled. "Who should I make this out to?"

"Sophie." Her lip piercing lifted as she grinned. "I loved this book. Can't wait for the next one."

"Thank you." As she wrote, the black ink turned gray. Mack snatched a new one from the pile.

The woman rested her palm flat against the table and leaned forward. "How do you like the city?"

"Seattle's beautiful. Loving all the trees."

She scribbled the same message as she did for all people. Their name, then:

Thx. M. Ryder

"Thx" was lazy. She knew it, and they maybe knew it, too. But after signing thousands of books over the years, the lack of letters saved her wrists.

The woman slid a card over. The fourth one today.

"In case you find yourself needing a tour guide." She bit the corner of her lip and the bookstore assistant motioned the next fan forward.

"Thanks." Mack put the card in her pocket with a smile—an automatic response meant to defuse a situation and ensure the other person didn't feel rejected. Even though it'd been a few months since she slept with anyone, and the hammock kiss from Charlie had her body screaming, she wouldn't call. Only one woman occupied her mind.

Ninety minutes later, Viviane called for a short ten-minute break.

"I need a massage." Mack rolled her fist up and down the tangled knot in her hip. "Next time, can we put that in the rider? Comped ass massage with peppermint lavender oil."

"Do you need me to rub your butt?"

"I thought this day would never come."

Viviane shook her head with a giggle. "You're doing great. We've got an hour and a half left. Not sure if we can get through the crowd in that amount of time, so it'll be up to you to call it. I'll let you know when you meet the obligatory time."

Mack returned to the table with fatigue interrupting her nerves. She peeked at her watch. 4:05 p.m. She stifled a yawn, and Viviane leaned in to ask if she needed more coffee. At this point, Mack needed something way more potent. A shot of adrenaline to the heart or a defibrillator might do the trick. She twisted her neck for relief when something caught her eye. Her pulse flew into her throat.

The red hair. The septum ring. The signature flowy dress, this one an emerald color that highlighted her eyes from a hundred feet away. Mack's eyes locked with Charlie's, and everything else faded into portrait mode.

She came.

"Mack. *Mack.*" Viviane gripped her forearm. "You all right?"

"Yeah. Sorry, no, yeah, I'm good. What was your name again?" she asked the confused-looking woman in front of her, and quickly scribbled a note inside the cover.

Mack squeaked the chair back and leaned into Viviane's ear. "My... ah... friend is here. I think for moral support."

"Where?"

"Red hair. Green dress. About twenty-five people back."

Viviane lifted herself a few inches from the chair and scanned the crowd. "Tattoos?"

Mack nodded.

"Damn, woman. She's beautiful."

Mack overheated again, but this time she welcomed the sensation. "I know," she whispered, and motioned to the store assistant.

SEVENTEEN

CHARLIE'S DRINK SPECIAL: SUPPORTIVE RED-GINGER TEA

What am I doing here?

The overworn hardwood floors beneath Charlie's feet absorbed all her toe-tapping. Her nagging, internal voice from this morning nudging her to see Mack turned into a screaming, pushy voice by noon. She had called Lena into work and tossed her apron at Ben, who solidified his Best Hype Man of the Year Award with howls and ear-splitting whistles as she dashed to her car.

The size of the crowd was totally unexpected when she pulled up, and over an hour passed before she stepped into the shop. And now every shred of fortified confidence she'd had earlier evaporated as conversation swirled around her about Mack. Not *her friend* Mack. Not *the woman she kissed a few nights ago* Mack. But *international best-selling author* Mack.

Seeing Mack like this, a star-like figure with her admiring, giddy fans and giant poster of her prominently displayed in the window, made Charlie's heart pound so heavily she was pretty sure the woman next to her could feel the vibration. No way was this the same woman who sat on the floor with her eating pizza after installing hardwood floors. Nope, this was *M. Ryder*. Best-selling author. Book club discussions. One hundred thousand social media followers. *One. Hundred. Thousand.* When she checked today, she nearly passed out.

She'd met her as Mack. An exciting outsider who asked great questions and made Charlie feel like the most fascinating person in the world. Charlie didn't forget Mack was a writer—she constantly typed on her laptop. But in the backdrop of the Seattle tech industry, where everyone had a laptop, Mack blended into the population. But here, a light shone on her. And Charlie felt ridiculous.

Charlie froze as Mack whispered something to an employee, who stared at her. What the hell was Charlie doing? Mack was totally out of her league. Did she even want Mack in her league? No, yes, maybe? Okay, *fine.* She had feelings for Mack. A huge, crushing number of feelings. She wanted her.

But so did this crowd.

Charlie shuffled her tote and moved to return to where she came from—the land of the safe. Surrounded by Colombian coffee beans, blackberry scones, regulars, and zero potential heartaches.

A pencil-skirt-wearing woman tapped her on the shoulder. "Charlie, right?"

Charlie gulped and forced a nod.

"Ms. Ryder would like me to escort you to the back room."

Wow. Even with a hushed voice, a dozen eyes shot her way, several containing scowls. Her heart soared like someone lifted their masquerade-ball mask and extended a formal invitation for her to join the Illuminati.

They ducked under the velvet rope and hurried past the line. Mack flashed a quick glance with the sides of her mouth lifted before she turned her attention back to the person standing in front of her.

The amplified paper and ink scent inundated her behind

the curtain. The energy of the shop and its history soaked in through her feet. The thin, worn, hardwood planks creaked with each step. Stacked books filled every nook.

Heaven.

"Go ahead and take a seat, and she'll be here in a bit. Help yourself to whatever." The assistant's hand flung toward a table with various grapes, cheeses, crackers, and flame-free candles.

"Thanks." No way could her coiled belly ingest any snacks. She fiddled with her dragonfly charm bracelet and tapped her boots against the floor.

Ten minutes later, the curtain swung open. Mack had zero hesitancy when she marched to Charlie and wrapped her arms around her.

Damn. Mack always smelled so freaking good. Today a citrus meadowy scent traveled to her nose. Charlie nuzzled in a little closer.

"You came!"

"Thought I'd stop by and check on you. Oh, and I brought you something." Charlie grabbed a container out of her bag.

Mack's eyes lit up. "You brought me the hostage scone?" She popped a chunk in her mouth. "Yum. So good. Thank you."

"How's it going out there? You look like a natural."

"I'm miserable." She swiped the corner of her lips with her pinkie. "I'm so tired. And my throat is on fire. I had no idea this many people would show, and I already spoke for a few hours at the conference."

"And how's your body?"

"My body?" Mack's dimples appeared.

Charlie's entire being turned red. It was like Mack could read every thought. "From yesterday... from the floor."

Mack laid her hand on Charlie's arm. And kept it there. "Ah. In one day, I've exceeded the maximum amount of Tylenol a human should have in a week. But I think—"

The curtain swiped open, and a stunning Black woman

with braids reaching to her waist peeked in. "Mack, we've got to keep the line moving."

"Okay, be there in a second."

The woman smiled at Charlie before she pivoted and closed the curtain.

"Come sit by me." Mack pushed her hands together in prayer hands. "Please."

"What? No. I can't do that." But the idea of being by Mack in any capacity sounded pretty damn good.

"I'm serious."

Mack's palm pressed into Charlie, and her entire arm went mushy. Mack tugged her toward the entrance, and Charlie followed.

When they stepped outside of the curtain, Charlie felt a hundred eyes look at her. The air-conditioning and fans couldn't keep up with the heat and she subtly fanned her dress at the thigh.

"Viviane, meet Charlie. Charlie—Viv," Mack whispered as she got settled back into her chair and fetched a pen.

"Hi, there. Nice to meet you. We'll chat more when this is all over," Viviane whispered back with a firm grip, brilliant smile, and effortless confidence.

Charlie liked her immediately.

The next hour zoomed by. People held their books out to Mack as she charmed each guest with generous smiles and quick conversation. Charlie did this in her shop—schmoozed—but she *loved* it. Watching Mack do this, knowing she cringed inside, impressed the hell out of Charlie.

"Hey, the contractual time is over. You wanna wrap this up?" Viviane asked Mack with a hushed voice.

"Nope," Mack said. "They've been waiting for hours. Least I can do is stay."

Viviane nodded and told the assistant to continue.

A man approached with three books under his arm, his

body bouncing as he held them out to her. "Your book kicked ass. I'm buying these for my family. Loved everything about it. Dude, the ending was killer. I mean, you know, not killer, but *killer*." His loud and rushed tone was more excited than dangerous, but Charlie's hair stood on edge.

"Thank you for that." Mack poised the pen over the book. "Who should I make this out to?"

"Can I get a hug?" The man plunged his arms forward without waiting for a response, and although he directed his reach to Mack, Charlie's backbone stiffened.

Viviane clamped her hand down on top of Mack's, her bangles tinkling. "Sorry, no hugging policy. I'm sure you understand."

Mack handed back the books, reached under the table, and gave Charlie's knee a squeeze. The tingles blasted to the top of her thigh. The overzealousness was aimed at Mack, and she comforted Charlie? *Swoon.*

When the last person left, the owner bolted the deadlock. He waved his employees over to the counter as Mack slid down the chair and rested her head on the back. "I'm so flipping tired."

"You did good." Viviane patted her on the arm. "Charlie, thanks for hanging out. You were everything Mack needed to not crawl under the table."

Viviane and Mack excused themselves to chat with the owner, and Charlie chipped away at her neon orange fingernail polish while she marinated in Viviane's words.

What Mack needed. Did Mack need her? Why, after only a short amount of time, was Mack needing her equally scary and wonderful?

The women gathered their items, and they all moved outside. The city streetlights illuminated the rocks embedded into the sidewalk as they walked to Viviane's waiting Uber.

"Been a heck of a day. Gonna head back to the hotel and

sleep off the success." Viviane tugged her bag higher on her shoulder. "Great to meet you, Charlie. Mack, give me a hug."

They both waved to Viviane and turned to stroll down the sidewalk. Cars honking, buses whipping by, and chirping crosswalk indicators funneled in the background. Mack dug out several business cards from her pocket, tossed them in the trash, and continued alongside Charlie.

"You hungry?" Charlie asked.

"No. The nerves frazzled my appetite." Mack pointed to a café on the corner. "You up for a coffee from your competitor?"

Charlie glanced up at the chain coffee shop nestled between two clothing stores. "Ah. My old stomping grounds. I used to go to this place when Ben and I skateboarded downtown."

"You skateboarded?" Mack held the door open. "You've officially leveled up yet another notch on the cool factor. My mom put the fear of God into me that I'd break some body part if I ever tried, so I never did."

The quiet, dimly lit coffee shop contrasted with Sugar Mugs's radiant energy, but the roasted coffee bean scent comforted her the same. They found a quiet corner table and sipped vanilla chai tea lattes. With the whirlwind afternoon shifting to a peaceful evening, Charlie took a deep breath.

"You have a perfect slope."

Mack's eyebrows furrowed. "Um, thanks? What's a slope?"

"This little spot right here." Charlie touched the middle point above her lips and below her nose. "The slope."

"Is that an actual term?"

"Yep." Charlie took a tentative sip. "You've never used that in one of your stories, huh? Better write more kissing scenes." A burn spread in Charlie's chest. They hadn't talked more about the hammock kiss, and now the subject hung in the air. Charlie's eyes drew toward Mack's soft mouth, then her perfect pink cheekbones, strong jawline, smooth neck, and dark eyes.

Focus on the chai.

"I'm in awe of you right now." Charlie tossed Mack a sheepish grin. "You're like... famous. I half expected TMZ to be outside on the sidewalk taking photos of us."

Mack laughed. "It'd be a very sad, very slow news day if I ever showed up online."

"You said before that it's tough to be around groups of people like this?"

Mack nodded.

Charlie twirled the drink. "Well, you were a natural with the crowd."

"It's all an act. I hate it. And I'm not just saying that. Do you know I didn't even make my first doctor appointment for myself until I was twenty? My mom, in Seattle, made the appointments for me in New York. Ridiculous, right?"

So, she's not perfect. Which made her even more perfect.

The sugared tea traveled quickly, and they resumed their trek toward Charlie's car. A light mist started, unearthing the metallic scent of rain against the pavement. Charlie looped her arm through Mack's and tugged her under the building's canopies.

"Here's a random question." Mack slid over to allow another couple heading towards them space on the sidewalk. "Are umbrellas sold in Seattle?"

Charlie chuckled. "Yeah. Wait, what?"

"I never see anyone with umbrellas. Or rarely. I only thought about it because the woman over there has one." She pointed to a woman holding a canary yellow umbrella looking in a shop window.

"Tourist, for sure. Locals just brave the elements."

An electric city bus drove by them as they waited at a stop light, and Charlie glanced at Mack through her peripherals. Mack's mouth twisted like she was deep in thought. Several moments of silence passed when Mack squeezed her arm.

"You have no idea what it meant to me that you came here today."

Charlie shrugged. "It was nothing."

"Charlie." Her lusciously raspy tone filled the air. "It was everything. I don't have a lot of people in my life, and you just showed up."

"You literally installed my floors yesterday. Like hard physical labor. Pretty sure I owe you a massage."

Mack's eyebrow lifted, and Charlie swallowed, and both remained silent. But Mack wrapped her pinkie around Charlie's pinkie, and she nearly crumbled from the sweet touch.

Thoughts escaped like a herd of cheetahs. She didn't want this, right? No. Yes. Unsure. *Ugh.* Surrendering like this opened her up for real, genuine hurt. Happiness bubbles floated just above her head but were still out of reach. Maybe she wanted this. But what was *this*? Was "this"... *them*? Her heartbeat picked up, and she slowly exhaled a silent breath. She'd invested so much time after the divorce to mend her shattered heart. Did she really want to risk going back to that place?

They crossed the street and stopped in front of Charlie's car. "Can I give you a ride?"

"Nah, thanks, though," Mack said. "I'm meeting my parents for dinner down here in an hour."

Charlie nodded, but her heart dipped. She beeped her key fob when Mack cupped her hands behind Charlie's neck. Charlie's breath hitched as she waited for Mack's velvety mouth to press against her.

Damn, she wanted this. All of this. A date. Sex. *Mack.* Flutters flew into Charlie's chest. She licked her lips with a shy grin and parted her mouth when Mack leaned forward and touched her forehead to Charlie's.

Mack closed her eyes and took a deep breath. When she pulled back, her expression was soft but undecodable, and

Charlie turned to Jell-O from the intimate act. But her lips ached to feel Mack's mouth on hers, and her brain shorted on the confusing signal.

Mack squeezed her hand. "Night," she said softly, and headed down the street.

EIGHTEEN

CHARLIE'S DRINK SPECIAL: BOOSTED EXTRA-TALL DRIP

"What in the white chocolate mocha hell is going on?" Ben guzzled a cup of water and slammed it into the garbage. "We have like triple the customers than usual."

"I know." Charlie scribbled a third sold-out tag over the display case. "It's bananas."

But amazing. With every single customer, her stress level reduced. The ordinarily quiet chatter in the shop took on a louder, more festive decibel, and her heart filled. Her vision board, energy work, and crystal rubbing played out in real time. People talking and laughing. The continuous till beeping. Coffee grinding in the background.

She darted to the storage room for more napkins, stopping on the way to straighten out the new area rug she bought to cover the different colored flooring. This weekend, she'd have to buy tape to keep it from slipping.

She returned to her favorite mother-daughter duo.

"Hi, Charlie!" Amanda held out a purple dragon stuffed animal with glitter wings. "Look at my new stuffy."

"Hey, kiddo. Love the dragon. New stuffy means you finished your summer books already, right?" Charlie smiled.

"Proud of you. But I've got some bad news. We're out of chocolate chip cookies. All we have is oatmeal."

Amanda's face scrunched. "Eww. Oatmeal cookies are like breakfast. I want my cookie like dessert."

"That's fair." Charlie glanced up. "Hey, Erica. Sorry you guys had to wait so long. No idea if some sort of block party's happening, and I didn't get the memo?"

"I'm not surprised." Erica dug a credit card from her wallet. "You're internet famous."

"What do you mean?" Charlie didn't look up from scribbling their drink order on the cup.

"Have you heard of the author M. Ryder?"

Charlie dropped the Sharpie and quickly snatched it back up. "I do. We're, um... friends."

Erica's eyes widened. "You're friends? No way! Anyway, she tagged Sugar Mugs in her socials last night."

Charlie froze. "What?"

Erica held out her phone with Mack's post displayed. "Seattle's reputation for coffee house superstardom is rightfully earned. Thanks to #SugarMugs for keeping me warm and caffeinated during my visit." A link to Charlie's half-assed website and Facebook page appeared below.

Mack did that? Charlie's neck turned hot and her smile grew.

For the next hour, Charlie rode an unforeseen high. Mack had brought nothing but good into her life—phenomenal conversation, friendship, and now customers. Were there a gazillion things she had to think through? Yes. Starting with Mack living in New York. Long-distance relationships almost always crashed before arrival. But Mack didn't seem in any hurry to leave. And her family lived here. And, well, maybe they could figure it out.

One time Jess described Charlie as having the loyalty of a golden retriever. When Charlie was with a woman, no one else existed. When she and Jess first got together, their relationship was all-consuming, addictive, and passionate. Charlie held an immediate, undying devotion to her, thinking how lucky she was to finally find someone who "got her" and was "her person." Everything revolved around Jess. If Jess was sad, so was she. If Jess was happy, so was she.

But being with Mack was different. The attraction ran deep through her core. Made her squirm at night, her hands pressed against herself, her fingers circling to release pressure. But the attraction wasn't dependent like it was with Jess. It wasn't an anxiety-ridden fear of constantly wondering how they felt, thinking they'd leave or hoping she was enough. This attraction was independent.

"I feel like I was just railed by a linebacker and need a hip replacement." Ben gripped the counter's edge and twisted as loud cracks released from his back. "God, that was a ton of people."

Charlie collapsed on the stool. "I can't even believe Mack did that."

"Super cool, for real."

"Might've been a fluke, though. We don't know if these people will come back."

Ben squished on the stool with her. "A bunch of people said they didn't know this place existed. If this keeps happening, you might need to hire more staff."

If this continues, I might not go bankrupt.

He pulled his cell from his pocket. "Remi texted that she drove over here earlier but couldn't find a parking spot, so she left."

She wiped her hands on a towel and leaned into his shoulder. "Dang. I haven't seen her for a while. She couldn't have parked a few blocks away and walked?"

He let out a puff of air though his nose. "It's like you've

never met my roomie before. She has the patience of a two-year-old. No way would she have waited that long."

The doorbell chimed. Andrew walked in with his cap flipped backward, hands in his pocket, and commanding footsteps.

"Oh, helloooo, daddy," Ben whispered.

"That's Mack's dad."

Ben straightened his back. "Hell yeah, it is."

"No." She bumped his leg. "He's Mack's *actual* dad."

His mouth dropped. "Shut. Up."

"I know, right?" She waved at Andrew and breathed a sigh of relief that Ben moved to the storage room and wouldn't be tempted to flirt. "Hey!"

"Hey there. Sorry I couldn't swing by yesterday. Some issues came up at work." He angled his head towards the flooring. "Looks like the area rug covered things up pretty good."

She rose from the chair. "No worries at all, seriously. I'm so grateful for everything you've done already."

"I know your shop's busy. Okay to pop over and take a quick look?"

"Of course." Sugar Mugs was still half-filled with customers, but no chance would Charlie send him away after everything he had done.

Andrew pulled out a tape measure from his pocket and knelt. After a bit of poking and prodding, he stood. "The gap is minimal. I gotta cut a strip, fix it with wood glue and a few floor staples, and we should be good. You girls did great. I'm really proud of you two."

Proud of you. Her chest spilled over with his warm fuzzy accolades. How many things had she done in the past in search of those words from her father? She thought back to when she sprinted up her splintered patio stairs and slammed into their trailer, gripping the paper that announced she got the solo in her freshman choir recital. Never taking his eyes off the TV, her dad rattled off those same words.

But Andrew's words were like marshmallow hot chocolate on a winter rainy night. "Please tell me what I owe you for this."

He waved his hands. "Nothing. The supplies were just sitting in storage taking up room." He stuffed the tape measure in his back pocket and slid out of the way of a customer. "I gotta tell ya, you've certainly created some spark in Mackey. Haven't seen her smile like this in a real long time, and that's enough payment for me."

Okay, no more. Her heart verged on full-on exploding.

Voices amplified as a few more customers entered, and Ben worked both the till and orders. She needed to hop back there before the guests mobbed him, but she wanted to elongate this conversation.

"Did Mack tell you I'm happy to look over the remodeling contract?"

She swallowed, not ready to have the whole "I'm proud of you" badge stripped away the second he looked at her delinquent bills. "She did, but I haven't had a chance to gather everything yet."

With the way his head bowed and the empathetic look he gave her, he probably read right through those words.

She tugged at her sleeves. "Um... I'm sort of behind on paying, and I just don't want you to think—"

"Hey, we don't worry about that kind of stuff. Late bills and things happen all the time, even with my clients. I'm gonna be honest here. The company should've known they didn't seal the floors properly. I don't want to make you feel bad, but the framing isn't up to standard. You might be eligible for some reimbursement since they didn't hold up their end of the contract."

Her home, her *dream*, wasn't built with the love it deserved. The environment she'd created, the family community, didn't deserve shoddy framework and leaky floors. But this might be exactly what she needed to climb out of her debt hole.

"You said they ended up charging more than double, right?"

She nodded.

"Did they give a reason?"

She bit her lip. The main guy on the crew word spewed every time they talked about the job, and by the end of their conversations she was normally dizzy and regretting she asked in the first place. "I think they just said unforeseen issues."

He stroked his chin. "Did they run into mold? Wiring? Termites?"

"No, nothing like that."

"Did you have a lawyer look at any of this?"

She shook her head. She'd looked for a lawyer to review the contracts at the time, but the fee was too much. Googling all the words she didn't know, along with searching online for similar contracts, lasted days. But not hiring a lawyer was a dumb decision. Stacked on top of more dumb decisions. She lowered her chin. "No... I did it all on my own."

He bent over and caught her gaze. "It's really impressive what you've done."

She shoved her hands in her apron to keep from hugging him.

"Listen, I'd still like to look if you don't mind. We'll keep the money stuff between us."

She nodded. Even though she told Mack about owing money, Mack had no idea the sheer amount of debt she was drowning under. "I appreciate it. I'll get everything and—"

"Hey, maybe you should stop ringing up all the orders and focus on making drinks," a woman towards the end of the line shouted out at a drowning Ben, who death-glared at Charlie.

"Oh no. Looks like that lady is trying out to be a guest manager today." She giggled. "I've gotta go help Ben."

Andrew dug his keys from his pocket. "Sounds good. I'll be back this afternoon."

The next hour flew by as more customers filled the space. When the rush turned into a trickle, and the conversations quieted, Ben slid over her daily Americano.

"What did Daddy McHottie have to say?"

Everything. Gave her the hope she needed that her dream wasn't a failure. Provided a splintered view of what a real dad should be like. Cracked the two-ton stress block she'd been drudging around for months with his fatherly jackhammer. "He was just looking at the work me and Mack did."

"Cool." Ben stirred his drink. "So... tonight's date night, huh? Know where you're taking her?"

A date. The words swirled like a cotton candy cloud. She'd have to say it in her mind at least twenty more times before the word sunk in. "Nueve's, probably."

"Ah, say hi to mi tía. You gotta get the arroz con dulce. She brought a sample over to Abuelita's a few weeks ago. So good."

"You need to tell your aunt to test more recipes. She used to hook you up. Which hooked me up. I'm dying for some authentic Puerto Rican food right now."

"Right? Hopefully, in the fall when the tourist season thins out, she'll whip something up." He set his drink on the counter and moved to restock.

Charlie grabbed the towel and sanitizing spray and wiped the counter. Was the dress she decided on the right one? The color was tricky, but she loved it so much. Should she wear the vanilla or pear perfume tonight? Or layer it? *Gah!*

Her phone rattled in her pocket.

Mack: So sorry. Head down on my manuscript today. Pick you up at 6?

Charlie: Actually, I'd love to pick you up. I know where I'm taking you.

Mack: You gonna give me a hint?

> Charlie: Wear something nice. Like a white t-shirt and jeans.

Mack: Those are the sexiest words I've ever heard. ;-) See you tonight.

A few hours later, Charlie tore up the stairs to shower, shave, and dress. She threw on some bangles, wing-tipped her eyeliner, and left her hair down.

A date. An actual date.

Was this really happening?

NINETEEN

"Charlie's gonna be here soon. Do *not* embarrass me." Mack
shot her mom a stern look, but her smile broke through. She
smoothed her palm down her shirt and tugged on the bottom—
for the gazillionth time in the last ten minutes.

"Aren't you more worried about your dad embarrassing
you?"

They both turned to her shirtless dad shaking his butt in a
horrible attempt at twerking.

"Okay, that's fair."

"So, this is a thing, though, right?" Her mom filled a pot
with water and grabbed noodles from the cabinet. "I mean,
you're wearing a button-down. I didn't even know you owned
anything except T-shirts."

"It's not *a thing*." Tonight was absolutely a thing. Full-on
doodling hearts on her notepad, scouring Charlie's Instagram,
no appetite *thing*. All day zings and zaps ping-ponged in her
body. In the last eight hours, the extra energy boosted her to
write four thousand words, take two showers, iron her entire
shirt wardrobe, and even contemplate for a hot second ironing
her socks. She didn't know all the dating rules and had no idea

170

how to act. But her confidence never wavered from one subject: She was going all in tonight.

If she and Charlie were about to embark on a potential relationship, she wanted to do it right. She'd tell Charlie she'd been her inspiration to bring her main character, Shelby, to life. And pray to everything that was good and holy in this world that Charlie would understand.

She'd understand, right? Charlie was reasonable. Kind. Mack would just blurt it out sometime during the night, Charlie would laugh and maybe even say she was flattered, Mack would shake her head at holding it in, and all would be good.

Or... she'd freak out. Throw water in her face and tell her to go to hell. Stomp out of the restaurant with her head held high, as the music would come to a screeching halt, and the entire restaurant would stop talking and simultaneously stare at Mack in disgust. Mack would be forced to leave with tossed water dripping down her face and wander aimlessly in the city with a wet shirt and bruised ego.

The sloshing of sauce in a pan snapped her from her spiral.

Her mom stirred and adjusted the heat. "I'm so excited to meet this girl you spend so much time with."

"Woman, Mom. We're adults."

The intercom buzzed, and Mack's breath halted. Several hammering heartbeats later, knuckles rapped against the door.

A human sunset stood in front of Mack. No other person could wear such bright oranges and yellows, with that red hair and that fair skin, and pull it off. She was *gorgeous*.

And that dress. *My God.* All of Charlie's fullness and curves and femininity overflowed from the fabric. If Mack could dive into all that right now, she'd die happy.

"Whoa, you look great." Charlie's radiant smile filled the room.

"I was going to say the same thing." Mack kissed her on the cheek, then immediately withdrew.

What were the rules again? Maybe Charlie didn't want to be kissed. And maybe she did. And maybe Mack was too all up in her head and didn't know what she was doing, and *God*, she just smelled so good, and her hair was just so...

Stop. Breathe. Breathe again.

"Come on in." Mack held the door open and escorted her to the kitchen. "Charlie, this is my mom, Kelli."

"Nice to meet you." Charlie shook her hand, not even looking the teensiest bit nervous.

Unfair. Clearly, Mack was the only one freaking out right now.

"I'm so happy to meet you!" Her mom looked like she death-gripped Charlie's hand and pumped it multiple times. "So, you're the one that my Mackey keeps talking about."

"Mom, Jesus."

Her mom waved her off. "Charlie, come in, come in. What can I get for you? A drink? Cookie? Soda?"

Charlie shook her head. "No, I'm good, thank you."

"Snacks? String cheese? Edibles?"

Mack scrunched her face. "Mom." A hole must exist somewhere that could swallow her. Having her parents there for a first date should've been a hard no. What was she thinking? But Charlie wanted to pick her up, this was her current residence, and she had limited options.

Her mom threw her hands up. "Sorry, sorry. I heard you have a great shop. I'll definitely make my way down, soon."

Her mom peered so intently at Mack that her face would likely implode, clearly trying to read any single micro-expression to decode Mack's thoughts. Probably already planning some grand wedding with lesbian cake toppers and too much food and wine and miniature salted caramels.

"I'd love it," Charlie said. "Anytime. Is Andrew around? I have a folder for him."

Mack lifted an eyebrow at the large envelope Charlie pulled

from her bag. Were these the bills she mentioned while stripping floors? The image of Charlie sobbing that afternoon bored into her memory. She swallowed back the urge to demand Charlie tell her everything so she could fix whatever needed fixing.

"Yep, he's just changing. I'll grab him for you. Mackey, watch the noodles." Her mom skipped away, leaving Mack and Charlie.

Alone.

These nerves were ridiculous. For weeks, she'd spent every day with Charlie. More than almost any human on the planet. But now, her heart raced so fast she didn't know if she should scream or dance or pass out, and every word formerly housed in her brain fled for other places.

"Sorry about my mom," Mack finally pushed out after too many quiet moments passed.

"She's great." Charlie smiled. "So... I'm super pumped for tonight. I know where we should go, unless you have some thoughts."

Mack shrugged. "I'm clueless. Seriously. It's your city. I'm at your mercy."

"Oh, this could get interesting." Charlie giggled. "Ben's aunt owns a great bar and restaurant downtown, and his roommate, Remi, bartends there. We're talking about the best Puerto Rican food in the city. Thought we could hit up Pike Place first, look around, then head there for a late dinner?"

Charlie could've suggested knitting in a retirement home and it would've sounded amazing. "Perfect."

A door closed in the distance, and soon her dad popped into the kitchen with her mom trailing behind. "Hey, Charlie."

"Hey, Andrew. Sorry it was so crazy when you stopped by earlier and I didn't get the chance to properly thank you for everything. Seriously. You have no idea how much all this means to me."

"Ah, you girls did all the hard stuff." He grabbed an IPA out of the fridge and twisted off the top. "You two kicked ass the other day. Put my crew to shame."

"Mack, I'm surprised you're not more handy in general," her mom said. "Your dad has always been good with his hands."

"Damn straight."

"Drew!" She backhanded him on the chest while Charlie giggled and Mack groaned. "Not what I meant."

A year ago, a month ago even, Mack never would've dreamed she'd be standing in her parents' beautiful new condo with her mom stirring pasta sauce, her dad doing whatever the heck he was doing, and the woman of her dreams laughing and soaking it all in next to her. Every part of her filled with warmth.

Now all she had to do was silence her conscience, untangle her knotted gut, and pretend she wasn't using Charlie to create.

"Charlie, did Mack tell you the story of how I convinced her mom to go out with me?" her dad asked as he dipped his pinkie into the sauce, and ducked to avoid another smack from his wife.

Charlie tilted her head. "No... but now I'm curious."

"I told her Winona Ryder was my cousin, and if she hung out with me long enough, we'd call her."

"Winona Ryder from *Stranger Things*? I love that show."

"*Stranger Things*? More like *Heathers*, *Reality Bites*, *Edward Scissorhands*."

Charlie gave them a blank stare, and Mack sucked back her smile. '80s and '90s movies were a staple in their house, an obsession passed down from her parents at an early age. Charlie was likely verging on the lecture of a lifetime over classic cinematic masterpieces.

"Doesn't matter. She's been around forever. Since my last name's Ryder, I chased Kelli around and made up these stories about family Christmas gatherings and summer BBQs with

Winona. Come to think of it, Mack must've gotten her story-telling talent from me." He elbowed Mack with a smirk. "Anyway, after promising her I'd introduce them, Kelli finally went out with me. And almost up broke up with me the second she found out it wasn't true."

Mack's mom turned off the stove and drained the pasta. "I knew he was full of it. I mean, how dumb did he think I was? But I had a crush on him for an entire year and was playing hard to get."

"Oh, I love this. What a cute story." A wide grin appeared on her face. "And I promise I'll brush up on my movie history by the next time I see you."

He pulled out some seasoning from the cabinet and handed it to her mom, then glanced at Charlie. "Did you bring something for me?"

A blushing Charlie handed over the folder and stared at the floor before straightening her shoulders. "I did. This should be everything."

Her dad nodded and tucked the paperwork under his arm.

Mack wanted to beg her dad to look at what Charlie handed him and take care of anything she needed immediately. She clamped her tongue between her teeth and inhaled. Charlie was a fighter, a survivor. Navigated a tough childhood, opened a store, and kept her smile bright. No matter how much she wanted to step in and protect her, tonight was *not* the time to satisfy her savior complex. "All right, now that we've gotten the awkward meet-the-parents out of the way, how about we leave?"

Charlie readjusted her purse. "Nice meeting you, Kelli. Does Mack have a curfew?"

"Oh my God, let's go." Mack laughed and opened the door.

The sweet, pine-infused air crossed Mack's nose as they walked to Charlie's car, and she shielded her eyes against the bright evening sun. When Mack opened the car door, she couldn't help but grin. The car looked exactly as she thought it would. A sparkly medallion hung from the rearview mirror, various lotions were stuffed in the console, and the steering wheel was wrapped with purple fuzzy warmer.

"You said Pike Place Market first, right?" Mack asked as she strapped the seatbelt across her chest. "The place where all the dudes throw fish at one another and yell?"

"Yeah, but it's so much more than that. The market's filled with local artists and farmers. Has this great view over the Sound. I can't wait to show you some of my favorite vendors." Charlie eased into traffic. "The market is really busy on the weekend afternoons, but since it's a bit later, hopefully it won't be too bad." Charlie grinned and squeezed Mack's knee before she pulled it back.

Tonight was already better than every night this past year, and it had only just started.

"For real, though, if the market gets too intense, we can go somewhere quieter."

At this point, she would've followed Charlie just about anywhere. Crowd-surfing in a mosh pit? Sure. New Year's Eve at Times Square? Sounds fun. Front seat tickets to Coachella? Perfect. As long as this bubbly feeling continued, Mack was invincible.

The car rumbled over a few impressive potholes as they drove through the narrow streets of Seattle. Mack caught Charlie's eye and shoved her hands under her knees. She was here, in a car, driving *on a date*. She should've gotten Charlie flowers. Damn it. Or chocolates. Or a pet bunny.

After parking and walking toward the market, Charlie leaned toward Mack. "Ready for this?"

"Obligatory selfie?" Mack pointed at the oversized, lit-up *Public Market* sign hovering above the building.

"For sure. We don't want anyone here to think we're locals or they'll start asking for directions."

The city buzzed around them, conversation and laughter mixed with the briny Puget Sound scent and fresh fish. A bookstore, flowers—*so many flowers*—and merchants holding slices of Pink Lady apples on the sidewalk bordered them as they padded down the hill.

A faint piano melody echoed in the distance as they strolled past cheesecake displays, humbows, and piroshkis near the original Starbucks. Mack's stomach growled. Down another block, passersby tossed coins and dollars into the open, scratched guitar case in front of a man strumming an Ed Sheeran song.

"Over there." Charlie pointed at a lively crowd surrounding burly men wearing orange pants and suspenders. They eased their way to the front and stopped near a sign that said: *Caution: Low-Flying Fish.*

The men tossed a fish and yelled something indistinguishable to one another. And the crowd dispersed.

"Wait—that's it?" Mack said. "That's the whole thing? Did they just throw a fish and yell '*ey!*'?"

"Pretty much. No idea why it resonates with so many people, but I get sucked into it every time."

Mack took out her phone to snap a few photos. In all the years her parents had lived in Seattle, she never once visited the market. New York was hard to beat for people watching. But this place might come in as a close second. "Maybe people like seeing teamwork? These guys seem happy. I heard they made corporate training videos."

"I should make Ben watch one." Charlie tugged on Mack's wrist. "Let's go over here. I love this booth."

Tables with bamboo jewelry, glass bongs, and artwork filled the space around them. Mack glanced at Charlie, who eyed a beautiful, jade-colored stone. The back of Charlie's hand brushed hers and Mack's insides heated. The hum of the crowd faded into the background, and Mack tapered her focus on Charlie. Everything about her was exquisite. The red lips. The hair that was so plush and full that Mack wanted to ask her if she could wrap it around her fingers but didn't want to come off like a total freak. That rose-and-vine chest tattoo...

Mack peeled her eyes away from the tattoos and brought them to Charlie's bubblegum lips. Jesus, she was hot. But the attraction was so much more. Her heart was as big as her hair. The way she froze and held her breath when a kid tripped in front of them. The way she made eye contact and chatted with the person behind the counter. The way she moved. *Damn*, the way she moved.

Charlie bit her lip with a shy, slow smile and interlaced her fingers through Mack's. Mack silently absorbed her through her skin.

Other couples walked by, pointed out things, laughed, and held hands. Were they feeling the same tingles as she was? Did they feel a surging rush up their arm? Was this what it was like to feel... whatever this was?

It was official—from here on out, Mack never wanted anyone else to touch her hand. No other hand could feel like this. Warm and inviting, and comforting.

So seamlessly. So naturally.

And so effing deceptively.

This ended tonight. From here on out, Mack wouldn't write anymore using Charlie's background without her consent.

TWENTY

CHARLIE'S DRINK SPECIAL: TRUTH SERUM
CUCUMBER SPRITZER

Well, she held Mack's hand. *Just like that.* Just like today was an average Saturday, with an average couple doing average things. But her heart knew differently and hammered against her chest. Charlie peeked from her peripherals at Mack to gauge her reaction. Mack grinned and swiped her thumb across her knuckle, and Charlie's shoulders loosened.

The market always held a soft spot in Charlie's heart. As kids, she and Ben would pool their money and pop down here to split clam chowder or Beecher's Mac & Cheese. Or, on random Saturday afternoons, she and Rosie would take the Metro to eat pork-filled humbows and watch cruise ships sail by.

Charlie's stomach roared like a gorilla. "Oh no. I made it angry." She pointed at her belly. "I'm so hungry. You ready for Puerto Rican cuisine?"

"Absolutely." Mack followed her to the exit, her grip firm and delicious against Charlie's palm. "Back home, Spanish Harlem has this tiny family-owned restaurant with the best mofongo in the world. But it's a solid subway ride to get there, so I only go once or twice a year."

"Ooh, mofongo's good, too." Charlie jutted her chin toward the street past Post Alley. "Nueve's up a few blocks and to the left. Parking sucks, so we have to hike it, okay?"

"Unfair advantage. You live in hiking boots. I'm wearing my flat Converse."

"Maybe we can steal an electric scooter from a kid. I'll drag on the back shotgun style."

Mack laughed. "Deal."

Midway up the hill, Mack stopped as her breath labored. "I need to rethink my stance on giving up running."

Charlie rested a hand on Mack's back. "You good?"

"Nope. Pretty sure this is a perfect, lung-crushing, forty-five-degree angle, designed by Seattle architects to punish tourists who are used to practical, flattened land. Like those offered by the New York City Department of Tourism." Mack tugged Charlie closer. "But you're the most beautiful, skilled hiking partner anyone could ask for."

"You're making me blush. Pretty sure it's because you think I'm a skilled hiker, though. Let's do Rainier sometime and revisit this conversation."

When they reached Nueve's, Charlie pulled open the heavy wooden door and a swoosh of hearty, buttery, roasted-pork-and-garlic air drenched her. A *super* friendly hostess who may or may not have had one too many chocolate-covered coffee beans asked them to follow her to the table.

"Charlie!" The bartender, Remi, waved at her with a wide grin as she filled up a line of cocktail glasses with mojitos.

"Hey, Remi." She smiled and kept following the hostess.

"That's Ben's roommate?" Mack glanced behind her shoulder. "She looks vaguely familiar, actually."

"You've probably seen her in the shop. She pops in every few days. She even helped me set up a Sunday Drag Queen Reading Hour for kids a few months back."

"Here you ladies go." The hostess motioned to the booth. "By the way, I'm dying for what you're wearing right now."

Charlie held out the side of her dress and curtsied. "Thank you."

"Like, what a fun dress. So pretty! If it weren't all legit inappropriate, I'd totes ask to touch it, but you know... Enjoy! Your server will be with you in like less than a minute."

Charlie flipped open the menu. Where did one begin? Coquito, tostones, pasteles... Her mouth watered. "You know what you want?"

Mack closed the menu. "Nope. I like to live life on the edge. When the waiter comes by, I'll make a game-time decision."

"Gutsy. I like it." Charlie sipped water and accidentally linked her foot with Mack's. She smiled when Mack didn't move.

"I didn't know you guys did a drag queen reading."

"When I started, I wanted to do it once a month, but I've been slacking at coordinating. Next time won't be until September."

Mack propped her elbows on the table. "Do the kids like it?"

"They love it. They all huddle down on the floor and look at the queen like she's a real-life fairy princess. After, they line up and take pictures with her. Super freaking cute."

Speaking of cute... Mack's button-down shirt was such a subtle change from her regular wardrobe. That, along with a layered necklace, and Charlie's pulse had not stopped thudding in her ears since she walked into Mack's parents' condo.

They locked eyes, and every cell buzzed.

Mack cleared her throat. "Do you want something to drink at all?"

"I don't drink."

Mack cocked her head.

"Does that surprise you?" Charlie asked.

Mack paused for a moment. "I don't know. Maybe a little? Did I just become my grandpa and assume with the sleeve tattoos and septum piercing you'd..."

"Lick salt off my wrist and toss back a tequila shot?" Charlie grinned. "I can see that. Gotta keep people guessing."

"For whatever it's worth, neither do I."

"Really? Well, they have a great cucumber spritzer made with fresh mint. Remi does this dramatic show of slapping it in her palm." Charlie tossed her head behind her shoulder. "Watch, she's doing it now."

Mack lifted her eyebrow. "Whoa. She has one heck of a smack for those who are into that kind of thing."

And Charlie hooked her finger in her collar to cool down from the flirt in Mack's voice.

The waiter scooted up to their table. "Ladies. What can I get for you?"

After giving their order, Charlie leaned back. "Can I ask why you don't drink?"

Mack played with the straw in the water glass. "I used to throw down, once in a while, on the weekends or whatever. Mostly when I was forced to be in social situations."

"You really hate people, don't you."

Mack chuckled. "I do! It's bad. I love humanity if that makes sense. But individual people make me itchy."

Charlie related to this on a certain level. She loved chatting and being around people. But individuals disappointed her on a deeper level.

"When I started writing my first book, I discovered that hangovers and writing don't mix. Even getting buzzed killed my creativity for a solid twenty-four hours." Mack tapped her fingers against the table. "After I was published, I traveled for book tours and meetings and tried to keep up my social media and author site. Everything became so much harder if I wasn't clear-headed."

The waiter delivered their mocktails, and the women clinked their glasses in cheers. The mint and cucumber spritz fizzled down her throat. Charlie soaked in every word as Mack told her about building her site, explained author brands and the marketing needed behind a book launch.

"What about you? Why don't you drink?" Mack asked.

Charlie unwrapped her silverware and put the napkin in her lap. "My dad's a raging alcoholic, and in case that gene got passed down to me, I didn't want to end up like him." Charlie delivered this with the same tone as if she rattled off her favorite dessert, but her insides cringed.

Mack's mouth twisted. "I'm continuously shocked at how open you are. I've just never met anyone like you."

"These are just facts, you know?"

Mack tore off a small chunk of bread from the basket. "Do you talk to all your friends about this kind of stuff?"

"You mean Ben?"

"No, your other friends."

Charlie reached into the breadbasket but played with the food. "I only have surface-level friends."

"What's a surface-level friend?"

"Like friends who'd say it was cute I wanted to name my dog Booger."

"You have a dog named Booger?"

Charlie giggled and bit into the bread. "No. I'm saying I'm not close enough with my other friends where they'd tell me that's a terrible name. These same people sent a sad-face emoji text when Jess and I got divorced, or just text to dig for gossip. So... surface level." Her voice dropped. "Now ask me how I felt about being raised by a single father who forgot to come home on the weekends, and we've got a different story."

Mack seemed to hold her breath. "Do you want to share that with me?"

Charlie fiddled with her silverware. So many years had

passed since she'd been on a date. Maybe the rules had changed, but she was pretty sure the dating playbook didn't constitute a deep dive into her childhood trauma. But Mack's gentle, dark brown eyes burrowed into her, and her body relaxed.

"It sucked. Sometimes when I think back and try to process everything that happened growing up, I realize the worst part was the waiting—constantly anticipating if he'd show up. And if he did, what condition he'd be in. At night, I'd sit for hours by our trailer window wondering with each passing headlight if they were his."

Mack put her hands on top of Charlie's but then quickly shoved them under the table. "I'm so sorry. I can't imagine how hard that was for a little kid. Were you ever in danger?"

Charlie bunched a napkin between her palms. "Hmmm. I guess? As much as a child being left alone is in danger. But my dad's a sweet guy, you know? Sometimes I think that makes everything harder. Like if he were evil, I could hate him and move on." The napkin was crushed by now, and Charlie tossed it on the table. "My sob story is probably not what you wanted to hear on our first date."

"No, I love it. I don't love that it happened to you, but I love learning about you." Mack smiled. "Do you think this affected you as an adult? I've researched this stuff for my books but haven't had this level of conversation before."

"God, yes." Hanging on to unhealthy relationships, check. Clingy, check. Worried everyone is leaving, check. "Gave me lots of trust issues—which were sometimes warranted."

"How so?"

Charlie fixed her gaze on the table. "My ex-wife cheated on me."

Mack flinched. "Are you serious? How the hell—"

"Wait." Charlie held up a hand to stop Mack from saying something that could turn this conversation. She rarely told anyone about Jess's infidelity, but when she did, they all had the same reaction—anger. Yes, it was wrong and hurtful and deceit-ful, but the situation was complicated. "She wasn't her best during that time. But neither was I. Every inch she pulled away from me, I gripped tighter. I was suffocating her and compro-mised myself. And technically we were separated..."

Through bites of their crispy empanadillas, Charlie contin-ued. She told Mack about her deep desire to lay down roots, which counteracted Jess's desire to travel. The catalyst of their relationship ending was when Jess couldn't understand why Charlie wouldn't sell the house Rosie left her to fund their trips. Jess couldn't wrap her brain around how a structure symbolized her childhood safe haven, and the memories of baking muffins and drinking cocoa were worth more than trips to Italy.

Another round of spritzers ordered, and while Charlie sunk her teeth into the most amazing pastelón de carne she'd ever had, she unloaded stories of her father's weekend benders offset with coffee dates, nail painting parties, and scouring garage sales for cheap toys.

"I had a come-to-Jesus moment with myself. He'd never be my version of a normal dad, and I could either walk away or stay. And if I stayed, then I needed not to try to change him." She wiped her greasy fingers off in a napkin. "What's that saying again? Expect the worst, hope for the best? When he gets sober, I cheer him on. When he relapses, I no longer consider it a personal reflection on me."

The waiter dropped off the dessert menu, and Charlie took a breath as she reviewed the flan, rum cake, and arroz con dulce. Talking to Mack over dinner was more than just easy. The conversation was downright therapeutic. Releasing the words simultaneously released years' worth of tension. Not the sexiest of conversations, but it was intensely intimate. An oncoming vulnerability hangover lunged toward her.

Mack folded back into the seat. "I hate that it took this conversation, right now, to kick me in the ass. My parents might do some annoying things, but my memories consist of betting on marshmallows when we played Uno or taking the subway to Central Park on the weekends. I feel like I need to hug them when I get back."

Charlie still couldn't fully wrap her mind around how Mack didn't bow daily to the universe in gratitude for winning the parental lottery. "I don't want you to think I'm miserable. But you know... I married someone who wasn't right for me because I was scared to be alone. But these last two years, I feel like a different person. Healthier. Happier."

"And now you have a shop."

Thankfully. Because she finally proved to herself that she could accomplish things on her own. Her dignity and self-worth did not have to link with someone else's. And Charlie would've never met Mack otherwise.

Charlie took another sip of the spritzer, the liquid calming her dry mouth. She'd been speaking almost exclusively for close to two hours. Mack didn't seem to mind and kept peppering her with questions. With every morsel she shared, Charlie's attraction grew.

"How did you end up with the name Sugar Mugs?"

"Ben tried to convince me to call it Sugar Jugs and do the whole bikini-barista thing."

Mack smirked. "Really? I mean, that's a tough one. Do I support women's empowerment? Yes? Female entrepreneurship? Yes. Do I think it has a deeply misogynistic history? Also, yes. But maybe the women are flipping the script?"

"Exactly. Like more power to the woman that wants to do that. I just couldn't. Not that I wouldn't kill it in a bikini." Charlie shimmied her shoulders. "But I'd get too cold and then cranky."

The waiter dropped off arroz con dulce, and Charlie savored the cream melting into her tongue. "Ben was right. This dessert is so good."

Mack took a bite and licked her lips, and Charlie focused on nothing else.

"Can you please add therapy to my floor labor bill I owe you?" Charlie scooped the spoon back into the rice dessert. "I cannot believe I talked that much about myself."

"I loved every minute of getting to know more about you. Besides, if I ever need to blackmail you, we're solid."

"Deal. All right, your turn. Did you always want to be a writer?"

Mack bit into the dessert and her jaw worked in a circle. "No. Well, yes and no. I used to write all the time, short stories and things."

"Poems?"

"God, no. The people who write poems are brilliant. I can't write a poem to save my life." She set the spoon on the side of the bowl. "Ever since I was young and had trouble falling asleep, I created stories. I could see every tiny detail. The character's eyebrow shape and if their pointer finger was taller than their ring finger. I heard their voices and pictured their smells. As I got older, the story evolved, and I'd get pissed when I'd fall asleep because I wanted to solve the mystery or figure out different twists."

"Did you do this for *The Edge of the Shadow*?"

Mack nodded.

"Robbery gone wrong, murder, and mistaken identity helped you fall asleep?"

Mack laughed. "Morbid, I know. I'm the same person who loves serial killer documentaries and podcasts."

"Oh, hell no." Charlie waved her wrist. "That stuff scares the crap out of me. I can't even do scary movies. I saw *The Sixth Sense* when I was a kid, and I'm still sleeping with a nightlight."

"The one with the cute little boy who saw dead people?"

"Exactly! Dead people!"

Charlie wanted everything in Mack's head implanted into hers. As Mack spoke, her heart grew, her limbs ached, and her mind wandered.

Mack. Was. Perfect.

For the first time in months, Charlie wasn't thinking about her shop, bills, or a pending bankruptcy. She wanted to know every part of Mack, to sink into her soul's wading pool, swim around, and uncover all her secrets. What made Mack happiest? Did she talk in her sleep? Did she ever have a dog?

She rolled the spoon in her mouth and glanced at Mack. "Where do you get your inspiration?"

"Ideas come from all over the place. I was at a conference in Minnesota a few months ago and drove by a sparkly billboard in the middle of a cornfield with a really obscure message. I don't even remember what it said. But it was so odd that I wondered if some ultra-rich, secret society of farmers lived there that spread mind-chip devices in the soil instead of corn. Or maybe some lonely farmer fell in love with Pluto and put this billboard up to beam a message to it. Random stuff."

How does that even happen? Just coming up with the name Sugar Mugs depleted her entire bucket of creative juice. "My brain could never go there. I love this stuff. Give me another one."

"Hmmm... let me think." Mack played with the straw. "Okay, the twist in *The Edge of the Shadow* came from watching the news. They had a story about the cops busting a woman for a string of armed bank robberies. I kept thinking, *But she's so pretty.* How does someone so pretty commit crimes?" Mack shook her head. "I know it's an asinine thought, but I never stop thinking those things because it often leads to something. So, I kept at it, like, oh, she's doing it for a different purpose. Or she isn't the real criminal but instead part of an elite squad hired by the bank to showcase security flaws. Then that morphed into what if she did it because an evil person kidnapped someone she loved. And it took off from there. But inspiration comes from everywhere. TV. A song, reading, overhearing conversations at coffee shops or restaurants."

"Writers do that?"

"Yeah, all the time. I call it mining for word gold."

Charlie crossed her arms. "I'd feel so violated if someone did that to me."

Mack's face went pale before it turned red. She coughed and took a sip of water. "You would?"

"Absolutely. Listening in on private stuff is like someone reading my text messages or diary. It'd feel so gross. Isn't that illegal anyway? Like recording someone without their knowledge?"

Mack shifted in her seat and tucked her hands under the table. "No, not illegal." She depleted the rest of her water and indicated to the waiter she needed more.

"It should be. Sorry! I guess you do that. I don't mean to insult your craft or research."

"No, totally understand." Mack gave her a weak smile.

Oh no. Why did she do that? If they were on a reality show right now, the audience would groan at the level of awkwardness Charlie just heaved on the table. A knot formed in Charlie's stomach. Mack had listened to her the entire night while she rattled off depressing childhood stories, and now Charlie talked crap about Mack's work. Amateur move.

"How long does it take to write a book?" Charlie kept her voice bubbly and light to try and defuse the obvious tension.

Mack shrugged. "Depends. Some people take years. Viviane represents one author who completes four a year. I can't even understand that level of sorcery."

A slow fire burned in Charlie. Besides the work-insult faux pas, tonight was one of the best she had in years. Ease flowed between them, and energy simmered in her body. She didn't want to change the dynamic, and a first date was probably not the best to talk logistics, but her heart ballooned with each passing second, and she had to address her concerns.

Charlie spun her trio of stacked rings. "When are you going back to New York?"

"I don't know." Mack wiped her mouth with a napkin and took a deep breath. "I first came here to escape the pressure of my publishing deadline. But I miss my apartment and space and the city."

Of course, Mack had an entire life outside this little bubble. She had an apartment, a bed, and maybe a cat that the neighbor watched. Charlie's face fell. No way this could be permanent.

"But I guess I'm here indefinitely." Mack reached forward and brushed the top of Charlie's fingers. "And right now, I don't want to leave."

Damn. Charlie liked this woman. A lot. The conversation. Those shoulders. Her accent and smile and quiet way about her. The feeling she got when they talked, like she was the most fascinating human in the world.

Mack paid the bill amongst Charlie's protests. Outside, the mist had stopped, and the moon peeked out behind the clouds, joining the glowing streetlights. Charlie linked arms with Mack, and Mack pulled her closer.

"Want to come back to my place for hot chocolate?" Charlie's raw, shaky voice gave away every internal sensation. "Or should I bring you back to your parents?"

"Hot chocolate with you or Netflix with my parents?" Mack put her mouth against Charlie's ear. "Easiest decision of my life."

TWENTY-ONE

CHARLIE'S DRINK SPECIAL: RAINBOW LOVE LATTE WITH EXTRA SPRINKLES

The walk up the loft stairs was slow and deliberate, every footstep filled with anticipation. A soft breeze flowed through the night air, enough to dry Charlie's damp, trembling palms. Her throat was both arid and wet. The nerves and anticipation collided, and her insides didn't know how to respond. She couldn't remember ever feeling this many conflicting emotions, even with Jess.

Was she sure about all of this? No. Absolutely not. But, at this moment, everything felt right, even if the speed scared her. She fell into a relationship so quickly with Jess. An instant connection, followed by a decade of sickening, heavy codependence. But she broke free from that addiction. Just because only a few weeks had passed with Mack, this was different. *Right?*

When Mack toed off her shoes and set them on the mat, Charlie moved to the kitchen. "Do you take whipped cream?"

"Only non-dairy."

"Oh God, not you, too." Charlie giggled and turned the stove on.

Mack strolled up behind her and laid a gentle hand on her waist, and Charlie's knee bent. An automatic reaction, like

Mack's touch rendered her limbs useless. Mack released and tossed her wallet and phone on the counter. As soon as her phone hit the granite, it buzzed. Charlie glanced at the screen, and Mack clicked it off.

"Viviane."

"I didn't mean to look." Flames shot to Charlie's face, and she grabbed the milk from the fridge to avoid Mack's gaze. "God, that's invasive. I don't even know why I did."

"The phone was just sitting there. I would've looked, too."

Charlie was sure Mack could hear her loud heartbeat. What was Mack thinking? She was quiet, in her cool and unfazed way, but she didn't look nervous. She pulled a stool next to the counter and rested her palm in her chin as she watched Charlie at the stove.

The milk bubbled, cocoa stirred, and they both took a slow sip. Charlie wrapped her hands around the mug, hoping to soothe the trembles, and pointed to the couch. She turned off all overhead lights on the way to the living room and flipped on the electric fireplace and lamp instead.

"Is it just me, or did that seem like a truth serum dinner?" Charlie fanned her dress out and crossed her legs underneath her butt. She said a lot tonight. Too much. Her insides were raw.

"You can tell Ben his roommate should add a warning that her virgin cucumber spritzer contains the same loosening effect as booze."

"I need to level this playing field. Okay, truth cocoa." Charlie blew into her mug. "Tell me something about yourself. Something embarrassing or random or something no one knows."

"Hmmm. You're going to make me think, aren't you? I mean, embarrassing, really? Pretty sure I have a million of those." Mack drummed her fingers against the mug. "Let's see. Random, huh? Um, I hate pickles."

"What? Who hates pickles?'

"Me."

"I mean, no one hates pickles. Okay, okay, give me more."

"More?" Mack tucked her legs underneath herself. "My favorite movie is *Fight Club*."

"Okay, Brad Pitt in that movie is the only time I questioned my sexuality."

"Right? The movie was so smart. The writing is incredible. And the more I watched it, the more it resonated with me. This sort of weird obsession with material items and things and how it ruins you."

Charlie set her mug on the side table and rested her head in her hand. "Okay. More. Rapid-fire style."

"Gah. The pressure." Mack chuckled. "I love clowns. I *hate* cats. My dad taught me how to drive a stick shift—in New York City. Picture that for a moment. Figured if I could handle that, I could handle anything. I got a D in my freshman creative writing course, and if you asked me right this second to explain participial phrases and dangling modifiers, I'd panic."

Charlie grinned. She had no idea what those words meant and didn't necessarily care to learn. But knowing that Mack didn't know, as Mack shook her head like she was disappointed in herself, tickled something. With every morsel of herself that Mack shared, Charlie inched closer, thirsty for more. She'd spent so much time with Mack over the last several weeks, but an entire person existed that she hadn't tapped into. Her striking cheekbones, and fresh haircut and firm arms, may have caught her attention immediately, but now uncharted waters needed to be explored.

"Interesting. And you're a writer? Okay, more."

Mack looked towards the ceiling and settled into the couch. "More. Oof. Okay, I hate country music. I love the old crooners. Frank Sinatra, Sammy Davis Junior, and Ray Charles are on constant rotation. Sometimes I wear noise-canceling headphones when I write with nothing playing. I sleep with a sound machine. And I made out with a girl in the bathroom at a Britney Spears concert."

Charlie's mouth dropped, before she giggled. "I have so many questions. You went to a Britney Spears concert? Bathroom? Like how does that happen? Ask her for a tampon under the door and initiate a conversation?"

"Long story. Let's just say I was on assignment for the college newspaper, and there may have been alcohol involved." Mack twirled the cocoa with a stirring stick. "Um... I'm scared of needles, so part of me thinks you have an immortal superpower because you willingly have tattoo needles stuck in your body. I love anchovies on a pizza, my favorite snack is freezing grapes with Jell-O seasoning, and my favorite candy is Fun Dip. I order it in bulk online. And... um..."

Charlie lapped up every single morsel of intel and squeezed Mack's knee. "One more. Come on. You can do it."

"I've never liked hot chocolate until this moment."

Charlie's face flushed, and she sipped. The warmth of the liquid matched her insides, and her body gravitated toward Mack. She wanted to pull her in and taste her, but yesterday on the street, Mack didn't make a move and left Charlie confused. But today, they held hands and sat *this close*, and Charlie's heart hammered.

Charlie nibbled on the inside of her cheeks. "Have you ever been in love?" *Jeezus.* Personal question much? But she couldn't help it. She needed to know everything. She said she never dated, but maybe that was a generalization.

"No," Mack said firmly, holding her gaze. "I used to think it wasn't in the cards for me."

A touch of sadness that no one realized Mack's awesomeness mixed with relief that Charlie wasn't competing against the memory of an ex.

"And now?" Charlie's voice cracked.

Mack placed her mug on the side table. "Now..." Mack's gaze traveled the lust triangle from Charlie's eyes and down to her lips and back again. "Now it seems like it might be in my future."

Mack's tender tone swam through Charlie. Everything in her body turned to liquid. She cupped Mack's face and swiped her thumb across Mack's impossibly soft skin on her cheeks. Doe eyes peered back at her, reading her soul, and her body tingled with a silky lust web that fanned from the top of her head to the tip of her toes.

Salt and blackberry drifted off Mack, and the back of Charlie's throat moistened from craving. Mack rested her hands on Charlie's thighs and inched closer. Charlie's internal temperature rose to a feverish level, and her oxygen vanished. Mack leaned in a little more, and Charlie's legs trembled. She was too close. She wanted—*needed*—to taste her.

Mack glided her hands up Charlie's arm, leaving a path of goose bumps. Mack's mouth hovered over Charlie's skin, sending a ghost breath up Charlie's neck.

Did she want this? Definitely maybe. If she did this, everything would change from this moment on. God, Mack smelled *so good*. The heat of Mack's hands seeped through her back as she ran her fingertips up and down Charlie's spine.

Oh my—she did want this.

So. Much.

She drew Mack to her and pushed her mouth against hers. Chocolate swirled with their tongues, and Mack firmed her grip on Charlie's hips. Her endlessly smooth skin was like satin beneath Charlie's fingers. Mack brushed Charlie's hair away from her neck and sunk her lips into the slope, Charlie's body buckled. She fell back into the couch and opened her hips for Mack to slide between her legs. Mack flattened her palms on either side, caging Charlie, as she kissed her earlobe and neck.

Wrapped in her protective arms, Charlie's body loosened.

She brought Mack's lips back to hers and sighed into her mouth as she yearned to explore. Everything was so good, so smooth, so flawless. She wanted to pinch herself to make sure she wasn't dreaming. She swept her hands beneath Mack's ass and tugged her closer.

"Is this okay?" Mack's breathy voice reached her ear as she inched Charlie's dress over her knees.

"Yes, everything... are you okay?"

Her tongue brushed across Charlie's collarbone. "Perfect."

Charlie's heartbeat kicked so frantically that she knew she'd burst. Tasting Mack's mouth, licking her earlobe, and whispering down her neck was the only thing on Charlie's mind. She shifted her hips and sunk deeper into the couch as Mack pressed into her.

The glow of the fireplace flickered as Charlie's hunger intensified. She slid her fingertips under Mack's shirt, raking across her back, as Mack pressed her thumbs on Charlie's outer thighs. She needed Mack closer. Her body begged for friction.

Mack licked Charlie's lower lip. "You're so beautiful, Charlie... the first time I saw you... I stopped breathing."

Charlie's hips twisted and reangled, but Mack still wasn't close enough.

Mack's fingers traveled higher up Charlie's thighs. "If you want me to stop, tell me, okay?"

"Don't stop. Please don't stop."

Skilled touches and controlled kisses covered Charlie. She gasped and abandoned all control over her limbs as their bodies collided and heat flushed through her core. She needed her. She wanted to know her, every part of her. Charlie's tongue slid across Mack's upper chest peeking out from her shirt as Mack kneaded her skin.

Heated skin pressed into Charlie's hands. She trailed Mack's belly, this warm, firm belly she wanted to squeeze because there was so much pressure everywhere and it collected at her fingertips. She feasted on the salt on her skin. Mack's mouth moved against Charlie's, captured it, and begged for more.

Moaning and breathing and whispering filled the air. The tension built in Charlie's thighs and center. Mack broke contact and sat back on her tucked feet. In two fierce tugs, she ripped her shirt open.

Damn.

"Gotta love snaps instead of buttons," Mack said with a small smile and threw her top in the corner. She paused, holding Charlie's gaze. One, then two, then three seconds went by, and Mack still didn't move.

Why'd she stop?

Charlie shoved an oversized pillow underneath her back and propped herself on her elbows. "Are you... we... good?"

Mack's beautiful ivory chest rose with a deep breath. Her cheeks flushed pink. "I want to look at you. Right now, in this light. I want to remember this moment." She reached for Charlie's hand and kissed her palm.

Oof.

Scooching up, Charlie took control and brought Mack in close. Mack's breaths became hers. Charlie shifted back, and Mack straddled her, and now Charlie couldn't think. Mack's porcelain skin brushed against hers, the glow of the fire highlighted the amber in her irises. Charlie gripped Mack's hips as she circled against her.

Swiping her fingertips across Mack's lower belly, Charlie whispered, "Your skin's so soft. It feels so good."

Mack's stomach muscles clenched beneath her touch. This was happening. And it was real and not scary but also *really scary* and wonderful and delicious, and Charlie couldn't even handle it. Mack slipped her hands through Charlie's mane, fisted her hair, and deepened her kiss.

Inside, Charlie's body trembled and laughed and cried. Too

many conflicting emotions drove through her, and she didn't know which path to follow. She pulled away and caught her breath. She peeked at Mack's flushed face, her moistened mouth, and couldn't stop. Charlie dove back in, Mack's tongue swiped hers, and now Charlie reached the maximum intensity where even her eyelids pulsed.

Desire filled Charlie, and tension spread to her limbs. Mack's thighs wrapped around Charlie's. The warmth of skin on skin, the internal flames, was everything she had dreamt of. Tonight was special. Beautiful. Mack's mouth grazed her lips, the tip of her nose, and the crook of her neck. Charlie gripped Mack's ass and dragged her closer. They rocked against each other, a gentle wave brewing.

Mack hooked her fingers on Charlie's waistband, and Charlie quivered.

"Can I touch you?" Mack whispered in her ear, her fingers patiently waiting, not moving, the warm breath of her mouth soothing Charlie.

Charlie nodded but couldn't speak.

"Is that a yes?" Mack's voice contained a hint of a smile.

"Yes... yes," Charlie murmured.

When Mack's thumb swept across her sensitive skin, between her legs, where she hadn't been touched by someone else in so long, her breath hitched. She was sure at this moment she may die from the sensations.

"Still okay?" Mack whispered as she massaged Charlie.

Charlie melted and captured Mack's mouth again. The kisses intoxicated her and left her hungry. Grazing her lips across Mack's neck, she felt fingers grasp on to her. Her hands lowered and cupped Mack's breasts, her thumb moving across Mack's covered nipples. She slid her fingers up and looped them under Mack's black cotton bralette.

"Can I take this off?"

"Mmmm... yes."

Charlie lowered Mack's bra straps, freeing her. She ran her lips across her breasts, her hands and fingers working together. She pulled Mack's nipple into her mouth, and Mack gripped her head and swiveled her hips.

The sensation of her mouth on Mack's skin magnified every desire. Charlie's body ached for release, for deeper points of contact. Mack skated her knuckles up Charlie's inner thigh, and the intense motion made her legs shake.

Fingers danced on her. Charlie squirmed, and her body begged to be touched deeper. Mack dropped her hands. *Come back!* She needed to feel Mack on her. Her cells sparked, pressurized, and Mack was the only thing that could relieve the ache. Clunky dress fabric constricted her, and she needed it off. *Now.*

As if she could read her mind, Mack wrapped a strong arm under Charlie and rested her fingers on her dress zipper. Before she said anything, Charlie whispered "yes" in her ear. A metallic *zwoop* sounded as zipper teeth released, and her dress fell to her waist.

Shivers flew up Charlie's spine and to her ears. She wiggled her dress over her head as Mack yanked it off and tossed it. Lying back in her favorite black lace bra and panties, Charlie trembled.

"Jesus Christ... you're so perfect." Mack's shoulders rose and fell in heavy breaths.

Mack tugged down Charlie's bra and latched her mouth on her breast, licking and sucking her nipple as Charlie gripped the edge of the couch, the sensation so exquisite that she whimpered. Her hips moved and rotated, and her center tried to make the deeper contact she craved. If Mack didn't touch her again soon, she wouldn't be able to take it anymore.

Heavy breaths and moans filled the air. Mack dropped her hand in between Charlie's legs and paused.

"No more asking. Just... everything... do everything... I'm so ready," Charlie moaned.

Mack leaped from the couch and kicked her jeans off. She hooked her arms under Charlie's hips and scooted her down. Her fingers peeled off her panties, and she angled closer to Charlie. Mack's delicate mouth kissed her stomach, side, and leg. Her tongue trailed up her thigh. Charlie surrendered to Mack's control.

With a flick of Mack's tongue against her knee, upper thigh, then stomach, Charlie understood how much Mack wanted her. As Mack's fingers circled, explored, and finally... *oh my, finally*... touched her, pushed into her, Charlie knew how safe she was. Mack slowed down and *indulged*.

"You feel so good." Mack's husky voice nearly shoved Charlie to the edge as her fingers and tongue danced on the heat pulsating between her legs.

Charlie gripped the back of Mack's head, her increased breathing matching Mack's. The butterflies were in flight, her heart full, her body alive, awake, comforted, and excited. She wanted more.

Charlie pulled Mack up, kissed her neck, and put her mouth to her ear. "Bedroom?"

Mack exhaled against her ear. "Bedroom."

TWENTY-TWO

MACK'S DRINK SPECIAL: MORNING-AFTER MOCHA DAZE

"Nooooooo," Mack whimpered at the shrieking alarm clock as Charlie smacked around in the dark until it silenced. She dug her knuckle into the corner of her dry eye as the room squinted into focus. "What time is it?"

"Five," Charlie's groggy voice muttered. She nuzzled in a little closer, her warm breath moistening Mack's chest. "If I could call in sick, I swear I would."

Mack breathed in Charlie's sweet scent and pink cheeks and wrapped her messy hair in her fingers. Her skin tingled underneath Charlie's delicate touch, and Mack snuggled the sheets tight around them.

I'm in heaven.

Last night. This morning. Their conversation. Sleeping in Charlie's bed. Them connecting, *really* connecting. Falling asleep together. Waking up naked. She thought she knew what it'd feel like. Dreamt of situations where she didn't scurry off the second the other person fell asleep. Watched a few rom-coms over the years and wondered if reality would ever be as good. But she wasn't prepared for *this*.

This was better.

Charlie peeled herself off Mack and dangled her feet off the bed. Yawning, she stretched her arms high above her head.

Mack crawled up behind her and kissed her naked back and shoulders. "Don't go." She gently tugged Charlie back down.

"I don't want to," Charlie whispered. "Why don't you sleep for a bit? I'm going to hop in the shower."

"Can I join?"

"Don't do this." Charlie dragged herself off the bed. "If you join, there's no way the shop's opening up."

Mack shuffled to her side. "Can't Ben do it?"

"He's not starting until seven."

Mack fell onto her back in defeat and watched Charlie's naked body tiptoe out the door. As the shower ran in the distance, Mack dragged a gentle hand over her fevered inner thigh that hadn't stopped pulsating since last night. Every part of her tingled with the memory of Charlie's mouth on her.

She's perfect.

Was this too fast? Probably. But right now, all she wanted to think of was Charlie beneath her, the roundness of her hips, the silkiness of her skin. She replayed everything from the previous night, from how Charlie buried her face and giggled during their conversations, to the sensation of her fingers gripping Mack's.

She didn't come clean, though. What was she supposed to do? Charlie said she'd feel violated if she knew a writer used her for intel. The date until that point was magic, and the idea of hurting Charlie felt worse than withholding the truth. But Mack's insides burned with guilt.

She had to tell her, eventually.

She *would*.

Just not right now.

The shower stopped, and Mack raised her arm over her head, purposely leaving the sheet down to her waist until footsteps padded near the door. Charlie's wet hair fell and framed her face. The sun rays poked through the blinds, illuminating her like a sun goddess, and Mack couldn't breathe. "Sure I can't change your mind?"

Charlie bit her smile. "Unfair advantage. You cannot show me all of that... gloriousness... and expect me to function normally."

"My evil plan is working."

With her fuzzy pink towel wrapped around her body, Charlie crouched onto the bed and gave Mack one gentle kiss before she backed up and got dressed. "You should go back to sleep. Preferably for the entire day so I can come back up and find you just like this during my breaks."

"Will you bring me hostage scones and caffeine?"

Charlie slipped her dress over her head. "Always."

Mack rolled onto her stomach and rested her head in her hand, her body both tired and relaxed. No other place existed at this moment that she wanted to be at more. In Charlie's room, watching her get dressed, smelling her vanilla perfume.

"Stay?" Last ditch effort. Couldn't hurt.

"I hate this. I want to stay. You know that, right?" Charlie clasped Mack's hands. She rubbed the tips of Mack's fingers and kissed each one. "I'm not running from this. I'm not freaking out. I just have to work."

The words nestled somewhere warm and deep. "I get it. I should probably go home and do the same. I have a ton of writing to do."

Charlie nodded, and moved toward the door. "I left an extra towel for you if you want to shower. Come say goodbye before you go home?"

"Of course."

Once the front door clicked, Mack stumbled to the shower. A miniature yellow duckie towel folded on the counter with a duck head attached to it.

A duck head.

She grinned and tiptoed into the shower. Good God. Why did one person need so many products? The pink-tiled built-in shelf held at least a dozen bottles. She twisted a few caps off, sniffed various shampoos and conditioners, and made a silent vow to never tell Charlie she sometimes used body soap for her hair.

The heated water beat down on her, and she closed her eyes. This was impossible, right? To feel so close to someone she had known, what, not even a month? Someone she actually had sex with? Beautiful, incredible, heavy, passionate sex. And long. *My God*, that woman had more stamina than anyone Mack had been with before. Even her calf muscles were sore. Every ache and tingle amplified her feelings. She didn't want Charlie downstairs. She wanted Charlie next to her. She wanted to taste her body in her mouth, feel her in her fingers. To learn how her mind worked.

...no one could replicate the flavor of her tongue, a combination of fire and sweetness, and I scream inside...

She was not writing romance, obviously. But these emotions stirred everything inside. She was alive. Energized.

The duckie towel was seriously cozy. She glanced at her reflection. If she didn't look quite as ridiculous, she might've taken a selfie.

In the bedroom, she spread out on the bed instead of getting dressed, not quite ready to leave. She nuzzled her nose into her arm and inhaled Charlie's body soap lingering on her skin.

Dewy skin scent lingers... feather touches send ripples down my spine...

She leaped up and powered on her phone, her mind swirling with inspiration. Multiple missed messages from Viviane blared back at her from last night.

> Viviane: You kill me that you never answer your phone. Can you give me a buzz?

Viviane: Woman. Hit me up, please. We need to chat about something.

Viviane: Seriously. Call me, please. Need to check in about something.

Viviane: Also, I made it home okay. My flight was great, thanks for asking. :/

Oops. Mack could be a terrible friend sometimes. She'd had every intention of texting to ask if Viviane got home okay, but she got red hair and full lips distracted. She clicked on her open page app and tapped.

I'm dancing. My feet planted, my straitjacket limbs glued to my side, but I'm dancing. She whispers to me, "Come here," and who knew combining those two words with the curling of an index finger could have the power of kryptonite. I stagger towards her, sober but somehow drunk. She slides her tongue onto mine, and I brace myself against the chair.

I ask, and she lets me in. Goddamn, she lets me in. I seize her, throw her underneath me, and hook one knee up high. I want to see all of her, share her body, feel her from the inside. She is my dream, laid out before me, the answer to my prayers. Right then, clarity grips me. Whatever it takes, I will protect her. She is mine as much as I am hers, and I will fiercely defend us. They will not rip us apart. They will fail in destroying our happiness.

I will roll naked on a glass beach to get to this woman.

She is my everything.

The phone was too tiny. Her fingers couldn't keep up with her thoughts. She threw on her clothes and raced down the stairs to the shop. Once she got to the bottom, her hand hovered over the doorknob, and her body stilled.

Why did she feel sheepish? An hour ago, she and Charlie were snuggling in bed, basking in... everything. And hours before that, Mack had never felt closer to another human. But a spell occurred among the darkened rooms and warmed bodies. Now the morning sun swallowed the trees and homes around her, and the cover of white sheets and a dusky sky no longer existed.

Mack shook out her arms and opened the door.

"Hey, you." Charlie's velvety tone melted every insecurity.

Mack quickly looked around the empty shop and pulled Charlie in for a kiss. Her mouth pressed against Mack's, freely, warmly. All right, it was settled. From here on out, every morning needed to start precisely that way.

"Hmmm... I could get used to this." Charlie sighed into Mack's mouth. "Coffee? Scone?"

"Only if I can have it upstairs, with you serving it to me naked."

Charlie blushed and moved behind the counter. The water hissed over the crushed coffee beans as a caffeinated aroma settled in the air. "I've never seen you with a wrinkle."

Mack glanced down at her rumpled day-old shirt. "My soul is currently dying a miserable, very disappointed, unkempt death." While reaching for Charlie's hand, she took a quick sip. The warm coffee traveled slowly as Mack brushed her fingertips across Charlie's knuckles. "We're good, right? Everything's good?"

"Yep. Are you?"

Mack nodded. She needed time to process. Sensations from last night and emotions from this previous month overstimulated her body. But the way a fiber of warmth linked her heart, mind, and body like connective tissue intoxicated her to the point that she never wanted to leave. "Yeah. For sure. This is all just new for me. I'm not sure what to say or how to act."

Charlie kissed Mack's hand. "It's new for me, too. We'll figure this out together, okay? Honestly, right now, all I'm worried about is taking a nap."

"Oh God, same!" Mack dug her beeping phone from her

pocket. "Ugh, Uber's here already. I have to head back to my parents' place. I'm gonna take a nap and come back in a few hours."

"Perfect."

"Kiss for the road?" Mack winked.

Charlie pulled her in. "Do you even need to ask?"

TWENTY-THREE

CHARLIE'S DRINK SPECIAL: EXTRA SWEETENED EVERYTHING WITH A DOUBLE PUMP OF SUGAR

Today's bakery delivery smelled a little sweeter than usual. The cinnamon from the coffee cake twirled above Charlie's head. The chocolate in the cookies wafted in the air. She stacked the items in the display and treated herself to one. Wiping her lip with her pinkie, she pictured Mack's mouth pressed against it.

The back door slammed, and Ben stomped into the shop. "God, what a night." He tossed his keys on the desk and grabbed the apron off the hook. "Hot boy summer needs to slow down. Met a poly couple last night. They did things I've only seen once in a—wait. Nope. What's happening here?" He swirled his fingers in front of Charlie's face.

"What?" Her attempted innocent voice faltered, and she fiddled with a paperclip.

"Something's different."

Not *something. Everything.*

After zeroing in on her for several long moments, his eyes finally widened, and he took a half step back. "Did you get laid?"

"Benjamin!" With the heat shooting through her body, her face was undoubtedly as red as her hair. She ducked out of the storage room and realigned perfectly straight chairs as Ben trailed her like a shadow.

"You have the worst poker face," he said. "You're blushing from head to toe. Probably other places, too."

The books on the bookshelf needed immediate realigning. "I'm not talking about this." She started pushing each one in to match them up until she gave up and wandered behind the counter.

"Who was it? Tell me it was that smoke show, Mack. I see the flirty-ass eyes you two make to each other."

She meant to glare at him. Damn the goofy grin that busted out with no regard for her attempt at subtlety.

"*Niiice.*" He gave her an approving nod. "Well done, Charles."

She rolled her eyes. "Don't you have a shipment to unpack?"

"You better spill the goods." He stuffed a few pens in his apron. "I live for this stuff."

She tossed a towel at him and pointed to the tables.

"I mean, she's hella hot. Obviously," he continued as if she wasn't blatantly ignoring him. "How was it?"

Amazing. Legs are still quivering. Want to close the shop, call her back, and recreate every second of last night. "I'm not saying anything." She needed to hang on to this euphoria for a few more hours before she got all up in her head.

She'd never felt like this before—not even with Jess. She had loved Jess with everything in her soul, but the nights of playing mindless solitary computer games because she didn't know how to be alone, combined with the continuous fear that Jess would leave, had changed her internal chemistry. She had yelled a lot. Cried more. The love she had for herself had only existed through the lens of Jess's love for her.

And this was different.

Saved from both Ben and her thoughts by the jingling doorbell, she greeted a customer. A few dozen lattes, mochas, and all breakfast sandwiches sold before the tidal wave of uncertainty brewed.

What did last night mean? Did it mean anything? Would things be weird now between them? And dear God, could Mack do that one thing again? Mack read her body like a Braille manuscript. With every sound, every moan, Mack knew exactly what to do. And yes, *God, yes*, she wanted to do it again. Would this afternoon seem too pushy?

Charlie could play off last night—and this morning—as a one-night stand with a friend. A release after an intense week of bills, flooding, first dates, and book signings.

But her mind couldn't calm the elation in her heart.

Dammit. Less than four hours away from Mack, she was already turning into a hot mess. Nope. She couldn't do this. She could never go back to being the woman she had been with Jess. Was she just processing? Or was this the beginning of a downward spiral into the dark world of codependency?

With a break in the action, Ben slid an Americano her way and leaned shoulder to shoulder. "Real-talk time." He fiddled with his straw. "How you feeling about this? It's kind of a big deal. Totally okay to flip out over it."

"Would you flip out over this?"

He lifted a brow. "Do you really want to compare our sexual comfort levels?"

"Fair." Charlie clicked her fingers against the cup. "Okay, it's definitely a big deal. But am I making it a bigger deal than what normal people make it?"

"Define *normal*."

She let out a heavy sigh. "You know, people that don't have trust issues based on a childhood trauma from borderline neglect. Like, people who used to eat Cheerios for breakfast and go school shopping with their parents?"

"Well, count me out, then." He nudged her with his shoulder. Several sips passed before he spoke. "I don't think you always trust your emotions, and that trips you up. After Jess, you questioned everything about yourself."

"I know my issues caused things to go bad with Jess and me."

"*Your* issues did not cause issues with you and Jess. Jess wanting something totally different than you caused issues with you and Jess. Jess doing what she did caused issues."

"I don't want to talk about that," she snapped. "We were separated."

Silence filled the air as she pictured herself sobbing into a towel in the bathroom, shaking from lack of food, dehydrated from the tears. She couldn't do it again. The breakup had ruined her for so long. Her broken-self shell finally fell off a year ago, and she'd cling to her newly found love and independence with everything she had.

Charlie cared about Mack a lot. But prevention was key. Maybe she should tell Mack they couldn't sleep together again, but she genuinely wanted Mack in her life. Charlie could say that her hesitation had nothing to do with Mack and everything to do with herself.

Or maybe she could have some fun. With an incredible woman who made her laugh, supported her, and kissed her like the promise of tomorrow didn't exist.

"Ah... there's that smile." Ben tossed his empty container in the trash. "Give me something good."

"God, you don't stop!" She grinned. "I feel okay about things. I think. I wish she were here right now if that indicates where my thoughts are."

"Okay is good. Bored, not good. Shame, not good. Wanting her to stay and sad she left, we can work with." He tossed a towel at her and handed over the sanitizing spray. "But where do you see this going? Is she planning on moving here?"

"Jesus, Ben. We've been on one date. I don't know. Probably not."

Her stomach dipped, and she aggressively wiped tables while shaking off the pending doom sensation.

"So this is a fling?"

Hope not. Damn Ben and all his questions. For the last twenty-four hours, Charlie tried hard not to dwell on what would happen if she continued falling for Mack while she lived in New York. Because really, how would that look? She'd pass through town every few months? FaceTime in the evening? Try to be cute and hip and send postcards with funny pictures? Ugh. She was doing it. Sex messed with her brain waves and had her acting like a fool. Tonight, she needed to do some serious meditation.

Ben tossed his hand in the air. "Chucky?"

"Can you just let me enjoy something for once?"

"You're right, you're right." He grabbed the spray from her and hung it back on the hook. "I'm happy for you."

TWENTY-FOUR

MACK'S DRINK SPECIAL: INSPIRATION ITALIAN ROAST

Mack yawned and stirred after crashing hard the moment she returned from Charlie's to her parents' condo. She flung her hands above her head and stared at the ceiling, her thoughts the same now as they were this morning.

Charlie.

No way was this warm, gluey snugness in her chest normal. Maybe not even healthy. But she didn't care. Everything in her was awakened. Thoughts she had never experienced before. Feelings. This pressure on her heart was both welcome and scary as hell.

Mack was a disaster. She knew it. Her parents knew it. And yet, the universe presented her a candy-pink-lips-and-red-hair-wrapped gift. She was the luckiest human alive. Now was the time to show her gratitude and make everything right. She cracked her back, stuffed pillows up to her neck, and reached for her laptop.

The night creeps upon us, but the menacing shadows are inviting. Stars and moonlight cast just enough light where I can see the glint in her eye, the outline of my reflection in her irises.

Her lips burrow into mine. Soft. Gentle. Almost like a butterfly wing, where you don't fully realize it touched you, but your skin lingers with the sensation. She pulls back and searches my eyes, my soul, looking for confirmation that I feel the same.

I can see it in her, and I'm not imagining anything. The realization, the complexity of what happened, and the consequence of what will happen if we go any further, hit us both.

I inch closer. Gentleness fades. Hunger takes over.

Inspired and motivated, Mack's fingers zoomed like lightning. Lost in her world, she created magic on the page. The words escaped so quickly that her fingers had difficulty keeping up. She adjusted her stiffened body and re-shoved the pillow behind her head.

Images interrupt my sleep, but for once, they're welcome. Nightmares of tsunamis and immobile legs, gone. Replaced by calm, crystal water, sand funneling between toes and a faint hum of a breeze off the coast. A voice whispers in my ear. Dream and reality collide. Warm skin touches me. Serenity consumes me. After all this time, it's staring at me. Without a doubt, without hesitation, I know exactly what needs to happen.

Mack's phone chimed with a message, then rang. She silenced it without looking. Her fingers continued to race, machine-gun clicking against the keyboard.

We're at a critical turning point, and tonight, no doubt things will change. God forgive me. I have no choice in what I'm about to do. The strawberry gloss is sticky against my bruised lips, but I smack them just the same. Tonight, I'll look my best. After this, doing what I need to do, our lives will cease to exist in their current state. From this moment on, everything's considered a "before" or an "after."

The pages stacked up. Layers upon layers of story burst from her, taking her down a road she never expected, but she let herself go there. Her outline tossed, for this moment at least, and her characters spoke through her, told her what she needed to do. She followed them through this journey and let herself get lost in their direction.

Her hyper-focused state pumped dopamine through her veins and staved off all other sensations until the nerves in her lower back beat out the competition and forced her to move. When she pulled her leg up to her chest, the burn shot from her hip to her spine. At some point, she seriously needed to consider chiropractic care. Or a proper desk. She flipped over and glanced at the clock.

3:45 p.m.

3:45!

She snatched her phone, nearly numb fingers scrolling through the message barrage.

9:21 a.m.

Viviane: we need to chat. Please call me

10:07 a.m.

Charlie: Drinking hot chocolate. Not because I want it but because it made me think of you

10:15 a.m.
Viviane (missed call)

10:16 a.m.
Viviane (voicemail)

12:29 p.m.

Viviane: Do not make me fly to Seattle. I will. I love you, but you need to call me ASAP. It's about the contract.

1:12 p.m.

> Charlie: So bummed you aren't here. You missed the cutest thing ever! A daycare brought the kids down here for steamers (for you not in the biz, it's warmed milk with a flavor). All the kids were holding each other's hands in a chain line. Freaking adorable.

1:50 p.m.
Viviane (missed call)

3:33 p.m.

> Charlie: hope everything is okay, and I totally didn't scare you off 😅 (insert hyper-paranoia, kind of needy, weird trust issues here)

> Charlie: 🤍

Mack buried her face in her hands. With everything Charlie had shared with her, abandonment, awful parenting, and a delinquent ex, the first thing Mack did was ghost her right after they slept together? Mack had to be better than this.

3:51 p.m.

> Mack: OMG. Sorry, I was super focused on my work. The day flew by.

> Mack: and now I want hot chocolate

> Mack: and more kisses

Mack exhaled and dialed Viviane.

She picked up on the first ring. "Seriously, you can't do this to me. We're a business partnership, you know that, right? And I'm laying down the best friend card, too."

Oh no. Only once in the last four years had Viviane laid that tone on her, when they had differing opinions about attending the largest NYC book fair of the year. Mack lost then, too. "I'm sorry. No joke, I really was in my zone this time."

"How close are you to meeting the deadline?"

"I'm going to be a little late getting it to you."

Her mind flashed to Charlie's face flushing last night as her protection wall crumbled, and she opened up about her past. Originally, Mack dug for details for a different reason, but Charlie steamrolled Mack with her innocence and vulnerability.

"I can't do this anymore." Mack flung back on the bed. "Using these stories from the coffee shop. So, I need more time. Do whatever you have to do, but let the publisher know there'll be a delay."

Viviane exhaled. "You're not writing a memoir. You're writing fiction. Really good fiction. Doesn't matter where it comes from."

It does now.

Hard stop. Mack needed additional resources. She shifted to her side and ran a fingertip across her mouth. Charlie's soft mouth left hers hours ago, but if Mack closed her eyes tight enough, she could faintly sense the imprint of Charlie's lips.

She sat upright on the bed. "I need a few more weeks to research."

"Your research is solid." The harsh, yet motherly, tone echoed through the receiver. "If hearing the coffee shop stories expedites your work, then you need to keep at it. The publishers called today."

"And?"

"Do you remember all the details of the contract?"

"God, no. That's why I have you."

The sound of an office chair rolling back and forth sounded through the phone. Which was not a good sign, as that was

Viviane's go-to when delivering harsh news. "Okay, part of the contract states if you do not meet the milestone deadlines, they have the right to rescind your advancement."

Mack's mouth went dry. "What? What do you mean?"

"You don't produce, you repay."

The sharp words cut Mack's breath. Repay? All? Some? What exactly did that mean? Not that the explanation mattered —the advance was gone days after she received it. Handed over in one lump sum to a hospital billing department, chemo center, and recovery facility.

Mack pressed her palm into her forehead. "There must be something you can do."

An uneasy silence followed.

"Sometimes we have some wiggle room," Viviane finally said. "During our call, I toed the waters, but their response was firm."

The team had set the publishing schedule for the next eighteen months. This shouldn't shock Mack, but Viviane's sharp tone blared all the alarm bells. Mack had precisely four weeks to finish an editor-worthy draft. Stomach acid vaulted to her throat. "I need more time."

"Firm, Mack."

She scooted up on the bed and dropped her head into her arms. Her heart thumped and she inhaled and released full breaths. Trapped under a deadline, again, the creative blanket she'd wrapped herself in since setting foot in Seattle disintegrated.

"No one's going to recognize themselves in your work," Viviane said. "No person ever reads a book and thinks it was based on a conversation they had with someone at a diner or a shop. You're going to be fine. You're panicking, and that's okay, but just head there tomorrow—"

"They're Charlie's stories."

"Charlie?" A long pause followed. "Oh dear."

Viviane's defeated voice matched Mack's insides. More silence followed, and if the gravity of the situation hadn't sunk in before, it sunk in now.

"Well, woman, I wouldn't want to be in your shoes." Viviane sighed. "Looks like you have a decision to make. But I don't want you to feel like you have to fly solo on this one. If you need me to help you with that decision, you holler immediately."

Mack had already decided. She just needed to come to terms with the consequences. Losing an advance was one thing. Losing her contract, career, and reputation was another.

But this wasn't just about Mack.

Viviane didn't need to say it. Mack knew Viviane well enough to know that she wouldn't say it. But Viviane's commission, a chunk of her livelihood, was also on the line.

After they hung up, Mack laid the phone on her chest. She barreled through every scenario, determined to find the one with the least carnage.

She couldn't let Viviane down. She couldn't pay back the money. She couldn't use Charlie. And she couldn't produce in four weeks what normally took four months.

So what *could* she do?

Her phone vibrated, and her heart soared and sunk at once with Charlie's name on the screen.

Charlie: want to come over tonight?

Mack: more than just about anything.

Mack: But I can't. I have to work.

TWENTY-FIVE

CHARLIE'S DRINK SPECIAL: CHANGES CAPPUCCINO WITH BLAST FROM THE PAST SYRUP

This was normal, right? This ache in her heart, a sort of mash-up between hurt, a touch of nausea, and desire. Charlie picked up the phone for the fifth time today to text Mack, then quickly clicked it off before she did something stupid.

Don't do this. Stop being so needy.

Only two days had passed since her and Mack's night together. What had felt so right, so secure, *so perfect* in that moment now filled her with borderline mayhem. So far today, she'd rung up several orders wrong and tossed a few botched drinks.

Sure, Mack texted her. But long delays passed between texts, and her usually snappy responses evolved to two-word quips. Was Mack already pulling away? Maybe she really was just busy. Maybe there were other women. Maybe Charlie liked Mack more than Mack liked Charlie, and now it'd be so freaking awkward when... *if...* she came back.

"Maybe you should get out of your head." Ben rattled a cup of iced coffee in front of her face.

Was she talking out loud? "No idea what you mean." How

long had she been standing there, staring at her bonsai tree with snippers in hand and no leaves falling?

"You go from all glazy-eyed to your face wrinkling like a dehydrated sloth and back again." He reached for the box cutter. "Want to talk about it?"

Nope.

She couldn't even properly articulate what was happening to herself. What would she say? After knowing someone for just a few weeks, she thought she was already falling in love? And that after the last few years of being celibate, one night of fantastic sex had her seeing visions of roses and dancing in her future? What about the fact that she was probably misinterpreting everything and that she should never have slept with Mack because now Charlie was overthinking and self-conscious, and...

"You thinking about Jess?"

"Yes. No. I don't know." Charlie dropped the shears into her apron and followed Ben into the storage area.

Ben ripped open the coffee bean boxes and stacked them on the shelf as Charlie slumped into the chair. She propped her elbows on the counter and relaxed her chin in her palm.

Jess, the person, wasn't what occupied Charlie's mind. It was Jess, the *situation*. The whirlwind of their relationship. The searing pain of their breakup. The amount of therapy and effort it took to reclaim who she was. One night with Mack had stripped back all her hard work.

Nope. She was not doing this. The person she used to be was gone, and she had evolved into someone else entirely. Someone better, independent, suited, and fit to handle her affairs. She would never mangle her identity with someone else's. Two years ago, she busted through the needy cocoon and soared out as someone new entirely. She refused to revert.

An unknown number displayed on her cell screen and she flung it onto the desk hard enough that she winced. The very last thing she needed was a cracked phone when she had zero funds to replace it. *Fan-freaking-tastic*. First, she swirled about Mack. Now creditors were calling. She couldn't keep her stuff together, and she was totally over it.

"Wait. Stop shelving." She drummed her fingers against her chin and focused on the inventory. "We need to order things better. From now on, Colombian on the right, Ethiopian in the middle, Kona on the left."

Ben stared open-mouthed.

"What?" she snapped as she pulled out a Sharpie and masking tape. "I'm sick of not being more buttoned-up. I need to gain some control over... everything."

He lifted an eyebrow but said nothing. Last week she found a five-thousand-count straw box shoved between the toilet paper supply, and today she was organizing the beans by region.

She scribbled *cup holders* on a piece of tape and patted it on the shelf. If her thoughts were spinning out of control, then perhaps organizing her supplies would make her feel more in control.

Ben shoved the beans into piles. "What's going on?"

She broke down boxes to avoid looking at him. Since they were kids, she told Ben nearly everything. He was the constant in her life. The one she trusted the most. Why couldn't she just spit this out? "I just... I don't know how much longer I can keep this place open."

Ben stopped moving and lowered his arms. "What do you mean, not keep it open?"

The concerned look on his face gut-punched her. If a dark black hole could open at any moment that she could fall into, she'd seriously appreciate it. She stared at the half-torn box and swallowed. "I screwed things up. Bad. I just... I put way too much into remodeling this place, and overspent. Creditors are literally calling all the time and sending things in the mail, and any second now they're going to bust down the doors and haul me away."

He paused for a long moment. "Why didn't you tell me?" His voice was more defensive than sweet.

"You're pissed, right? 'Cause I'm failing?"

"What are you talking about? Pissed, yes. But not because the shop might go under. Pissed that you didn't trust me enough to tell me. You know I've always got your back. Why did you keep this from me?"

She dropped the box and pushed her palm into her forehead. "I don't know. I just... I didn't want you to think I couldn't handle it."

Ben shook his head and sighed. "Don't ever do this. I'm here always. Good, bad, whatever. We're a team." He brought her in for a rare but warm hug. "Now what?"

"I honestly don't know." She'd given Mack's dad all the contract information several days ago and hadn't heard anything. Not that he owed her anything, but *still...* She had to make a decision soon about Sugar Mugs. "Can you hold down the shop for a bit? I've gotta run upstairs to do some paperwork."

Ben nodded and she ran up to her loft.

Taking a seat at her desk, she pulled in a full, deep breath and opened her laptop. No more running. Time to face this head-on.

She scoured the inventory spreadsheet with the product costs. What was the profit margin on coconut milk? Maybe she could eliminate that. What if she upped her charges? Although that felt icky to do to her regulars and after being open less than a year. Maybe she should stop using fair trade coffee. Although that felt even worse than raising prices.

She opened the drawer of unopened bills and failure-to-pay notices. One by one, she laid them in a pile and pressed out the wrinkles. Putting them in order from *Final Notice, Sent to*

Collections, and *Third Notice*, her stomach coiled and she thought she was going to throw up.

An hour in, she texted Ben to say she needed more time. Two hours in, she started to cry. Three hours in, she put her game face on. She could do this.

Her phone pinged.

> Mack: Hey, beautiful

> Mack: so sorry, totally MIA. This deadline is gutting me with a razor-sharp butterfly knife like I was a rat paying for talking to the cops.

> Mack: sorry, my head's still on the manuscript

> Mack: and if you tell anyone about that scene, I'll deny it until the day I die

> Mack: how are you?

Charlie's fingers suspended over the screen. She held the phone in her hand for a full minute before she stuffed it back in her pocket without responding.

Yep. She could do this independent thing.

The afternoon rush slowed, and Charlie waved at Ben as he left. She reread Mack's message, started to respond and stopped herself.

Stay strong. She could message Mack after work. Like what an independent person would do. Like what a healthy, well-put-together, fully organized person would do.

The motivational quotes calendar on the wall caught her eye, and she studied the Mark Twain quote: *"The secret of getting ahead is getting started."*

He was right. She could do this. Time to take charge and

regain control. The last customer had left over an hour ago, and even though no one else stopped in, today was still a better day customer-wise than most. Charlie flipped the sign to closed and wiped her forehead with her arm.

Audit slips and receipts littered her tiny desk. Multiple notepads scattered the storage room and were stuffed God-knows-where. Post-it notes covered both the corkboard and half the mirror, bearing messages like: *Ben needs July 14-22 off*, *a decaf espresso should be called a depresso ;-)*, *June 17 shipment missing forks—follow up!*, *Best advice of the Year: Don't be a Dick*.

She pulled in a deep breath and clapped her hands. One by one, she plucked the outdated Post-it notes and tossed them in the trash. Ten minutes in, she couldn't help adding one more note: *Cleanliness is next to godliness*.

Next, the notebooks were all found, including one shoved behind the box of old phone chargers in the corner. She flipped through each page and tore out anything outdated. She grabbed her fat purple Sharpie and labeled three notebooks: *Recipe Ideas*, *Inventory Issues*, and *Random Notes*.

Labeling! Utensils and office supplies banged against the side of drawers as she searched for the label maker she purchased months ago. She finally found it buried under a stack of towels in the supply closet.

"Aha, you little stink-rat. I got you," she said when success-fully printing her first label after nearly twenty minutes of clicking buttons. She stepped back and admired her work. Okay, okay, the space did look more professional. Maybe those online articles about "decluttering your space will declutter your mind" weren't completely bogus.

What a day.

She climbed on the stool to grab parchment paper, and when the bell jingled, she almost hit her head on a box. Didn't she lock the door? She was sure she did.

She bolted out of the supply closet. "Sorry, we're closed —Dad?"

Her heart flew into her throat, and she nearly choked. Five, maybe six, months had passed since he last visited. The salt-and-pepper scruff on his cheeks indicated a shave from a few days ago. His red-orange hair had faded a bit, and gray seeped in at the temples, but the rosy cheeks and familiar dark circles were the same.

"Hi there, princess," he said with a crooked grin while gripping a small paper bag.

"Oh... hey." She leaned in for a brief hug. The stark spice scent of his generic aftershave and the burn-off from day-old whiskey and unwashed clothes oozed from his pores.

She gauged the redness of his eyes. "What are you doing here?"

He shook the bag. "Wanted to stop by and bring you a little gift."

Her heart dipped at the salted truffle See's candies. Over the years, he forgot so many things—school functions, birthdays, to come home on the weekends. But he was great on minor details. Salted truffle chocolates were her favorite. "Thanks."

"Those still your favorite?"

"Sure are." She popped a chocolate in her mouth and offered him one. "You should sit down. You thirsty? I can fire up the machine, make you a coffee."

"Nah. You don't need to do all that fussin' on me. Maybe just a quick water will do." He slumped onto a barstool and glanced around the room. "Ya got some new stuff there, huh? Don't think that couch was here last time I was here."

It was. "Hmm. I don't remember, either." She passed him the water and sat next to him.

"Oh, forgot. Brought ya something else." He slapped at his various pockets until he pulled a bottle of used purple nail polish with a fifty-cent garage sale sticker affixed to the side. "Thought of ya when I saw that."

She gave him a soft smile. "Thanks. That was sweet of you."

He folded his arms across his chest. "Rosie woulda been real happy to see what ya did with her place."

The words struck fast and hard. She blew out a quick breath. "Yeah, I think so, too."

A tug of war erupted inside. Visions of her spending hours in her room or sitting in front of the TV with a box of cereal and a cup of water because he always forgot to pick up milk, juxtaposed with him letting her polish his toenails, spraying whipped cream in her mouth, and talking about the Seahawks.

"So... I gotta job down at the pier. Haulin' crab from some local guys."

She sighed and clicked her fingernails together. "That's great. Make sure you're careful with your back. That's tough work."

She said that because that was what polite people said when given news about a job. The job would last a day, maybe a week, if a job even existed. Her father had a knack for weaving in enough truth to not tell a bald-faced lie.

He scratched at his scruff. "Yeah, well, to make an honest livin', sometimes you gotta do an honest man's work."

What did that even mean? He needed to spit out why he was here and stop doing this ridiculous dance. Confusing signals flushed her body like a wet, weighted blanket. Relief that he was alive and moderately healthy, melting that he remembered her favorite color and chocolate, tension from an inevitable disappointment slam that would surely hit her before he left.

The section of the floor she and Mack had spent hours on last week caught her attention, and the feeling when Mack's dad said how proud he was of them marched through her.

They'd only met a few short times, yet he showed her what it was like to have a parent who loved and nurtured their kids.

"I was hopin'... just to hold me over until the first paycheck comes in, if ya could spot me a few greens? I'll pay you back."

The tension in her shoulders evaporated when he asked. It always did. The apprehension of when and how he'd asked caused the strain. Yet, her heart sunk into an unfamiliar space, low and deep. All these years, she held on to a sliver of daughterly hope that her father was something he wasn't. That pancake dad, hot chocolate dad, joking dad was her real dad, and this other dad was an imposter.

She had to stop chasing the delusion.

Her shoulders straightened, and her chin raised. She marched behind the counter and dug her purse from under the till. Her fingers trembled as she tugged out every dollar she had in her wallet and repeated the same steps with the tip jar.

She had no idea how much it was. At this point, it didn't matter. Had she not already counted down the till she would've given him her entire daily earnings. Her breath was choppy, but her pounding heart eased.

Determined footsteps padded across the floor as she gripped the wad of cash in her hands and bit her quivering lips. As his eyes dashed between her face and money, a mix of desperation, excitement, and regret seemed to cross his face.

He knew it was wrong. And so did she.

They spoke no words. She laid the cash in his open palm, and his fingers curled around the bills. He nodded with his eyes cast down and shoved it in his pocket.

"Dad." Clearing her throat didn't clear the sickness in her stomach, and she stumbled a few steps back. "I love you, and I want you to be safe and healthy. But the cash stops." She wanted to turn around, run away, or apologize and suck back the words. But she forced herself to stay firm.

Various emotions reflected in her father's eyes. Pain. Remorse. Regret. Maybe a touch of defiance. He opened his mouth and closed it, and then dropped his head. "This is who I am."

And just like that, it hit her. He'd never change. Nothing she did could make him change. But the beauty was that she could take or leave him, but it was *her choice*. Not his. His issues had nothing to do with her not being a good enough daughter. His problems were his own.

She was a double, extra-large cup of cappuccino, and he was a short shot of espresso. He probably gave her everything he had... gave her his entire shot of espresso. But it wasn't enough, and it would never be enough. Her cup needed more.

She took a lifetime of deep breaths and looked at him. *Really* looked at him. Saw him for who he was—an addicted single father who struggled to raise his daughter. A man who lost his sister, Rosie. A man abandoned by his wife. She saw the missed teacher conferences and the broken park-date promises. She saw her coloring book drawings taped over the entire kitchen wall and leading to the hall because he said the colors made him happy. She saw her new sparkly dress shoes he had saved up for when she was eight. She saw vomit in the bathroom, empty bottles, regretful smiles, and pancakes.

She. Saw. Him.

But also... she saw herself. Her desperation to be needed. Her compromising her morals and her need to fix him and support him to make her feel complete.

Something about this day, this moment, this second, crashed down.

She was enough on her own.

The chair squeaked when he stood, and he pushed it under the table. His head hung a little lower as he walked to the door. When he reached the exit, his hands hovered on the door handle.

He barely glanced at her, and his mouth parted. "Ya did good, kid. Real proud of ya."

Her heart both shattered and filled at the words. Years she waited to hear these words, and her younger self collapsed. But her adult self knew it was too late.

"Hey, Dad?

His spine straightened. "Yeah?"

"I forgive you."

He expelled a breath as his chin fell to his chest. And then walked out the door.

And she broke down.

TWENTY-SIX

MACK'S DRINK SPECIAL: LAVA-HOT LATTE

Mack frowned. Charlie had been Quick Draw McGraw these last few weeks with text messages, and now the time tipped on five hours since she sent her text. Should she message again? The shop would've closed almost an hour ago. Was Charlie okay?

A few rings, and Mack's call went to voicemail. She nibbled on her bottom lip and checked the time again. Not knowing if Charlie was okay made her legs jumpy and hands sweaty. She paced the room and bit the cuticle on her pinkie. Maybe Charlie was in the shower? Or went out with friends? All were likely scenarios. But... what if someone broke into Charlie's home, and used razor-sharp zip ties to bind her wrists to the pantry shelf?

Okay, okay. Maybe Mack should take a break from her manuscript.

Still... something felt off. Jesus, was this what Mack's mom felt like when Mack ignored her messages? Starting now, Mack would stop being a jerk, and when her mom called her, she'd respond immediately.

A full glass of water consumed, another billion pacing steps, and ironing her shirt eased nothing. Her belly turned sour, and she opened her laptop.

The stillness unsettles me. I strip off my coat and toss it on the dusty, pale pink, Victorian sitting chair near the fireplace. The only sound I hear is a faint clanking of the radiator upstairs and the muffled hum of old house wiring.

It's too quiet. "Hello?" I call into the vacant space, and my voice bounces back. "Hello?" I repeat, already knowing silence will be my response.

They wouldn't, would they? Families were off-limits. A code brokered between them months ago. An honest handshake agreement between two dishonest criminals. My tiptoes turn into thuds as I search the rooms, open closets, and look under beds. Days ago, I would've welcomed the calm. But now... now things are different. Too much is at stake.

Mack wrote. Pages and pages developed, feeding off her belly's sickness.

Who thinks of impending loss to this nauseating degree? Apparently, me. We've all read the articles on anxiety and fear, worrying about our loved ones, but I'd been exempt. Until now. Sure, I take precautions. But my precautions are ironclad. I think. I *hope.*

I should celebrate my success from earlier tonight, but my mind races, flashes to an impending void, and my heart squeezes so hard in my chest that I grip the chair in front of me to keep from passing out.

Her fingers cramped. Her parents arrived home, and she requested silence. She continued.

They can't take this away from me. For the first time in my life, I feel it. It's so close, a ghost whisper of a touch away. I can capture it. I know I can. My scalp throbs so hard, so heavy, but I push through. It's right there. All I need to do is stretch... reach... Once my fingertips make contact, I'll latch on forever.

Her phone rang, and her breath hitched at Charlie's name. "Hey!"

"I don't know what I'm doing." Charlie's hoarse, rushed voice boomed through the phone. "I'm making up all sorts of stories in my head, why something is one way, and maybe it should be another. And I'm scared, Mack. I'm so scared... and I know maybe it's not a big deal to you, or maybe it is, or maybe I don't know anything, but it's a big deal to me, and..."

"Hey, hey. It's okay." Mack sat up and flung her laptop to the side. She hated hearing Charlie like this, but relief spread that she called. "I'm here. You want to talk about it?"

"When you didn't text or sounded all disinterested in your messages, I got all weird, and I said I would never get weird again, and I did it after one date." Charlie sniffed. "*One. Date.* My healing, therapy, growing, all destroyed in a snap."

Oh no. Mack didn't respond to anyone, ever, in her zone. But she actually sent a few messages to Charlie. She remembered tearing her eyes away from the manuscript to jot a quick note. To Mack, it was huge. But Charlie clearly needed more.

"I think you're too hard on yourself. Growing and healing don't mean you're not allowed to feel anything," Mack said. "I'm sorry that not texting or calling immediately caused that anxiety. Not answering you has nothing to do with you and everything about me being trapped in my zone."

"Huh?"

Mack pulled her knees up to her chest and placed the phone on speaker. "It's like if I called you during your morning rush. You'd probably ignore me."

A cry-giggle sounded. "Oh... God, that totally makes sense. And then my dad came here, and things feel so different, and maybe there's light—"

"Your dad came to see you?"

"Yep, and it's like, for once, it's all good. I mean, it's not, but the weight lifted, but then it amplified the weight with you, and it's hard, you know? It's all really new and scary."

"It's scary for me, too."

Several seconds of silence followed. The sound of a sniffle and blowing nose came through the receiver. "It is?"

"Of course it is. I don't even know what to do with myself." Mack twirled her index ring. "I have feelings I've never had, and my body doesn't know how to decode them. Is it anxiety? Is it happiness? Is it—"

She stopped herself. Was it love?

"I just... I need to know how you feel." The vulnerability in Charlie's voice burrowed into Mack.

"I'm all in." Mack's unprotected heart kicked frantically against her chest. Excruciating, slow, silent seconds passed.

"Want to come over?"

The drive to Charlie's took a million years. Mack tapped her thumbs on the steering wheel. She turned the music up and back down again. She sped through yellow lights. And when she pulled up, she withheld from sprinting up the stairs.

Charlie ripped the door before Mack even knocked. Mack was prepared to talk things out, sit there all night if they had to, make sure they both felt secure and heard. Whatever it took, Mack was committed.

But Charlie gripped her from behind her neck and pushed her lips onto Mack's before Mack could squeak out a word. Charlie kicked the door shut behind her and latched the lock. The wall pressed into Mack's back when Charlie drove her against it as her tongue pushed into Mack's mouth.

Charlie stood back for a second, wide-eyed and flushed. "Is this okay?"

"Everything's okay. Everything."

The relief poured in. Indecision poured out. Mack kicked her shoes to the side, and Charlie reached for her. The heat in Charlie's hands soaked her skin as Charlie pushed Mack's shirt up, her lips only leaving Mack's to graze her neck. Mack held the swell of Charlie's ass, pulled her in tight, and rocked against her.

A frenetic energy inundated the air. An urgency pushed on Mack like she'd lose everything if she didn't share her body with Charlie right this second. She needed to connect to Charlie. To prove to herself, to prove to Charlie, that everything was real.

Mack wanted it messy and dirty but needed it sweet and comforting. She craved being held and pinched and soft fingers and whispered to that they'd figure everything out and would take this ride together.

When Mack sucked on Charlie's bottom lip, the sweetness of tea and vanilla filled her. She skimmed her thumbs across Charlie's nipples and melted with each moan. Fingertips dug into her back, and Mack crumbled against the sensation.

Zippers undone, bras unfastened and tossed, skin turned warm, moist. They stumbled down the hall like neither one could lose contact with the other, or the spell would break. Mack trembled, fear and happiness colliding. She had *no idea* that everything could feel this good. Her heart, her mind, her body. All synchronized swimmers in this pool of...

Yes, she had to say it. She *loved* Charlie. And she was pretty sure Charlie loved her, too. She'd protect Charlie. And she'd let herself be protected.

They fell on the bed, the headboard banging into the wall with a vibrating thud, and the urgency broke. Mack pampered herself with Charlie's silky skin. Her mouth begged to experience every piece of her. Charlie slid down, and Mack sat back on her knees. Tonight, every part of Charlie would receive the attention it deserved. She brushed her finger across the birthmark on Charlie's upper thigh. She kissed the daisy tattoo on Charlie's calf. She glided her tongue across Charlie's wrist.

"Does this feel good?" Mack asked as she swept her tongue across the lily on Charlie's lower belly.

"Yes..."

How did she get so lucky? How did she stumble into Sugar Mugs and meet Charlie and get to *be* with her? Got to know her, understand her, and love her. Was any of this real? Did she dream Charlie up, create this perfect being in her mind?

None of this made logical sense.

But she didn't need it to make sense.

Mack pushed her thumbs against Charlie's thighs, trailing from the knee and higher as Charlie's limbs shook beneath her. Mack's fingertips sunk into Charlie, and her back curved. They rocked together, slow, steady, rhythmic. Heartbeats matched. Breathing matched. Mack cupped Charlie's body, held her close, and they moved together. Mack never wanted to leave.

Charlie flipped Mack over, her skin glistening, her breaths heavy. Charlie kneaded Mack's skin and feathered her fingertips so delicately that Mack thought she'd die from anticipation. She quivered underneath Charlie's smooth touch.

Time was inconsequential. Words weren't needed. Everything outside didn't exist. There was no manuscript. There was no coffee shop. There was just them. Connecting, genuinely connecting, in a way she'd never connected to anyone before.

Exhausted and dreamy, Charlie laid her head in Mack's lap, and Mack twirled her silky locks with her fingers. When Charlie's breaths shifted, turning heavy with sleep, Mack looked down at her. The angel in her lap. The heaven she didn't know existed. Her heart swelled, and she blinked back tears.

Confident Charlie was asleep, Mack whispered, "I love you."

Charlie's thumb, hazy and light, swiped against her leg. "I love you, too..."

TWENTY-SEVEN

CHARLIE'S DRINK SPECIAL: EXTRA-LARGE LITE EVERYTHING

Crumpled sheets swaddled Charlie as she rolled over and drew Mack closer. Mack softly raked her fingers through Charlie's hair, sending shivers up her spine. Only a week had passed since Mack stopped by and cracked the "I love you" seal, but eternity could pass, and Charlie would never get sick of how they ended up every night: snuggles, massages, and sexy time.

"I'll give you a thousand dollars not to go to work today." Mack's drowsy voice funneled in the dark.

"Deal. Same goes for you," Charlie said with a grin, knowing it'd never happen.

This past week, Charlie focused on her customers and organizing the shop while Mack holed herself up at her parents' condo, burying herself in writing for twelve to sixteen hours a day. But every night, she showed up at Charlie's with takeout and an overnight bag. By day two, Charlie's chest stopped sinking every time the jingle sounded, and it wasn't Mack. By day five, Charlie's body turned into Pavlov's dog whenever she heard Mack's footsteps up her stairs.

Mack nuzzled into Charlie's neck. "My parents have been

up my ass all week to have you over for a movie night. Sorry, they're relentless. You good with that?"

Not only good but spending time with parents who treated her more like a daughter from Day One sounded incredible. "Yep. Tonight work?"

"Unfortunately." Mack groaned with a chuckle.

Charlie dragged herself to the shower and her thoughts swirled. When she and Jess first got together, their relationship combined the thrill of sneaking away from Jess's parents, the passion of exploring sex for the first time, and constant conversations about what it would be like when they were adults and away from their miserable parents. Everything with Mack differed.

When Mack kissed her, Charlie's toes curled. Her heart skipped. She wanted to see Mack smile, to hear her moan. Charlie wanted to feel Mack on her fingertips, to bathe in her breath. She wanted to giggle at Mack's dry humor and listen to her read passages from her book. But the sensation wasn't frantic, or addictive. It was stable.

She tugged the towel around her and moved back to the room. "You gonna go back to sleep?" Charlie whispered, and planted a kiss behind her ear.

"Only for a little. Then I need to get back at it."

After she finished getting dressed and put her hair up, Charlie leaned against the doorway. She took a moment to marvel at Mack's bare back and messy, black hair as she lay flat against the stark white sheet.

Mack peeked out of one eye and patted the bed next to her.

"I wish," Charlie said, and then trotted downstairs to the shop.

The machines warmed, supplies refilled, and her first cup of coffee downed. Ben strolled in with a half-attached apron and a yawn.

"Morning, sunshine." He patted his hands in his apron with

a frown and opened a desk drawer. "What the hell's happening here? Did you label the *inside* of the drawer?"

She grinned. "Who knew labeling would be so gratifying? I'm thinking I'm gonna do my linen closets next. Rows for shampoo, conditioner, and curl cream. Oh! Ponytail holders, fingernail polish, cotton swabs, towels—"

"What have you done with my bestie? Bring her back, please." He grabbed a Sharpie for the orders. "By the way, Lena will be here at 8:00 instead of 8:30. She's super excited."

Since Mack posted about Sugar Mugs, took over as Charlie's self-proclaimed social media manager, and started posting regularly on all the channels, business had picked up. Today, Lena officially bumped up from a "once-in-a-while" employee to a "part-time" employee.

"She's been killing it. Did she talk to her friend last night about picking up leftover hours? I only have a few more months with you here and need to make sure I've covered everything."

Ben laid a hand on her arm. "It's gonna be okay. You know that, right?"

Charlie nodded but maintained her denial about Ben's approaching graduation date. For the first time in over a decade, they wouldn't be working together every day.

"Chucky, look at me." His voice was firmer than usual, and she paused. "You got this. I *know* you got this. And pretty soon, you're gonna realize you got this, too."

She wrapped her arms around him in a rare, warm embrace. "Maybe you're right."

"Pffft, please. I'm *always* right." He bumped her with his hip and moved to greet the incoming customer.

The beeping-till-and-steam-milk-screeching DJ mix boomed through the shop as customers poured in. Macklemore's latest track thumped in the background as coffee cake and chocolate cookies flew off the shelf. Nearly three hundred customers served—a record for a Wednesday—and finally,

Charlie flipped the sign to *Closed* and dashed to her loft to shower before heading to Mack's parents' condo.

Never in her life would she have thought she'd be this excited to have dinner with parents.

When Charlie stepped off the elevator at Mack's parents' condo to find Mack waiting in the hallway, her heart soared.

"You know you're the best girlfriend in the world, right?" Mack pulled her in for a kiss.

Girlfriend. Gah! She said it so casually, so easily, like it was any other day. And Charlie couldn't shake the smile.

"I can think of a few ways to compensate for this." Mack's low, raspy tone sent a blush through Charlie.

"Movie night with your parents sounds kind of fun. And I brought your dad a goody bag." She lightly rattled the bag of blackberry scones.

"You're going to spoil him. You know he's like a chihuahua. He'll just keep barking for more."

Charlie stepped into the condo and took her shoes off on the mat. The space was beautiful, with tall ceilings and a vast stone fireplace. She noticed this when she picked up Mack for their first date, but she was so out of her element at the time that very little of the place stuck. She remembered leaving with a feeling in her stomach, one she couldn't place. But now, warm fuzzies replacing first-date jitters, it struck her—the place was homey, filled with love. Family photos covered the walls: Mack swinging in a park, eating pizza with sauce over her face, blowing out birthday candles, buried in a book.

Mack's mom rounded the corner with her arms stretched out for a hug. "Charlie!"

"Hey, Kelli!"

Mack whispered loud enough for her mom to hear. "You don't have to hug her if you don't want to."

"Stop." Charlie giggled and accepted Kelli's warm embrace. "I'll gladly take hugs from your mom any day."

"Mackey, you should follow Charlie's example," Kelli said. "Give it a few more visits, and maybe I'll convince Charlie to let me French braid her hair."

Mack gaped at her mom. "You've officially stepped into creepy lady territory."

"What? You always kept your hair so short, and all I ever wanted was to braid someone's hair." Kelli bounced her gaze between Charlie's giggles and Mack's stone-cold glare and tossed her hands in the air. "Okay, *fine*. Maybe that's a tad creepy."

Booted footsteps approached the kitchen from the den. "Hey, kiddo," Andrew said with a grin.

Mack rolled her eyes. "She's not a kiddo."

He clicked off his phone off tossed it on the table. "Yep, yep. Got it. Still working on my language. Women, not girls. Women, not kiddos. Hey there, woman."

"You have a truly special gift to do a little worse every single time," Mack joked, grabbing a bowl and crackers from the cabinets.

"I'm not as picky as Mack. You can call me whatever you like." Charlie handed him the bag. "Brought you a treat."

Andrew's eyes lit up. "Blackberry scones?"

"Sure is."

"Well, you may be my new favorite daughter."

Mack pinched his triceps. "God, you're the worst."

Everything about being there was what Charlie had envisioned a family looked like. The goofy dad. The mom futzing with crackers in the kitchen. Mack pretending she was annoyed, but her grin busted her. The sting of jealousy was muted by a warmth developing.

"Would you mind helping me bring these into the living room? I wanted to talk to you about something." Kelli handed

Charlie a few sparkling sodas and napkins. "Mack and Drew, you two are in charge of popcorn."

Oh no. Was this the dreaded parent talk? The "you better treat my girl right or else" conversation?

"Sounds good. Extra butter, extra salt, extra goodness," Andrew said.

Mack furrowed her gaze at her mom. "I guess I'll supervise?"

Charlie followed Mack's mom into the den, where stacks of paper, notepads, and pens started from thickest to thinnest, perfectly lined in order across the cherrywood desk. "Whoa. This is like next-level organization. I've been cleaning my place lately but never thought of putting pens in weighted order."

"Finally, someone appreciates my attention to detail." Kelli reached for a black leather-bound portfolio holder. "I'm telling Drew this. He's so cocky, always thinking his way of shoving stuff wherever it lands is better."

Kelli's smile faded.

The energy in the room immediately shifted, and Charlie felt like she was in the principal's office. Her cheeks heated. Even though she only met Kelli one other time, the idea that she did something wrong, or let Kelli down, made Charlie's stomach turn.

"Is everything okay?" Charlie croaked.

Kelli tapped her fingers on the portfolio she held like a shield. "I don't know how else to say this... without just saying it."

Oh God. She didn't know Kelli well enough to decode her expression—flat lips, a rigid posture, and a crease cutting across her forehead. But all signs indicated this wasn't good.

"I overstep. Always have. Mack's been on me for years to knock it off," Kelli said. "I started down a rabbit hole when reviewing your paperwork and emails from the contractor.

There was a ton of information, and it took me a while to understand what I was all looking at."

Charlie's stomach fell to her feet. "Sorry... I know... it was so disorganized, but I'm trying to get better."

Kelli put her hand up. "Stop that nonsense. I'm not talking about the organization. You did this all on your own? When Andrew and I took over an *already established* business, we hired consultants, money managers, advisors, everything. How you did this on your own is beyond me."

The heat in Charlie's face now felt more like a blush.

Kelli gave her a firm nod. "Be nothing but proud of what you've done."

Oof. Twice now, Mack's parents said this to her on different occasions, and twice they produced the same reaction. "Thank you... That means a lot."

Kelli leaned against the desk and motioned for Charlie to do the same. "So... back to me overstepping. I probably should've let you handle this on your own. I didn't intend to take the reins. But when I read the emails you forwarded and scoured the contracts and bills, things just didn't add up. I didn't want to give you bad advice, so it took longer than I hoped to make clarifying phone calls."

She paused and scanned Charlie's face, which probably looked like a ball of confusion.

"Okay..."

"I got into it with this guy, who was a jackass when I questioned him about the amount you owed. Not going to bore you with all the details, but it turned ugly. I threatened litigation, said I'd tell all the people in the business about their ethics, call the Attorney General and Better Business Bureau... you get the picture. I laid the damn hammer down."

"Yikes." A sweat bead accumulated above Charlie's lip. Was this good? Bad? Litigation? Charlie had nightmares like this, that a judge would slam down a settlement, and she'd arrive home one day to find it wrapped in red tape and locks on all the doors and windows. She snapped her beaded bracelet against her wrist. "Um, am I in some kind of trouble?"

"Trouble? No." Kelli unzipped the leather pouch and slid a paper across the counter. "All that being said, here's your new bill and monthly payment."

Charlie's fingers trembled as she scanned the numbers. *What?* This couldn't be right. She held her finger at the number to ensure she saw it correctly. She read the number a dozen times more before she glanced at Kelli again, who crossed her arms with a satisfied smile.

"I... this, this is less than half of what I owe. Like *way* less than half... I don't even understand. This doesn't make sense." The room swayed in the background. Her pulse pounded in her neck. She blinked and focused on the paper. *Less than half.* If this was true, it changed everything. The stress, the pending bankruptcy, the fear that she'd have to give up her home. Less than half was not only doable, it was life-changing. "Is this true?"

Kelli nodded. "Drew and I chatted about your place, and some of the contractor's work was not up to snuff. They should've immediately offered you a discount for botched features, not doubled their rates with bullshit charges for labor costs and things. Looking back at all your previous statements, they trickled in fake costs from the beginning and probably figured since you didn't say anything, they could keep doing it."

Her stomach clenched. Why would anyone do this? How did they go home at night and feel good about themselves? "I didn't know... I looked every night at their work, and it all seemed okay."

"The contractor are the professionals. Not you. You're not gonna beat yourself up for this. They took advantage. Stuff like this makes me sick. And you can bet your ass I'm gonna check into other places they worked on *and* I'm reporting them."

Charlie's lips trembled. "This amount here? This is what I owe?" Her shaky pointer finger hovered over the red circled number. "Are you positive?"

Kelli nodded. "Sure am. I'll email you the official paperwork later for your records. And Drew said he could come by at the end of the month and fix some of the framing stuff."

Charlie's mouth parted, but she couldn't form any words. Hot tears sprang to her eyes.

Kelli put a gentle hand on Charlie's arm. "I truly am sorry for overstepping. I tend to do that, and Mackey gets so pissed sometimes and—"

Charlie wrapped her arms around Kelli and melted into her tiny frame. Her shoulders shook, and tears saturated Kelli's shirt. Charlie only met her once and barely knew her, yet Kelli did this for her. Just like that? How... why...

Sobs escaped, and Charlie was helpless to stop them. Months of hiding, pushing things down, denial, bubbled up. The tightness she'd carried evaporated, and gratitude replaced the vacant spot.

"Shh... shh. You're all right. Everything's gonna be okay," Kelli whispered as she patted her back.

Footsteps grew louder from the hallway. Charlie lifted her head and wiped her eyes with her forearm when Mack entered the room and froze.

"Jesus, Ma... what'd you do?" Mack's tone was only slightly kidding as she beelined to Charlie. "You okay?"

Charlie shifted to hugging Mack. Drenched in support, tears sprang back to the surface. "I'm good. Your mom just really helped me out."

Kelli patted her back once more and stepped away from the women. "Well, I better help Drew with snacks. God knows what sort of seasoning he'd try on the popcorn. Charlie, I'll tell you later about the time he thought oregano and cinnamon would make a good mix."

Charlie hugged the paper against her chest as Kelli left the room. With trembling fingers, she swiped a final tear from her cheek.

"You sure things are good?" She glanced between Charlie's eyes and peeked down at the paper. "Is this about the bills?"

Charlie sniffled. "I was so worried. Even though I told you some, I didn't tell you everything." She pulled in a deep breath. "I thought I was going to lose my shop, and in a snap, your mom fixed everything. I can't even believe it's over. It's like for the first time in a year I can fully breathe."

Mack scooped her back into her arms and kissed the top of her forehead. "I wish you would've told me the depth of this sooner. I could've talked to them right away, or given you money, or made some calls, or something."

"Stop. You did so much already, and *God*, I'm just so relieved." Her chin trembled again, and she buried her head in Mack's shoulder.

Andrew came into the room, juggling an oversized bowl and several sodas. His eyes dashed between their faces, and he took two steps back. "I... uh... I'll come back."

"No, no. Please! It's your home." Charlie wiped a last tear and scooted over to him to grab the drinks. "It's all good."

He looked hesitantly at the women. "I don't want to interrupt lady stuff."

"Drew." Kelli raised an eyebrow.

"Sorry, sorry. I shouldn't joke." He gave a weak smile. "I'm thinking you told Charlie the good news?"

"She did," Charlie said.

"Well, okay then." He jutted his chin toward the coffee table, and the women followed him. "Come on. Movie night needs to start."

TWENTY-EIGHT

MACK'S DRINK SPECIAL: BUSTED BROWN SUGAR BREVE

"Mack." Her mom pounded on the door and charged into the room.

Mack's neck cracked when she whipped her head up. "Jesus, Ma! Privacy much?"

Yikes. Mack straightened. Stiff from a full writing day, she slowly adjusted her spine and closed her laptop. She couldn't decode her mom's invasive glare and heavy breaths. Her mom wasn't pissed. But she wasn't happy, either. More... stern. Somber. She had flashbacks of when her mom told Mack she was sick.

Mack's stomach coiled, and she swallowed. "Is Dad okay?"

"Yes." Her mom pulled a chair beside the bed. In a significant shift from her normal MO, she looked at a loss for words as her mouth opened and closed multiple times with nothing coming out. "We're changing insurance in November, so I wanted to review the plan we were on a few years ago during the chemo and stuff."

"Okay..."

"So, I started digging. And I found some old files."

Shit.

The chair squeaked on the floor as her mom crossed and uncrossed her legs. "And I kept digging. 'Cause you know me... a dog with a bone." She took a breath and exhaled. "Some things didn't add up. *Literally didn't add up.* The high deductible. Claims. Multiple capped items."

Her mom rested her elbows on her knees and stared into Mack's eyes. They burned so hard that Mack turned away as her neck grew hot and itchy.

"Tell me what you did."

Mack tugged on a thread on the comforter. They were never supposed to find out about this. Her parents were the proudest people she knew. They'd be mortified, not think of this as a gift. She kept her eyes on the thread to avoid her mom's gaze. "I don't know what you mean."

"Mack." Her mom leaned forward. "Mackenzie."

Mack's head flew up at the blunt tone. She held her shoulders firm for a second before they collapsed. "I paid for it."

"Jesus Christ." Her mom dragged her hands down her face. "That was almost—"

"I know how much it was."

Her mom stood up, and paced in a circle, biting her thumbnail. "How did... how did you even get that kind of money?"

Mack clamped the inside of her quivering lip before she spoke. "The advance for my second book."

Her mom's chin dropped to her chest.

Was she mad? What happened now? They *couldn't* tell her dad. He'd be mortified, then humiliated, then very, very angry. His purpose in life was to take care of "his girls."

Mack was on the verge of throwing up. The thick yet near-silent tension in the room was worse than any fight or screaming match she and her mother had in the past.

The evening sun poured through the cracked blinds. Her mom opened the blinds fully and stared outside. She stood in silence as her shoulders lifted and lowered with deep inhales. "Why did you come here?"

Huh? "What do you mean?"

Her mom faced her and crossed her arms. "Mack. Stop, please. Right now. No more lies."

Mack rested her chin on the pillow. "I had writer's block."

Her mom nodded. And remained silent.

The dense energy in the air made Mack squirm. "I panicked, okay? I thought being away from my surroundings, being around you and Dad, maybe that would... you know... spark something."

"You waited a year to visit. Why?"

Did she actually want to hear this? Probably not. Mack could barely acknowledge the reasons herself.

"Why," her mom repeated with a hardened voice.

Mack's chin trembled. "I couldn't look at you."

"Because of my hair?"

"It wasn't because of your hair." Her voice turned shaky. "It was because of what I did."

Her mother's stern face swapped to confusion. "What do you mean, what you did?"

The words simmered below the surface. Three years of holding everything in... Lies. Guilt. Shame. Mack scratched at the back of her neck. She didn't want to say it.

Her mom took a few steps closer. "Tell me."

"I ran! I totally deserted you, okay? You gave up *everything* for me. High school. College. Living in a different city. Your freedom. And what did I do when you got cancer? I focused on my book. I was more interested in writing, editing, and going on submission than seeing my own mom in the hospital. I'm such a selfish ass. I don't even understand how you love me some-times." The last words barely came out as Mack started sobbing.

Her mother must hate her now. Every horrible thought Mack had about herself about how she responded to the diagnosis tumbled forward. She was an ungrateful, terrible daughter. Literally deserted her mom and dad to fight this battle on their own.

"Honey." Kicked-off shoes hit the dresser. Her mom crawled onto the bed and pulled Mack into her chest. She rubbed Mack's head and stroked her arms until her cries slowed. "You're not selfish."

Mack sniffed and dried her eyes on her sleeve. "I think I am."

"Well, you're wrong."

Mack sat up and plucked a Kleenex from the box on the nightstand. "But I didn't see you because I was too worried about my book. Like, who does that?"

"Do you really think it was about your book?" she asked. "Or was it maybe about not wanting to see me sick?"

Mack's heart sunk. She didn't know. When her parents called and said "cancer," everything changed. Multiple stages of grief blasted her within that first hour, but her body held on to shock and anger until denial consumed her. Focusing on her book somehow seemed more urgent than her sick mother.

After several minutes passed, her mom pulled back and looked at her. "I wish you could have met my nana. All fire and spunk, like a sugar-glazed jalapeño popper," she started. "I used to visit her every Saturday, for tea and cookies, even though tea's disgusting."

"You must've really loved her," Mack said quietly, but cracked a smile.

"I did. But the second she got sick, I stopped visiting. Every week morphed into every other week, then once a month, until she finally passed. I couldn't stand to see her like that. I wanted to remember my vibrant nana, not a sick woman in the nursing home. I kept saying it was because I had homework or chores, but that was a lie. I was protecting my heart."

Mack looked up at her and kept quiet.

"I'll bet my life that you were doing the same."

The words hung in the air as Mack exhaled and thought back to that time. Maybe her mom was right. Maybe the idea of her mom dying was too much for her.

"Now." Her mom clasped her hands together and laid them in her lap. "We talk about repaying you."

"You don't have—"

"Not a word. This is non-negotiable."

With how firm her mom's voice was right now, Mack knew there'd be nothing she could say to change her mind.

"Tonight, I'm gonna talk to your dad, and we'll figure out a plan."

A final tear ran beneath her eye and Mack ran her thumb across her cheek to catch it. "He's going to be so mad..."

"Yes. He will be. But he'll understand." Her mom slid out of bed and pulled the cover over Mack's legs. She laid her hands on Mack's shoulders and squeezed. "What did I ever do to deserve such a good kid?"

She scooped her heels off the floor, and left the room.

And Mack breathed out three years' worth of trapped air.

TWENTY-NINE

MACK'S DRINK SPECIAL: CLOSING CAPPUCCINO

The end.

I can't believe I did it.

A year of stress and agony shoved behind Mack. A month of brutal rewrites. A mad case of carpal tunnel radiating white lightning pain through her wrist, and one begrudging trip to her mom's chiropractor. But she did it.

Saying she strayed from the outline was the understatement of the year. The finished product was a one-eighty turn. When her brain flipped and latched on to this new story, the words gushed. This last month was the easiest writing in her career.

She'd have to defend her decision. And she hated admitting it, but with her parents already transferring over a sizeable chunk as part of their repayment plan, she had the luxury of freedom. If the publishing house and editor hated her latest direction, she'd let them rescind the offer and find a new publisher. She believed in herself. She believed in her agent. But mostly, she believed in her book.

She loved her first novel. *The Edge of the Shadow* was a dark, windy, joyless ride filled with agonizing turns and cliffs. The book reflected Mack's desire to chase the impossible.

But this one, newly titled *Crooked Roots*, elbowed itself into the top spot. She prayed her fanbase would ride along with her, no matter how much the style departed from her debut.

She stepped outside and saw the Olympic Mountains behind the scattered clouds. Soon enough, snow would cap their tops. She interlaced her fingers, stretched, and pulled in a full breath.

The self-induced isolation was complete. The book was done. Time to remove herself from her "cat cave," as her dad referred to it. She needed to return as a semi-regular functioning member of society and enjoy a bit of peace before they potentially terminated her contract.

First stop, reconnecting with her girlfriend, whom she'd seriously neglected the past several weeks. Even though Mack slept there most nights, she was so mentally exhausted by the end of the night that she typically crashed upon arrival.

She grabbed her phone and FaceTimed Charlie. The second the red hair and glowing smile popped on the screen, Mack's shoulders loosened. "Guess what?" Mack stepped back in the room and slid the patio door shut.

"Did you do it? Did you finish?" Charlie's eyes were wide and expectant as she walked into her office space in the shop. "Let the record show I haven't contacted you for a horrific seventy-two hours. Three whole miserable days! I ate an entire box of mint Oreos. Although that was the highlight, and I'm not ashamed."

Mack ran her finger across the screen like she could touch Charlie's face. One month in, and Mack swore every day she could not love her more.

And every day, she was wrong.

"I'm done!" Another surge of tingles flew through her from saying those words aloud, and she flopped back on the bed.

"Oh my God, yay! How do you feel?"

"Like I gave birth to a thesaurus." Mack pulled herself up

on the bed. "I'm going to send it to Viv after we hang up. Then I hope to God the editor gives me a two-week break before the heavy revising starts."

"Not a month?"

Mack grinned. "I think I used up any remaining goodwill by getting my two-week extension. I'm not going to push it."

Charlie leaned against the wall. "I had no idea how much a book had to be edited before it was sent to the universe. I pictured writers sitting down, popping it out, giving it a once-over, and calling it good."

"Can you imagine? I'd be a millionaire." Mack rolled over and propped herself up on her side. "Tell me everything I've missed in your world this last week."

"Let's see. I tried a new gluten-free cookie sample that didn't suck. I might end up carrying it. Oh! And my linen closet is officially at a Navy SEAL level of organized."

Charlie's voice was like smooth, velvety chocolate, layering Mack in goodness. "I might have to see that one to believe it."

"I'm serious!" Charlie's mouth twisted. "So, since you're done, can we do a celebratory dinner?"

"How about we celebrate in the bedroom?" Mack tried to keep her voice low and sexy, but it cracked, and she laughed.

"That was seriously cheesy. Come on, I'm hungry."

"Me too." Mack attempted a growl. "Okay, I'm done. Yes, yes, dinner sounds amazing."

"What time can I see you?"

"Now. Literally now. I can't wait a second more."

The phone shook as Charlie walked back out to the lobby. "Okay, I'm going to close up early and head your way."

After they hung up, Mack plugged in her earbuds to pace the room and FaceTimed Viviane.

"Tell me something good," Viviane said when she answered.

"It's done."

"Thank you, Jesus." Viviane slapped her hand against her heart. "Woman, you had me a little nervous there. How you feeling about it?"

"Good. But it's sort of like someone qualifying for the Boston Marathon after two years of training. Like how they might not be sure that once they got there, they'd actually complete the run."

"Not sure I'm following. You mean because the editor still needs to review?"

Mack bit on the corner of her lips. "I, uh, changed way more than what we chatted about last month."

Viviane kept the phone on her face as she walked to her den and sat down. "Exactly how much?"

"Ah..." Mack tugged and twisted on the bottom of her T-shirt. Heat flushed her face. She hated that she kept this from Viviane—her cheerleader, her agent, her *business partner*—but she had to do what she did. "Quite a bit. Shelby's still an entrepreneur—"

"Drug dealer."

"Yes, fine. She still deals, but I flipped it from the rivalry between Shelby and her competitor..."

Mack propped the phone on the nightstand and paced as she talked. The speed of her words matched the wildness of her flinging hands. When she reached the climax and nearly knocked the lamp off the table, she flinched and sat back down. Ten minutes later, she described the finale as Viviane remained silent.

When Mack was done, Viviane stayed quiet.

Too quiet.

"Viv. You still with me?"

"Yes." Viviane took several breaths. The moments ticked by, one by one. "The book sounds interesting, Mack. It really does. But this isn't some minor character flaw or setting change. This is a complete departure from what you proposed, and what the publisher paid for."

Mack sucked in her bottom lip. All the ballooned elation of finishing slowly depleted. Even though Viviane was right, what the publisher chose to do didn't matter. She had made the best decision for herself and her future.

Viviane leaned on her elbows and brought her face closer to the screen. "You really believe in this story, huh?"

Mack nodded. "I really do."

Viviane took a deep breath and paused for a moment. "Well, I believe in you. And honestly, I don't know what the publisher will say. But this is what I know. I got you. If this is what you want, even if we lose the contract, I've got you."

THIRTY

CHARLIE'S DRINK SPECIAL: TRAUMATIZED TEA

Macklemore's latest hit thumped in the background as Charlie darted around Sugar Mugs, banged chairs on top of the tables, and mopped at record speed.

"Dude. You're gonna break a hip or something," Ben said while wiping the display glass. "Where's the fire?"

Charlie slapped the dripping mop across the room. "Mack finished her book! Which means I get to spend actual quality time with my girlfriend. I literally cannot wait. I just want to... ugh... I just want to squeeze her."

"You're both sweet and kind of terrifying." He grabbed the mop from her and bumped her toward the door. "Just go. I got this."

"You sure?" She drummed her feet against the floor in a tiny dance. "I really love you sometimes, you know that?"

"Yep." He grinned and blew her an air kiss.

The dusting of clouds in the sky did little to dull the bright sun as she sprinted to her car. She tossed her apron on the back seat and gave herself a quick sniff test. Usually, she would take a shower after work before seeing Mack. But tonight, everything took second place to getting to Mack. She slapped some vanilla-scented lotion on after she pulled off the highway and popped a mint into her mouth.

The last month had been a master class in self-reflection. Mack warned her she'd be a ghost for several weeks as she finished her manuscript. But during those nights, instead of repeatedly checking for messages, Charlie refocused her energy. Home organization shows became her obsession. She ordered a stupid amount of containers for her pantry—that she could now afford thanks to Kelli—and Marie Kondo'd the heck out of her closet. She created a new seasonal drink menu. And she finally coordinated the fall Sunday reading hour schedule with several local drag queens.

She speed-walked from her car to Mack's parents' condo and almost skipped down the hall to their place.

Kelli swung the door open and tugged her in for a hug. "Hey, you! Wow, you're early. I think Mack wasn't expecting you for at least another hour."

"I couldn't wait any longer." Charlie removed her shoes at the entrance. "How are you?"

"Good. Drew's working late tonight. *Thank God.* I need a moment to myself. Promise you'll never tell him I said that." She chuckled. "We still on for manicures on Monday?"

"Absolutely."

"Someday, we'll force Mack to go with us. You'd think with how sore her wrists are she'd like the massage... but she never listens to me."

Knowing what she knew about Mack, it'd be a cold day in hell before she'd let someone groom and polish her nails. "Let me see what I can do. Maybe I'll promise to take her for Puerto Rican food after."

"Good." Kelli nodded her head towards the hall. "Mack's in her room. Go ahead and head in there."

Charlie bolted and knocked on Mack's partially open door.

The desk chair nearly knocked over when Mack jumped up

and raced over to Charlie. She wrapped her arms around her and nuzzled into her neck. "God, I've missed you."

A faint whisper of rose and mint drifted from Mack's skin, and Charlie melted as she inhaled. She cupped Mack's face and pressed her mouth against hers.

"Never again am I going this long without seeing you." Mack locked their fingers together and brushed her lips across Charlie's knuckles.

"Babe," Charlie whispered. "It's been three days."

"I know! I hated it."

Charlie grinned at the irony. A lifetime of codependence, and the three days apart was the most secure she'd felt in a relationship. She didn't love being away from Mack. This entire month she missed her. But she was okay. Thriving, even.

Charlie trailed her gaze up Mack and lifted her eyebrow. "Oh my."

"What?"

"You're wrinkled."

Mack patted her shirt with a frown. "I am. And un-showered. And disgusting. Sorry, I thought I'd have time to clean up before you got here. Mind if I hop in real quick? No one needs to see me in this condition."

"You still look beautiful. Messy hair and all."

"See! I'm an embarrassment." A cheeky grin flashed across Mack's face. "Wanna join me?"

It took every ounce of willpower for Charlie to be respectful in Mack's parents' home and decline the invite. "Um. Yes. But no. Your mom's here. I'm not adding that type of karma to my world."

"Seriously? No fun. We're adults. I'll just tell her to turn the TV up."

"I sincerely hope you're kidding. 'Cause ewww." Charlie shook her head. "So, bad news... I called Nueve's, and they're booked up tonight. We gotta choose somewhere else."

"Anything." Mack tugged off her slippers and lined them up underneath the foot of the bed. "Literally anything. As long as I'm with you, we can lie in bed and eat naked takeout pizza for all I care."

"No chance. This is a celebration. We're going somewhere great." Although pizza and a bedroom sounded kind of amazing.

Mack's wide grin set Charlie in motion. With her heart filled and her body ignited, she pulled Mack into her and pressed her lips onto Mack's. Her mouth parted with Mack's tongue. Mack firmed her hold and walked back towards the bed as every cell in Charlie's body charged.

Mack pulled herself away. "Nope. I'm seriously so stinky and gross. Twenty minutes, okay? Be right back."

Charlie collapsed back on the bed and caught her breath. After dinner, they needed to go back to Charlie's *immediately*. Her body was on fire. Even her skin tickled.

But first, logistics: Find a fantastic place for dinner. Sushi? Thai in Edmonds? A bistro in Bellevue? She patted her pockets, then dug into her purse for her phone and found nothing but too many pens and a wallet. "Crap." She tiptoed down the hall and knocked outside the bathroom door. "Hey, I forgot my cell in the car. Can I use your phone or laptop?"

"Yeah, laptop's unlocked. Go ahead," Mack called over the sounds of water running.

Charlie returned to the bedroom and pulled the laptop open. *Jesus*. And she thought she was bad. Perfectly ironed, coifed, and the same outfit every day, Mack seemed way too buttoned-up to have at least twenty-five tabs open. Charlie minimized the current screen to not screw up whatever hot mess Mack had going on when exactly two documents appeared: *Crooked Roots* and *Charlie*.

A spark singed up Charlie's neck. *Charlie?* Gah! How

freaking sweet. Was Mack writing her a poem? Planning a surprise?

Ooh!... If she planned a surprise, Charlie would need coverage at the shop. God love Mack, but she never fully grasped how being the owner, manager, and head employee was not something—at least for now—that Charlie could just walk away from.

She clicked open the document and scanned it for a date. A metallic, sticky sensation curdled underneath her mouth's surface before it went dry as she read from the file.

- Alcoholic father, waiting at the window. Ask if she drew pictures. Did she have a stuffed animal/blanket, maybe a doll?
- *Storm*—use this! Perfect. Trembling as the wind howled, very scared; she seemed to distract herself with tea and fairy lights
- Brownie story—cute. Add a choking scene?
- Trust issues, smiling with a butterfly purse, holding something in
- Best friend—need more on how they met; what bonded them? Were drugs ever involved?

Unblinking, Charlie continued to scan. A small bead of sweat formed on her upper lip, and she swiped it off with the back of her hand. What was this? Mack did this? But... why?

She kept reading. Another page and another as her stomach muscles tightened so heavily that acid shot up her throat.

- Divorce, codependency
- Find out why she left, who left who, and what were her internal reactions when she signed the papers.
- Aunt dying—someone special to her—was this a catalyst for change? Ask about what a weekend

with the aunt looked like (movies? Cookies? Shopping?)

- Voice inflections when she speaks
- Cross-reference everything with the Mayo Clinic article on children of addicts
- Besides the storm, were there other memorable incidents of neglect; does she remember the weather around those times, the color of a dress, or what she ate that day? Need to determine triggers.
- Bonded over equally awful upbringings
- A mysterious package with the mail carrier

Tears and bile and heaviness wore on her. In front of her was her nightmare laid on the page, exposed, like fodder. Like entertainment.

Her limbs trembled. Her chin trembled. Her entire body, from her scalp to her toes, trembled. The words turned fuzzy as she stared at the computer until her fight or flight response kicked in.

And flight won.

THIRTY-ONE

MACK'S DRINK SPECIAL: DESPERATION DECAF

Man, she felt better. Shower for the win, and now Mack could focus on nothing besides Charlie. The book was done, delicious food was on the horizon, and a whole night of reconnecting awaited. Mack moved down the hall as she squeezed the last bit of water from her hair into a towel.

She stepped into the bedroom and glanced around. "Charlie?"

Huh.

She peeked out onto the patio.

Nothing.

She tossed the hair towel in the hamper and walked into the living room, where her mom was flipping through paperwork at her desk.

"Is Charlie in your bathroom?"

Her mom looked up with a furrowed brow and popped her reading glasses to the top of her head. "No... she just flew out of here, said sorry and thanks for everything. I just assumed something happened at the coffee shop."

What the hell?

Mack's face felt feverish. "Why wouldn't she have told me

that when I was in the shower?" she mumbled as she went back to the bedroom to dial Charlie.

No answer.

A slow pulse began in her neck that grew into throbbing as she looked around the room for a note, or clue, or *something*. She redialed Charlie.

Voicemail.

What could've been that awful to leave like that? Ben? A fire? Didn't matter at this point. She'd just drive over there, figure it out, and help her. Maybe her dad showed up again, or water was left on or something. She quickly threw on clothes and reached for her wallet when the laptop screen caught her eye.

Oh, God. No.

No!

Facing her was the *Charlie* document. Twenty-plus pages of notes from her interactions with Charlie since they met. The cursor was right above:

- Review medical journal studies on the long-term psychological effects of divorce with lesbian couples, and cross-check with her story on Jess. Maybe weave in hints of psychosis by abandonment or displays of violence.

"Fuck!" Mack slammed the laptop shut and gripped the back of the chair. This wasn't happening. Not now.

She'd planned on telling Charlie someday. Her confession was always a matter of when, not if. But things were good. *So good.* And Mack never had this before, a relationship... *love*... and now Charlie saw it... and... *dammit!*

Mack had to fix this. An image popped up of a distraught, sobbing Charlie flying down the highway, gripping her fuzzy steering wheel, swiping at the tears with her sleeve. What if the tears blurred her eyesight, so she pulled over and was in a one-person accident in a ditch, and no one saw her, and she was bleeding out but still crying and...

Running out the bedroom door with one shoe tied, she tripped as she tried to hop and tie the second one. She banged into the wall with a thud.

"Mack? What's going on?" her mom called from the living room.

"Not now," she yelled, pulling the front door open and slamming it shut behind herself. She didn't even bother with the elevator. She raced down the stairs and beelined for her car.

City lights zipped by in a blur. She dug her phone out of her pocket as she swerved to the left and tensed when the person behind her blared on their horn.

"Pick up, pick up."

At least a dozen times, maybe more, she called. She fumbled as she voice texted while navigating rush hour traffic. The air blasting in from all the windows down did nothing to dry the sweat collecting at the base of her back, or her wet hair. She swallowed, slammed her hand against the steering wheel, and screamed at a driver who pulled out in front of her.

What felt like a thousand hours later, she parked outside of Charlie's place. She ran up the stairs to Charlie's loft and banged on the door. She pounded so long that her knuckles began to feel raw.

"Charlie!" she yelled, over and over. "Please open up. Let me explain."

The high of finishing her book earlier nose-dived with the low of this moment, and Mack's body twitched with emotional whiplash. She called Charlie's phone again. After one last weak knock on the door, she slumped against the steps and buried her head in her legs.

. . .

Mack dragged herself down the hall and opened the condo door. Her shoes felt like lead when she kicked them off. The keys weighed a thousand pounds in her fingers as she hung them on the hook. The pit in her stomach grew into a flaming boulder, burning her from the inside out.

Charlie hated her.

Once in her room, she leaned against the wall and stared at the ceiling. How did she let it go on this long? Everything in her ached, and she deserved it. Tears sprang into her dry, crusty eyes as she moved to her closet.

After pulling in a large breath, she ripped off all the clothes from the hangers and plugged in her iron. One by one, she ironed each piece within an inch of their life and rehung them. She tore the sheet off the bed and tossed it in the hamper. She snapped the new sheet in the air and tugged and pulled until the lines were sharp and crisp.

Sweat beaded above her brow as she reached for an extra toothbrush and cleaner from the closet. Kneeling down, she gripped the brush and pushed it in frantic circles around the border of the room. Spraying and scrubbing, over and over, shaking her cramped fingers out, and pushing again until the bristles bent and finally the brush snapped in half.

She whipped it across the room and it hit the wall with a dull smack. "Ahhhh!" She slid down to her bottom and wrapped her arms around her knees.

Footsteps sounded outside of her open door. "Mack? You okay?"

She kept her back to her dad and nodded. He'd be disgusted with her if he looked at her. At this point, she was running on fumes. If one more person she loved started hating her, it would throw her over the edge.

Why didn't she just tell Charlie at the beginning? Right away and own up to the consequences? Once again, she put her need to succeed in front of the people she loved. Her shoulders shook before the rest of her joined in. She tried to swallow back her silent cry, but the high-pitched squeal escaped, and she buried her head in her hands.

"Whoa. What happened? You okay?" Her father's concerned voice made her shake even more. He knelt down and held out her arms like he was inspecting for damage. "Mackey. Did someone hurt you? Talk to me."

She folded herself into his soft T-shirt and muscular chest and sobbed. She was unworthy of his care. Reading his tone and tense body, she knew he verged on splitting someone's jawbone thinking someone had hurt his daughter.

"No one hurt me," she croaked.

But I hurt them. In the worst way imaginable.

"Come on, let's grab you some water." He pulled her up to her feet and followed her down the hall.

In the kitchen, she slumped on the stool and rested her head on the kitchen island. The granite was cool against her burning forehead, and she took multiple deep, shaky breaths. Her dad patted her on the back and pulled a stool next to her.

"What the hell happened?"

No words formed. Her insides burned and she kept her eyes down to avoid looking in his eyes. "I screwed up so hard, and I don't know what to do."

He angled his head. "What did you do?"

Where should she start? Ruined the one and only chance she ever had with the love of her life. Put her own needs above others' like she did all the time. Destroyed her chances at happiness. "I can't even tell you."

He exhaled. "You gotta tell me, otherwise I can't help."

"I don't deserve your help."

"Enough with the bullshit, kid." He placed his hand on the counter next to her. "I'd bury bodies for you. Tell me."

Her mouth felt like she'd been chewing on sawdust. "You know how I go places to observe, right? Get fuel for my stories.

267

When I met Charlie, she just provided so much good stuff. Like, inspired me to work."

His eyebrows furrowed. "What am I not following here?"

"I didn't know I'd fall in love with her and ruin everything."

"Mack, you gotta stop speaking cryptically. Just tell me what happened."

She pushed her knuckles into her temple and unloaded. Confessed to him like he was a priest, and she was on her knees regurgitating her sins. "But the night we slept together, I stopped."

Her dad failed to hide the grimace on his face.

"I was going to tell her. A million times. But everything was so good and pure, and I didn't want to ruin it." She pulled a paper towel off the rack and blew her nose.

He slid his baseball cap backward and drummed his fingers against the counter. Several long moments passed. "You really love her a lot, don't you?"

Dabbing her eyes with her fingertip, she nodded. "So much. I never thought I'd have this, and I just... I don't think I can fix this."

A firm, serious look passed as he held her gaze. "I didn't raise a quitter. I raised a fighter."

Her tank was empty. She lifted her shoulders in a sad, defeated shrug. "I don't know what to do."

Her father took a hard look at her. He sat back with his arms crossed as he seemed to study her face. "Maybe you should do what you do best."

A lone tear fell, and she flicked it away. "Yeah, what's that?"

He leaned in towards her. "Write."

He walked out of the room, probably exhausted from the most emotional support he'd given her in the last decade.

Write.

Silently sitting with her thoughts and slouched posture, she absorbed his words. Her dad was right. East Coast tough—not some punk who cried in defeat—was how he raised her. She needed to fix this. Charlie deserved to know everything, and if she hated Mack after that, at least she'd have the truth.

Her bent posture morphed into straight. She ran down the hall and whipped open her laptop. Buzzed with frenetic energy like she was racing against time, her fingers flew across the keyboard.

8:32 p.m. A doom lurked behind her. If she didn't get this on the page or in Charlie's hands, she'd lose everything. Forever.

The words flowed. It was the easiest, quickest thing she ever wrote.

She grabbed a flash drive and sped to the store.

The line nearly reached the door. Why the hell were so many people at a printing place at this time of night? Sure, the store was open twenty-four hours, but it was after 9:00 p.m. Her foot tapped against the floor as she waited. At least four other people filed in after her, and several people loitered to her side. They probably had important things too. College papers, or maybe work presentations. But not even one looked like their insides would explode like hers.

"Next." The guy behind the counter smacked his gum and looked like he wanted to be anywhere but here. "How can I help—"

"I need this printed off. Rush order." She slid the flash drive across the counter to him.

He barely looked up. "We can have it ready on Tuesday."

His uninterested monotone clearly showed that he did not care that this was the difference between relationship life and death. This object represented any fighting chance she might have of explaining her behavior and he barely glanced at it.

A simmer started in her stomach. "Tuesday?" Her voice grew a little louder. "I know you do rush orders. I've been to this chain before."

He looked up with the speed of a sloth and blew a small,

unimpressive pink gum bubble. "Well, we're backed up." He waved to the multiple customers waiting in line.

"Do you have more help?" She glanced at the two guys with name tags that were playfully pushing each other in the corner.

The simmer turned into a boil.

"We're all a little busy right now."

"Bullshit!" She skyrocketed from an inside voice to an outside voice.

Skimming the store, she searched for any other worker. A man behind her made a snarky comment, and she scowled so hard that he tossed his hands up and stepped back.

"Look." She flattened her hands on the counter. "I appreciate that you're busy, but this is really important. Your sign says any rush job done in two hours or less."

He raised an eyebrow. "Our sign also says we have the right to refuse service to anyone."

She was three seconds away from throwing something. A stapler, a profanity-laced tirade, *something*, if he didn't hurry the hell up. Her hands clenched into fists and she pushed them down on the counter. "No, it doesn't. That's a bar, not a printing place."

Jackass. She had zero time for this. All stress and regret ballooned to the surface as she planted her feet firmly into the ground. "You'll do this now."

"It'll be ready Tuesday."

Enough! She was done with this shithead. All of her internal boiling turned into a Death-Valley-level explosion. She narrowed her eyes. "I need to speak to a manager."

"He's on break."

She seized the skinny microphone in front of him in a screech and pushed the on button. "Need a manager to the front!"

"What the hell, lady!"

The manager emerged from the back room and stopped

mid-step when he saw Mack's face. His scowl turned to an expression of "I don't get paid enough for this crap" and he shooed the other employee aside with a heavy sigh.

Forty-seven minutes later, she marched to her car with a box holding 365 pages of all her hopes and dreams. "Tuesday my ass," she muttered, and climbed into the driver's seat. The car started with a roar, and as soon as she took a left out of the parking lot, she floored the gas and took off towards Charlie.

THIRTY-TWO

CHARLIE'S DRINK SPECIAL: COLD BREW WITH WHIPPED HEARTACHE

Well, here she was. Again.

Two years post-divorce, Charlie assumed the sickly, familiar position of crying into a pillow as Ben performed his best mother-hen impression. The sounds of clanking mugs and banging cabinets from the kitchen echoed through her place.

A few hours ago, Mack's broken voice pleaded outside the loft. Charlie had slid down to the floor, the cold metal of the doorknob wrapped in her fingers as she debated opening the door. Once Mack left, Charlie realized she couldn't power through on her own, so she reached out for her best friend to battle the shattered-heart storm with her.

"Here. This'll help." Ben handed her a cup of chamomile tea and motioned for her to scoot over on the couch. He scooped her legs onto his lap and squeezed her foot.

She hated this. Sitting on the couch, warm drink in hand, the salty, dried tears making her cheeks feel like they verged on cracking. She had more than one flashback of when she split with Jess, and she and Ben pulled multiple all-nighters.

"God, tea tastes like shit. Seriously, how do you drink this?"

His words were a joke, but his tone was sweet. "You ready to talk to me about it?"

The chamomile slowly settled her nauseated stomach. "I found a document on Mack's computer. About me."

Ben cocked his head to the side. "Uh... okay. Like naked pictures or something?"

"No... not *of* me. *About* me." She took a slow sip. "Stuff about my life, my dad, my fears. Everything. Like a journal." She paused and thought for a moment. "No, I guess, like an investigative report."

He stared at her. "Sorry, babe. You're gonna have to spell this out for me."

She clutched her tea and explained everything as Ben sat quietly next to her with an unreadable expression. "I literally wanted to throw up, looking at my life written out like a shopping list."

"Okay, is that super creepy or super sweet?" He seemed to pick up her death glare and cleared his throat. "Creepy. Definitely creepy. What did she say when you asked her about it?"

"I didn't ask her. I bolted."

Ben set down his tea and folded his arms. "Why wouldn't you ask her?"

Because she didn't want to admit that she had fallen into a trap. Her chest tightened. She was angry and shocked and heartbroken and should never trust anyone again for the rest of her life until she shriveled up and died.

"I already know why she did it. She told me a while ago how writers use people for intel. I just never thought... she'd do that to me." She dropped her head back onto the couch and stared at the twinkling fairy lights. "I knew this was too good to be true. What was the one rule I made when me and Jess split? Never again. I was happy single. *Thriving*, even. And now... now I remember why I like to be alone."

A long silence followed. The clock inched towards

midnight, and the full moon's glow seeped through the cracks in the window blinds. She yawned and curled up on her side.

Ben stood and moved to the window. He tapped his fingers against the pane, his shoulders lifting in a deep inhale. "I never liked Jess."

Her head snapped up. "What?"

"Sorry. No. Let me rephrase." He turned back. "I didn't like who you were with Jess."

"Um... we were together for like a decade."

"This isn't coming out right." He settled back on the couch. "This is me doing feelings. Stay with me for a second."

She tried to smile but couldn't. Everything was so heavy, including her lips. Her eyes were dusty, her mouth was tacky. She rested her head against the couch and trailed a finger across the fabric.

"We have the Charlie I know and love, right? Fun, full of life, vibrant." He moved his gaze to the wall. "But when you were with Jess, you were always sort of needy. Anxious and unhappy."

Really? Maybe he should've spoken up at some point during the last decade. Although, admittedly, it couldn't have been easy for him to bite his tongue for so long. "Is this supposed to make me feel better?"

"I know, sorry." He patted her on the leg. "But when you were with Jess, it was like it scared you to be who you were. You were her shadow. But after the divorce, you transformed and became *you*. All of you. And when Mack came into your life, you stayed that way. You haven't changed one bit. You don't frantically check your phone. You're not constantly talking about her like you don't exist if she doesn't exist. When she had to focus on her book, you weren't all pissy and anxious. You are just you—with a partner."

The weight of his words lay heavy on her. "Okay..."

"But I'm going to be straight with you. Your first inclination is to run. You dodge and smile at horrible customers. You put up with a ton of crap from your dad. And you're the current reigning champion for avoiding confrontation. So, now are you just running because it's comfortable? 'Cause that's your go-to? If so, cool. I'll be your bouncer. We don't have to let her in. I'll even run with you wherever you want to go."

She tugged the pillow into her chest and ran her fingers through the fringes. Ben wasn't wrong, even though his words stung, and she kind of wanted to kick him in the shins. Was she not giving Mack a chance? Was her MO really running and avoiding confrontation? Sure, she took hell from customers because that was her livelihood. And she didn't address things with her dad 'cause, well, that was her dad. And she didn't challenge Jess 'cause that was her wife. And...

Crap. Maybe she did run.

Ben scooted lower on the couch and draped his legs on the side. "I just want to make sure you're giving yourself a chance at authentic love."

Damn. Ben could be freakishly insightful. She exhaled and lowered her head. She gave herself a chance. *Right?* What Mack did was awful. Wrong. Unethical... *right?* She was tired, had been up for too many hours, and her body and brain were fatigued.

"But it really, really, hurts."

He nodded. "I know."

A knock on the door jolted her upright.

Ben got off the couch and looked out the peephole. "It's Mack."

She froze, then shrunk down under the covers. She couldn't think. Words probably couldn't even formulate on her tongue at this point. If she opened the door, no good outcome could possibly happen. She'd either scream, cry, or forgive her in a snap, and none of those options were acceptable.

"I can't see her." Hot tears sprang up. "Please, Ben. I can't."

"All good. I'll take care of it."

A pounding in her ears grew in intensity. She crawled off the couch, grabbed her lucky jade stone from the side table, and dragged herself behind the half wall to listen. Clutching the rock in her fingers, she held her breath as she waited for Mack's voice. She wanted to see her. She didn't want to see her. She wanted to scream and cry and swear and crawl into a ball.

She heard the door unlatch, and she rubbed the stone between her fingers like a cricket.

"Can I talk to her?" Mack's voice, though raw and shaky, was determined.

"No," Ben snapped.

No matter what gentle voice he'd given Charlie all night, Brother Bear was not playing. She wished she could see Mack's face right now. Was she red from crying? Scalding from anger? Fidgeting?

"I know it looks bad. And... it was bad. At first. I need to explain what happened."

Charlie's limbs froze. She could just step out. Talk to her. Be an adult and have a sit-down.

But Mack lied!

"I can't lose her." Mack's voice cracked.

"I don't know how you can fix this," Ben said.

There was a long pause, and Charlie imagined a standoff between them. Maybe Ben folded his arms, refusing entrance, while Mack tugged on her clothes or shifted her feet.

"Can you give this to her for me?"

The sound of something rustling and then footsteps fading away floated in the air.

"Whatever it's worth," Ben called out, "I'm rooting for you."

The door clicked shut, and Charlie peeked around the corner. Maybe Mack's scent would still be lingering in the doorway. Maybe Mack was standing outside the window, and she could get a glimpse of her as she walked down the stairs.

She stepped into the room, and her chest dropped. No scent. No Mack.

With a sympathetic smile, Ben held out a cardboard box the size of a paper ream. His hands hung in the air, the heavy box probably weighing on them. He waited a moment then handed it over. "She left this for you."

The box remained between the two of them until Charlie finally took it and held it to her chest. Mumbling a quiet "Thank you," she finally met his gaze and noticed how red his eyes were. "You're tired."

"Nah." He rubbed the edge of his eye and moved to the couch. He slipped off his shirt to his tank and shoved the pillow under his head. "If you need me..."

"I know where to find you."

Clutching the box to her chest, she dimmed the fairy lights on the way to her bedroom. Once alone, she sat on the bed with the box laid down on the blanket in front of her. One deep inhale later, she removed the lid and revealed a stack of papers with a letter on top. Her fingers shook as she lifted the first sheet, and read the first line: *Charlie, My heart is heavy as I write this...*

By the second line, a warm mist filled her eyes and she brushed a fallen tear from her face. The words turned fuzzy through her unfocused gaze. Was she really in the emotional state to see whatever it was? Strumming her fingers on the bed, she considered just tossing it. Or burning it. At the bare minimum, sleep on it and review it tomorrow.

The paper stared back at her, egging her on.

Gnawing on her lower lip, she considered all the options for a few seconds longer.

Then she read it.

Charlie,

My heart is heavy as I write this. I wanted to say this to you in person, but I understand why you don't want to see me. What you read was all true. I used you to build my manuscript. I had never met anyone like you, and I was instantly drawn to you like a flame. You inspire me.

But what started out as learning about your background through your stories changed to me learning about *you*. I used your strength. Your courage. Your beauty, grit, and resilience. I took all the best pieces from you and built something.

I'm asking, begging really, for you to read the enclosed manuscript. The heartache you will read on these pages, it's not yours. It's mine. It's what I feel when I'm not with you and when I picture my life without you.

Falling in love was never in the cards for me. I've never loved before, and if you'd asked me a month ago, I would've said it's probably not worth it.

But now, I would say yes. It was worth it. A lifetime of pain of being without you was worth the days of loving you.

Please read it. And if you never want to talk to me again, I'll understand. Out of respect for you and your need to process, I won't contact you after this. You hold all the cards. However you want to play this out, I'll honor your decision.

I love you.

Mack

Midnight had nothing on Charlie as a surge of energy shifted her crumbling body upright. She tucked her knees to her chest and opened the document with trembling fingers.

Crooked Roots by M. Ryder

For Charlie.

She shines, that's for damn sure. Not like a diamond. Nah. She's so much more. The cosmic universe exploded and sprinkled down a moissanite star that landed directly at my feet.

I watch her through the crowded room. The drunk business suits, crystal champagne flutes, and pianist at the white baby grand in the corner are nothing but a mild, amusing backdrop.

She makes her way, and I swear everyone turns to look at her. Maybe they do, maybe they don't, but that's what it feels like. And I struggle because I don't want them to look, but I don't blame them. She's a goddess, a mirage. How can anyone not look?

I'm nervous. Like straight up shaking, trembling, sawdust mouth, nervous. Any second now, she'll see me, and she'll know. To the depths of her core, she'll know she's too good for me. And it's not like I'm chopped liver, or fried pig skin, or whatever gross food analogy people use to put themselves down. I got some shit working for me. But it's just that she's too good for anyone. The rest of us are mere mortals, genuflecting at her feet, blessed with the opportunity to breathe in the same air she does.

I'm still watching her from afar. Like a goddamn creeper. But how do you approach someone like that? This divine being that floats across the room. And yet, she looks my way. She's staring at me, and for a second, I do the thing. You know the thing. I turn to see what's behind me. It was a wall before, but surely there's someone behind me who's the intended recipient of her light.

Nope, still a wall. My brain refuses to accept that the smile is meant for me.

Oh God, she's coming towards me, and my heart is kicking in my chest, wailing like a trapped animal. I'm sure it'll explode in the middle of this bougie-ass party, but I'm okay with it.

If I'm gonna go out, I wanna go out with that smile being the last thing I see.

Tears sprang from Charlie's eyes. Page after page, chapter after chapter, she consumed the work. The full moon beamed brightly into her room, then moved across it. Her legs fell asleep, and she stood and stretched.

The story was good. Great, in fact, but so much different from what Mack had described a few weeks back, when she said the novel was a thriller about a young, single mom drug dealer. The main character was still a drug dealer, but the story was more... personal. Deep. A heartbreaking account of a woman who made bad and good choices. A story of loss and love and redemption and forgiveness.

Her eyes officially turned to dust, and Charlie hopped off the bed to search for eye drops in the bathroom. She splashed water on her face, grabbed a snack, and returned to her room. The moon had now moved over to the other side of the house. The sun would break through the night sky in a few short hours. But she wasn't tired.

What have I done? There's no way this is my reality. After all this time, after what we've worked for, she's gonna leave?

I'm too stubborn to admit that it was my fault. Like a crooked lawyer in a cheap suit, I throw any fact I can scrape up at the wall to justify my action. "It was for her!" "It was for us!" "I was trying to change our lives!"

She glares at me with the strength of a thousand poisonous dart pens and calls me on my bullshit.

I shake my head. I refuse to accept this is over.

And just like that, she pulls on her sunglasses, grabs her purse, and her red stiletto heels stomp across my heart on her way out the door.

Charlie lay back on her bed. Lost in the beautiful story, her pain from earlier tonight... yesterday... whatever time it was... dulled. She reread the letter from Mack and threw her arms over her head. *Ugh.* Now what? Hints of Charlie's life were in the novel, but they were written so seamlessly that they could've been about anyone.

The bed creaked as she rolled over to her side and checked the time. Only one hour left before she had to get ready for work. *Oof.* But no way would she not finish this book tonight. She rested her head in her hands and continued.

I look at the house for possibly the last time. Crooked roots, backyard beginnings, chandelier endings. The home that we shared with love. The bonds we made, the family we raised. Do I have regrets? Of course. Some. But everything I did led us to this moment.

This is what I know. I will die for this woman. Melodramatic, perhaps. Truthful, absolutely. Because without her, what is there? She is my whole. She is my spirit. She is my home.

She is my forever.

THIRTY-THREE

MACK'S DRINK SPECIAL: DEFEATED DARK
BLUES DECAF

Mack flipped the oversized pillow to the cool side and cuddled it. Sobbing for this long left her eyes crusty with day-old tears, her lips dry, and her body sore. Add that to a lack of food and a giant cup of anxiety, and she was totally depleted.

Forty-eight hours.

Forty-eight hours since Charlie fled the condo. Did Ben give her the manuscript? Did she read it? Mack picked up her phone and put it down. No new messages. Maybe she could just reach out and ask—

Nope. She could not call Charlie. The timeline from here on out had to be up to her. Mack refused to break this promise, like the billion other promises she'd broken before. She knew nothing about relationships and certainly didn't know how to handle a breakup. But a baseline would probably be to honor her no-contact commitment.

She dug her thumbs into her throbbing temples. What if Ben never gave her the manuscript? She was pretty sure she had put the letter in there. She double—triple—checked it, but maybe it fell out while walking to her car.

Or... what if Charlie took the letter and threw it into the

fire? What if the torn shreds of paper flew out, the embers fell on her hammock, and it caught on fire? Was Charlie the type of person who made sure the fire alarms worked and—

Stop. Enough.

Mack's hip bone burned from lying in the same position the last two days, and she rolled to the other side. The room was darker today. Her parents' analog clock screamed from the living room. Plotting contingency plans for worst-case scenarios no longer provided the same level of comfort it had in the past.

Because this *was* the worst-case scenario. Charlie was gone.

A light knock rapped on the door, and her mom cracked it open. "Honey? Can I bring you a sandwich or protein shake?"

Mack mustered all existing energy to respond, "No."

"Dad said he could pick up teriyaki or sushi?"

Her throat hurt. Her eyes hurt. Everything hurt. She returned to facing the wall.

"Mackey... this isn't good. You've been here all day. Can I at least come in and open the patio door or bring you water or something?" After several moments of silence, her mom inhaled sharply. "I know it hurts, baby, but I'm scared you're going to get dehydrated or sick or something, and—"

"Go away. Respectfully." That was the last word she'd say today. After a bit, the door clicked shut.

Another hour, maybe two, maybe three, passed. Dizzy and stiff, Mack sat up and dangled her legs off the bed until the blood circulated. Heavy with fatigue, she slogged down to the shower.

Admittedly, the shower, a bottle of water, and the sandwich that her mom not so subtly snuck into her bedroom helped. Mack cracked open the patio door, and a slight breeze carrying a hint of the salty Puget Sound traveled in.

Her phone rang, and her pulse launched up to her throat.

She dashed across the room, and the adrenaline drained from her body when she saw Viviane's name on the screen. A split-second contemplation of ignoring it passed before she answered.

"I hate you," Viviane said in between sniffles. "*Crooked Roots*. I read it in two days. I neglected my kids, neglected the hubby, and now I'm bawling like a toddler who's up past their bedtime."

"So... you hate me in a good way?"

Viviane exhaled. "Mack. You *killed* it. It's beautiful. Heartbreaking. Thrilling. I just... dammit, woman. I'm still processing."

Praise from Viviane was a hot chocolate during a blizzard. Not knowing how she'd respond to the manuscript had weighed on Mack more than she realized.

"What's the publisher going to say?" The book, at this point, was so deeply personal that Mack almost didn't care. *Almost*. But at the end of the day, her work was also her business, and she needed to prepare herself for a potential disaster.

"I think they're gonna love it. I really do. I'm going to schedule a meeting for Tuesday," Viviane said. "But if by some chance they don't, guaranteed we'll find another home for this. Stellar work."

Even with her heart shattered, Mack wanted to hug Viviane through the phone. After they wrapped up, Mack ached to call Charlie and tell her the good news. She rested against the patio railing and watched the city below. The faint buzz of people and cars traveled up the fourteen floors. A small breeze carried a hint of fern and wildfire smoke, and goose bumps erupted across her skin. She gripped the edge of the rail, leaned all the way back to stretch, and tried to pinpoint precisely when everything in her life went to shit and what she could do to get it back on track.

Armed with a shot of confidence from Viviane's approval, Mack's focus shifted.

New plan: Recovery Mission.

She had told Charlie she'd give her space. But that was Mack assuming she knew what Charlie needed. Maybe Charlie didn't want space. Maybe Charlie wanted to see she was worth fighting for. Maybe Mack wouldn't lie back and take this like a punk.

She refused to surrender without a fight.

After stepping back in the room, she tied her shoes and shoved her phone in her back pocket when there was a tap on the door.

"Knock, knock," her mom said. "Honey... Charlie's here to see you."

Mack's stomach dropped. Her heart lifted. Everything started sweating, even her earlobes.

She's here.

She flattened her hair against her scalp and reached for a water bottle at the edge of the bed.

"Thanks, Kelli." Charlie's voice was timid behind the door. She tiptoed into the room. Dark circles lined her eyes, her face was pale, and her lips were absent of her signature red lipstick.

She looked the way Mack felt.

"Hey," Mack finally said, her mouth simultaneously dry and wet.

"Hey."

Mack didn't know what to say. Of all the times in her life for her words to fail her, now took the prize for the single most inopportune. "I'm so sorry."

Charlie's eyes lowered to her fingers and she picked at her blue nail polish. A deep breath was pulled in and released. "I wanted to hate you. *So bad.* Analyzing me like that, like research, like some sort of detective case... I wanted to stay pissed at you forever." Charlie crossed the room and took a seat on the bed. She plucked at her dress and paused for several long moments before she glimpsed at Mack. "I read your book."

Mack's breath halted. "You did?" And? What did she think? Not about plot lines or typos. Mack crossed fingers, toes, and a few internal organs, hoping to God the words translated Mack's struggle.

"It's fantastic." Charlie resumed her nail polish picking. "The main character, Shelby, was incredible. The story was beautiful."

Speak, Mack.

A loose tendril popped from Charlie's ponytail, and she tucked it behind her ear. "I'm really hurt."

The soft, sad tone crushed Mack. Of course Charlie was hurt. She had every right to be. To know that someone used you, at least at first, would destroy anyone.

No more delays. Mack had to tell her everything. "The second I saw, you were like... a painting. I was so drawn in by you." Mack leaned against the wall, unsure if she should sit on the bed by Charlie. "You were everything I wasn't. You have this aura and joy that radiated from you, and I was obsessed with finding out how a human like you existed."

Charlie stopped picking at her polish.

Mack's chest tightened. She wanted to shut up and dive under the covers. Charlie's silence was more than a little unnerving, and Mack couldn't read her solemn expression. She scratched the back of her neck and choked back a cough.

No more waiting. Go time.

"I got blocked when I started writing because Shelby wasn't real. Something was missing with her... some authenticity. And the more you shared your heart with me, the more I absorbed your energy and life, and the more Shelby became real."

She pushed herself off the wall and paced the room. The floor absorbed her heavy footsteps as the word tsunami in her head took shape.

"In the beginning, I used your stories. And God, I'm so sorry. I thought it'd be a few weeks, and I'd go back to the city, and you'd just be some person from a coffee shop." Mack's lips trembled. "But for the first time, I felt something so pure and real, and I finally understood love and loss. That's where the inspiration comes for how Shelby feels about her love, and the lengths she went through to save her. To save them. Being with you, feeling all this, I know what it's like now to be willing to lose everything to save one thing."

The bed creaked as Charlie slowly stood, her eyebrows folded and tears welling.

Oh God. Was she done? Mack froze, unsure if Charlie would stomp out of the room or stay. Mack raced to every plausible scenario to salvage what might be left. Drop to her knees and beg. Run down the hall chasing after her. Bury herself in a blanket and never return.

But instead of stomping out of the room, Charlie rushed towards her with open arms. She cried on Mack's shoulder, her body folding into Mack's. "I love you." Her hoarse voice was barely above a whisper.

The relief was something Mack could write about for years. A dam that broke. A balloon that burst. A geyser that fire-hosed love and tears propelled her off her feet. She lifted Charlie to her toes and buried her head in the crook of her neck.

"I love you so much." Mack exhaled the fear of the last several days. "I'm so sorry... so, so, sorry."

Charlie's breath was warm against Mack's neck, and Mack didn't let go until her arms quivered. She held Charlie's hand and stumbled back to the bed. Cradled in each other's arms, minutes ticked by before anyone spoke.

"Not all of this is on you. I shouldn't have run. That's not what committed people do," Charlie whispered as she trailed her fingers across Mack's arm. "I loved the character Shelby so much. She is strong and fierce and amazing."

Mack kissed the top of her coconut-scented head. "She's everything you are."

Charlie shifted up onto her elbows. "No. She's everything *you* are."

Mack cupped Charlie's face and pulled her in. Charlie's soft lips against hers was everything she'd ever needed. Nothing in her life had prepared her to love someone like this. From here on out, Mack planned to spend the rest of her life savoring these moments and fiercely protecting their happiness.

"I know it's kind of late..." Charlie whispered. "But do you want to go get a latte?"

Mack snuggled in closer and put her mouth against Charlie's ear. "I thought you'd never ask."

EPILOGUE

CHARLIE'S DRINK SPECIAL: THE HAPPIEST HOT COCOA

Nine months later

A cherry blossom-scented breeze combined with the sunny spring day was the whipped cream topping to Charlie's incredible week. She'd tried playing it cool all day but was currently at a golden-retriever-puppy level of hyper.

The soggy grass squished between her feet as she gripped Mack's hips and steered her to the side. "Cover your eyes!"

"You literally have me blindfolded," Mack said, slapping at the air in front of her. "I'm just wondering where the pink fuzzy handcuffs are at this point."

"Ooh. Good call. Adding that to the list."

"I love that list."

Charlie put her mouth up to Mack's ear. "Me too."

When Mack moved in six months ago, she'd only brought clothes, books, and pictures. Charlie had said a silent prayer of thanks to the home gods because her place was already busting at the seams. No matter how much she decluttered over the years, it wasn't enough.

Mack obviously knew her dad was building a shed in the yard. He or one of his crew had been there daily for the past three weeks. The shed would be for storage, or at least that was what Charlie told Mack. And she made Mack pinkie promise to not look inside because Charlie wanted to surprise her with her mad organization skills.

A rock got in their path and Mack stumbled. She clutched at Charlie's hand while she toed around the ground. "Am I gonna die?"

Charlie giggled and held her steady. "Trust me."

Mack twisted her mouth in feigned disbelief. "I once had a scene that started exactly like this. Blindfolds and an unsuspecting woman. And the serial killer said the same thing."

After the editor at the publishing house read Mack's story and loved it, Viviane immediately barreled in and negotiated a three-book deal. Mack spent the last six months writing in Charlie's bedroom, the coffee shop, or sometimes at her parents'. A half dozen times she even cheated and went to a different coffee shop. Mack was a trooper, for damn sure, but Charlie knew Mack craved her own space. And honestly, Charlie did, too. Being in a relationship: awesome. Being alone: also awesome. Neither of them was giving up needed personal time.

She kissed Mack on the cheek and firmed her grip on her side.

"If I trip on something, I swear to God someone's gonna pay." Mack grinned.

Charlie giggled and loosened the blindfold. "Ready? Open!"

Mack blinked multiple times and squinted into the space. The "shed" was a creative area with stark white walls, one bamboo plant that Charlie was mildly confident Mack couldn't kill, and a custom bookshelf with books lined up in rainbow order. If she would've had the space, she would have added a custom hammock, massage chair, and pet unicorn. Sadly, a 20 ft x 20 ft structure didn't allow for those things. But one last surprise remained.

"Do you like it?" Charlie asked after too many moments passed of Mack not saying anything. "I didn't buy the desk or chair because I didn't know what you'd like, and we can paint the walls and remove the bookshelf and... whatever you need. I know you need a quiet and freakishly clean space, and I can't always give that to you, so I thought—"

"Wait. Is this for me?" Mack's mouth popped open in shock. "This isn't for storage?"

"Nope!" Smiling so widely made Charlie's jaw begin to ache. She bounced on her toes and clasped Mack's hand to tug her inside.

Placing her hands on her hips, Mack looked around for several moments before she moved to the bookshelf. She traced her hands across the perfectly aligned books and inhaled. "For me?" she repeated.

"Yes! For you." Charlie wrapped her hands around Mack's waist and kissed her on the cheek. "You've put up with my mess for months, and I thought you'd want a disaster-free station."

Mack briefly rested her head against Charlie's. "Oh, come on. It's not that bad. And you've perfected the art of hospital corners."

That statement was actually true. Over the crash course of *really-getting-to-know-you* since they moved in together, Mack learned how to make every drink on Sugar Mugs's menu, how to use the multiple products in the shower, and that no one would die if the shoes were not evenly lined up against the wall. Charlie learned the difference between iron settings, that joy in cleanliness did exist, and that color-coordinating her closet was more valuable than she'd realized.

She also learned how to love without fear.

Charlie tugged Mack's hand over to a cabinet, her heart thumping. She was damn near giddy with excitement. "I have one more surprise. Ready? Check this out." She swung the door open to showcase a wall-mounted ironing board with an *M & C* emblem.

"An iron board with our initials?" Mack squealed and ran her flatted palm against the base. "Okay, you're seriously the best. Do you know that?"

Lips pressed against Charlie's cut her off from all other words. Her knees buckled—they always did—until Mack pulled back.

"God, I love you," Mack said, and kissed the top of her head.

Charlie rested her head on Mack's shoulder. A year ago, she'd never imagined she'd be standing in a shed on her property with the love of her life, a successful business, and her soul filled. After an unhealthy relationship, coming to terms with her father, and fighting to learn about herself, she finally found what she needed.

A partner.

A LETTER FROM THE AUTHOR

Hey there!

Thanks so much for reading *Not in the Plan*. I hope you loved getting to know Charlie and Mack as much as I loved writing their story. When I set out to do my first (of many!) sapphic romances, one thing I was pretty set on was I wanted the books to be sparkly, fun, and celebrate queer joy. I'd love to keep you posted about my new releases and bonus content. Please sign up for my newsletter, below. I promise I won't spam you or sell your info.

www.stormpublishing.co/dana-hawkins

If you liked this book and wouldn't mind leaving a review, I'd be so grateful. Even a short review can make all the difference in encouraging a reader to discover my books for the first time. Thank you so much!

Not in the Plan was inspired by combining a few of my favorite things: queer joy, sapphic romance, Seattle, and coffee. I wanted to bring alive this amazing city as a backdrop to this story, while touting the joys of coffee. So much of me is in both characters: red hair, tattoos, coffee lover, and crystals—check. Social awkwardness, introverted, the near obsession with writing, and the deep love of family—check. I think these women represent what many of us feel at times: overwhelmed, a sense that we are "not enough," and difficulty finding our own path.

The queer community continues to live in fear and is subject to discrimination, violence, anti-inclusive legislation and more. I intentionally created a world where my characters live in a safe, affirming, and celebratory space while navigating their relationship and real-life issues. I wanted, just for a while, for us to escape reality and enjoy a hate-free world.

Places all over are creating an inclusive space for folks, and it's inspiring. I'm looking at you, Korppi Coffee + Bakeshop in St. Cloud, Minnesota, the Cedar River Starbucks in Renton, Washington, the elementary school teachers at Briarwood, my neighbor who put up a pride flag right next to their American flag, the librarians in Florida who are fighting to keep LGBTQ+ books on the shelf, the grandparents down the block with a rainbow bumper sticker, and more. Goodness exists everywhere. Let's all be part of the good.

Thanks again for being part of this amazing journey with me! Please stay in touch—I have so many more stories and can't wait to share them with you!

Dana Hawkins

www.danahawkins.com

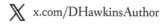 x.com/DHawkinsAuthor

ACKNOWLEDGMENTS

Ever since I was little, I created stories in my head while falling asleep. One night during the pandemic, I wrote down a story that had been floating in my mind for a few years. I had no idea the rush I would get from creating, or the joy it would bring me. I pinch myself every day that my dream of publishing these stories has come true.

Where do I even start to say thank you to all those who have supported me during my writing journey? When folks hear the term "it takes a village," it truly does.

To my spouse (my forever). Your unwavering support and cheerleading from day one is something I will never forget. You bought me a laptop and a rainbow coffee mug, and stepped in to do extra parent duties. You have no idea how much it means to me.

To my kids, Tanner, Kianna, Joey. Thank you for understanding when I needed quiet time and for jumping up and down with me when I signed a book deal. You are all so beautifully, uniquely perfect, and I am beyond lucky that I get to be your mom.

To my parents, Dave and Esther Dusha. Your love for your children, encouragement, and support are for the record books. Thank you for always encouraging me to follow my dreams.

To my writing community. Buckle up, friends—there are a lot of you.

Amy Nielsen. A couple of years ago, you quietly raised your hand when I was a beginning writer and offered to look at a few pages of mine. Your praise, guidance, and spot-on feedback gave me everything I needed to get started. Fast forward to five books later: podcasts, interviews, book trailers... the list goes on. I cannot imagine a world where I would be here today without you.

Jennifer Gatewood. You did not know me, and yet you offered to read my pages and give me feedback. Your kindness and grace know zero bounds. You are an amazing critique partner, an incredibly gifted writer, and I am so very lucky to have you in my life.

Dana Renee Green. From the second you and I exchanged emails, and then chatted on the phone, your positive energy and beautiful spirit filled me. Thank you for being in my corner, and reminding me that everything is happening exactly how and when it should.

S. E. Reed. Thank you for your constant guidance, quick feedback when I send you random "does this even make sense?" messages, and uplifting me on the daily.

Amanda Sauvageau. Years and years before I ever wrote down my stories, you encouraged me to share them with you. I will cherish forever spending so many hours reciting these stories to you. You gave me the foundation I needed to turn this dream into a reality, and I am forever grateful for you. I love you!

Erica Dusha. You are the best beta reader ever. Thank you for calling out when something doesn't work. I have changed entire scenes, even a book ending, based on your feedback. Thank you for always reading my work and jumping in to offer encouragement or advice. I love you!

Katharine Bost. You are such a kind and gifted editor! Thank you for helping me with this story and providing your amazing feedback. I would have never gotten this book deal had you not gotten me there.

Emily Gowers. Thank you for believing in me and taking a

chance on me. Your kindness and professionalism are unparalleled. You have made my dream come true, and I am forever indebted to you.

Jenny Hale. The time and energy you spent in answering so many of my questions, especially when you didn't even know me, was so incredibly kind. Your mentorship and guidance have meant everything, and I am confident you have a bucket of good karma heading your way.

Addy Hammond and Marnie Fischer—my auntie warriors. Thank you for believing in me and reading my stories.

Chad (my real-life "Ben"). Thank you for always having my back and providing me with years' worth of humor. I love you.

Bryn Donovan. Thank you for offering amazing feedback on my first few chapters.

And finally, thank you to Storm Publishing for giving my story a home.

Made in United States
Troutdale, OR
02/19/2025

29124060R10184